MAGGIE

Marie Maxwell

This first world edition published 2015
in Great Britain and the USA by
SEVERN HOUSE PUBLISHERS LTD of
19 Cedar Road, Sutton, Surrey, England, SM2 5DA.
Trade paperback edition first published
in Great Britain and the USA 2015 by
SEVERN HOUSE PUBLISHERS LTD.

British Library Cataloguing in Publication Data

Maxwell, Marie author.
Maggie.
1. London (England)–History–20th century–Fiction.
2. Nineteen sixties–Fiction.
I. Title
823.9'2-dc23

ISBN-13: 978-0-7278-8476-3 (cased)
ISBN-13: 978-1-84751-581-0 (trade paper)
ISBN-13: 978-1-78010-629-8 (e-book)

Except where actual historical events and characters are being described for the storyline of this novel, all situations in this publication are fictitious and any resemblance to living persons is purely coincidental.

Typeset by Palimpsest Book Production Ltd.,
Falkirk, Stirlingshire, Scotland.

One

'I don't care! I don't want her there – I don't want any of them there. I just want my friends! I don't want them spoiling it all. I'm old enough not to have to have them here every single birthday,' Maggie Wheaton said, the words pouring out quickly. 'Ruby and Gracie, Ruby and Johnnie, that's all you care about! Ruby and Johnnie and their bl—' She paused. 'Ruby and Johnnie and their blooming kids and friends.'

She was wide-eyed and very angry, so angry that she was on the verge of tears, but her stubborn streak wouldn't let her cry. Maggie was a determined and confident girl who was so used to getting her own way that she was finding this sudden denial of her wishes hard to accept.

Barbara Wheaton sighed and shook her head as she dried her hands on her apron and made her way across the kitchen to the long pine table where her daughter was sitting. Her movements were laboured as, leaning on a wooden walking cane, she pulled out a chair and carefully lowered herself down before wriggling slightly to get comfortable.

'Oh, dear me, this hip is getting worse. I'm going to have to go next door and get something for it; it aches all the time now. Maybe Dad is right. Maybe I *will* have to have something done to it before I end up not being able to walk. Or drive. We'd be lost if I had to give up driving.'

Maggie didn't respond; she simply folded her arms on the table dramatically and buried her head down on them.

'I'm sorry, darling, I know you're upset, but this really is the last time we're discussing this. I'm simply not going over it any more.' Babs reached across and touched her daughter's arm. 'I've already invited Ruby and her family. They always come over for your birthday, and I can't possibly change that on one of your whims and fancies. As it happens, Gracie isn't coming this year, but Ruby and Johnnie and the boys are and that's final,' she said calmly.

'It's not a whim or a fancy. I've been saying it for ages, and you just ignore me. It's my birthday, and I should be able to have a proper party with who I want, with my own friends, not yours.' Maggie's head was still buried in her arms and her voice was muffled, but the sulky teenage sarcasm was loud and clear.

'You're simply not old enough to be having the sort of party you're asking for,' Babs continued. 'Maybe in another couple of years. Now, weren't you going off to the tennis courts? Isn't there a tournament?'

'It's not fair! you never let me have any fun.' Maggie looked up and flicked her head to get her newly cut fringe out of her eyes. 'And now you want me to have another baby party. You're probably already planning the rabbit jelly and musical chairs. Well, that's not what I want,' she said, her voice rising with every word. 'I want a real party. In the evening, with music and punch and snacks . . .' Frustration was written all over Maggie's young face as she failed to talk her mother round and get what she wanted, the way she always used to be able to.

'I'm sorry you feel like that, darling, but Ruby is family, and she wants to be here for your birthday,' Babs reasoned firmly. 'However, Ruby is beside the point here. Daddy and I both think you're too young to have that kind of party anyway.' She paused and shook her head. 'Now, I'm not discussing this again with you. You're not having a party, and Ruby and Johnnie and the boys are coming here on Saturday for the usual birthday buffet, and that's the end of it.'

'But I'll be sixteen; that's old enough to have my friends here! You and Dad could go and visit someone, take Ruby with you, or I could have a party on a different day. I promise we'll all behave and—'

'Stop it. You're beginning to sound whiny, and that's not nice,' her mother said, cutting her off mid-sentence. 'The answer is no, and it's going to stay no. Maybe next year we can think again. Two or three of your friends are welcome to come as well, of course – you can have the record player in the front room and we won't interfere – but it's going to be in the afternoon on Saturday, and Ruby and Johnnie and the boys will be here, and that's that.'

Maggie glared again at her mother. 'How can I ask friends round to a birthday tea at my age? They'll all laugh at me. I hate you. You just want to ruin my life,' she screeched before storming out of the room and slamming the door so hard that it rattled on its hinges for several seconds afterwards.

She ran out into the large square hall, wiped the back of her hand fiercely across her eyes and sat down on the bottom stair to try and think of another way to get round her parents. She was determined to manage it somehow. She always had in the past, and this time she was desperate. She had to have a proper party on Saturday night! She'd already written the guest list, chosen her clothes, compiled the playlist for the records and found a recipe for punch. Young Maggie Wheaton was determined not to be thwarted because she was in love for the first time and wanted to have a good excuse to invite Andrew Blythe, the focus of her attention, to her house. A party would be perfect, but she couldn't do that if it was going to be a childlike party with all the family wheeled out.

She was a confident and self-assured young woman who had been loved and cosseted all her life and brought up to believe she was clever and beautiful and could conquer the world. But sometimes this self-confidence tipped over and she could come across as almost arrogant in her self-belief. As the adored only child of older parents, she had always been the centre of their world, but although she had definitely been indulged, the need for good manners and behaviour had also been instilled in her.

Despite her young age, she had an appreciation of her fortunate upbringing which had allowed her an excellent education, private dancing and singing lessons and expensive school trips, but sometimes, when her parents did say no, she found it hard to accept. Especially when it seemed unreasonable, which was how she saw their decision over a party.

Already five foot eight, she was tall for her age, with naturally blonde hair and fair skin which tanned easily under the summer sun. She was clever and attractive and she knew it, readily accepting that the boys in the village all wanted to go out with her and the girls all wanted to be like her.

But now she was hopelessly in love, and Andy Blythe had taken over her thoughts to the extent that she wasn't concentrating at school and was becoming increasingly frustrated at home because she didn't want to be anywhere other than around him. So far the new boy in the village – the boy all the local girls were hanging around at every opportunity – had barely noticed her, but she was determined to change that.

As she leaned back against the dark wood banisters she sighed and thought for a few moments, before standing up and opening the front door carefully so that her mother wouldn't hear.

'I'm going out,' she shouted loudly over her shoulder as she ran through the porch, snatching up her tennis bag on the way. She pulled the heavy wooden front door hard behind her and raced off down the driveway to the road before her mother could respond and call her back for the apology she knew she owed.

The Wheaton family home was at the top end of the close-knit village of Melton in Cambridgeshire. It was a large rambling house on an extensive corner plot and had always doubled as the doctor's surgery. The Wheatons owned the whole property, so a permanent division between home and surgery had been made after George Wheaton had finally retired and a new GP installed. It was the only home Maggie had ever known, and she loved it there, but she was starting to feel stifled by her sometimes overly protective parents.

As soon as she knew she was well out of view, she stopped and got her breath back. She carefully straightened the pleats in her tennis skirt before turning it over at the waist to make it shorter, tucked her blouse in as tightly as she could and tied her jumper casually across her shoulders. She ran her fingers through her hair and tugged it as straight as she could, then she pulled a pale pink lipstick from her pocket and, with her back to the road, did her best to apply it without a mirror.

Hoping she looked OK, Maggie walked purposefully down the main high street that cut right through the village; she looked straight ahead to avoid getting caught up in any conversations, and then at the bottom she turned into the narrow side road that led to the local tennis club. The nearer she got the more nervous she felt, as she hoped that the young man her attentions were absolutely focused on would be there.

The tennis club had been at the centre of village life for as long as anyone could remember. It had served many purposes over the years, but it had always been a meeting point for local youngsters, especially during school holidays. The small club served several of the outlying villages as well as Melton, and it was a good place to meet boys and girls from other schools. Evenings and weekends were strictly for the adults and private events, but there was an unwritten rule that the younger members could use the clubhouse during the day in the holidays and after school on weekdays; they were even allowed to play their own music on the club record player and bring their own refreshments.

She paused at the gates for a moment then, doing her best to look casual, she shrugged her tennis bag on to her shoulder and tucked her hands into the pockets of her skirt before sauntering casually up to the wire that enclosed the four perfectly maintained grass courts. She glanced around the players on the courts but quickly realized Andy Blythe wasn't playing, so she walked around to the clubhouse that overlooked the courts from the far end and tried to peer in through the small, grimy window without being seen. Although it was grandly called the clubhouse, it was little more than a large shed that had seen better days. Moves were afoot to have it replaced with something better, but meanwhile the villagers just accepted and loved the decrepit old building as it was.

She stood back a little from the window and squinted. Yes. Andy was there. She could just see him, leaning back in a rickety hard-backed chair with his feet up on another chair, a bottle of coca-cola in one hand and a cigarette in the other. He looked relaxed and casual at the table he was sharing with three girls and another boy, all of whom Maggie recognized but who she knew were slightly older than her; she was disappointed that none of her own friends were there, but nonetheless she steeled herself to go in alone.

Just looking at him made her catch her breath. He was the boy of her dreams, tall, handsome and worldly wise, and from the moment some weeks before when she had first set eyes on him she'd been besotted with a boy for the very first time. It was a feeling she couldn't explain, but she'd read enough magazines to know what it meant.

Before finally pushing the door open, Maggie took a deep breath to overcome the feeling of butterflies flapping around under her ribcage; usually self-confident, she found the feeling so alien that she had to concentrate hard to stay in control.

'Hello, everyone,' she said, putting on her widest smile as she approached the table. 'Have you all been practising for the tournament tomorrow?'

'The others have; they've only just dragged their sweaty bodies off court,' Andy said, laughing, and he paused to draw on his cigarette. He made a big show of blowing perfect smoke rings up into the air before continuing, 'But I don't need to practice. I'm probably going to win; I'm the best one here. That's if I enter, of course. I may not. I haven't decided. I might step back and give the others a chance. Fair play and all . . .'

Although the response sounded arrogant, it was also true. Andy Blythe was an all-round sportsman who was especially brilliant at tennis because, as he constantly told everyone, he had the advantage of playing both at his private school and on the private tennis courts at his own home.

'Do you fancy a knockabout now then?' Maggie asked, looking straight at him. 'I saw there's an empty court, and I need some practice. Not that I'm likely to get far; I'll be out first thing.'

'Actually, I'm whacked. I've had a hell of a day so far, what with driving lessons and things.' Andy shrugged and grinned. 'But come and join us. We're talking music . . . My dad brought a whole pile of records home from London for me. All the latest top twenty hits! I brought them with me and was going to play them, but the record player here is kaput. I'll have to ask Dad to buy the club a new one.'

Delighted at the invitation, Maggie dragged a chair across from an adjoining table, and they all shuffled round to make room for her. She dumped her tennis bag on the floor and kicked it under the table before sitting down opposite Andy.

'I love music and singing. I've got heaps of records at home but nowhere near as many as you . . .' She nodded her head in the direction of the two stacks of forty-fives on the table in front of him. 'You must have as many there as Woolworths in town.'

'I can get you some if you like. Dad brings them home all the time – all the hits and lots of new ones that haven't even been released. I always get them first. It's the advantage of being the only son and heir to the family business.' He looked at her for a moment with his head slightly on one side and then grinned. 'It's Maggie something, isn't it? Sorry, I'm no good with names. I've met so many new people since we moved here.'

'Yes, it's Maggie, Maggie Wheaton. I live up at the doctor's house. My dad used to be the village GP, but since he retired we live in the house itself and Dr Banbury runs the surgery next door in the annexe. He lives in one of the new houses out the other side of Melton.'

Maggie stopped and surreptitiously tried to breathe. She knew she was speaking too fast and saying too much. She leant back in her chair and hooked her hair behind her ears as casually as she could, hoping against hope that her face wasn't going red.

'Oh, yeah, I remember now, the doc's daughter. Anyway, I'll let the others introduce themselves – that's if you don't know them already.' He stopped and shook his head. 'Sorry, all. I keep forgetting that everyone knows everyone round here or else they're related. I'm used to living in Cambridge. It's a university town, you know, people coming and going all the time. Melton is so kind of archaic by comparison.'

'I know Cambridge really well – my dad went to university there, and we sometimes go to the shops there – but it's never going to be as friendly as somewhere like Melton. I've always lived here, and I rather like it.' Maggie bristled slightly as she responded, hating the idea that he might be thinking they were all country bumpkins in the village that had been her home all her life. But she quickly excused him in her mind, telling herself that it was only because Andy and his family were newcomers to the area and hadn't really had time to fit in.

But no one seemed to have taken any notice of what she'd said, and as the conversation moved on to something totally different, Maggie just sat quietly, feeling oddly out of place in the clubhouse she had known all her life.

Instead of joining in, she studied the boy opposite her. Andy

Blythe was an attractive and very modern-looking young man with longer than average dark-brown hair that flopped over his forehead and hooded hazel eyes framed with long thick lashes. Whenever she saw him or even fantasized about him, Maggie thought he looked like a pop singer or as if he'd stepped out of the pages of her favourite *Honey* magazine. Tall and athletic, he was always immaculately turned out in expensive, fashionable clothes that he wore well, and he had an air of confident entitlement way beyond his seventeen years.

Maggie had never met anyone quite like him before. Some of the local young men had tried hard to find something to criticize him for, but mostly they had failed. The main comment was usually: 'Who does he think he is?'

There was also an undercurrent of jealousy and distrust in the village towards the Blythe family as a whole, mainly because they were complete outsiders who no one actually knew anything about. And not only were they outsiders, but outsiders who had moved into the old Manor House, the most coveted house for many miles. Their biggest crime of all was that they didn't have the same perceived breeding as the previous aristocratic owner, who was allegedly connected to the royal family.

The old Manor House had always been spoken of with deference and in hushed tones, and many were upset that it was no longer in the hands of locally born and bred landed gentry. The expression 'new money' was often used when the older villagers were discussing the new family, and it always made Maggie wonder what it was about new money that meant it wasn't as good as old money.

The removal trucks had barely started to unpack at the Manor when the village gossip mill had whirred into action with rumours of dodgy dealings and the possible incarceration of family members. They saw something dodgy in the fact that Jack Blythe worked in show business and spent most of the week in London, leaving his wife Eunice to play the role of lady of the manor while their only son was away at boarding school. Whispers echoed around of shady relatives living there in secret, adultery, lovers, and second wives and husbands, but Maggie didn't know or care about any of it. All she was interested in was the son of the family: Andy.

From the first moment she'd seen him in the local newsagent shop she had been besotted and had sought him out at every moment she could, but now she watched curiously as the other girls stared and hung on his every word. She hoped that *she* didn't come across as shallow and daft. She was almost in a trance, and it took her by surprise when he suddenly jumped up and started scooping his records into his duffel bag.

'Well, I'd better be off. I'm under orders to be home for the latest house-warming; I think this is the third so far. It's taken Mother so long to arrange, and guests are coming from all over, so I'll be dead if I don't get back in time for lift-off!'

He held his arms out wide to the side of him; he shrugged his shoulders and stretched his back, before hooking his jumper on his finger and flipping it over his shoulder. He was dressed all in tennis whites, even though he hadn't been playing; his shorts and shirt were pristine, and his shoes were the best on the market. He looked more like a walking advertisement for tennis clothes than a young man at a village club.

'Ciao, everyone. See you all anon . . .' He bent over in a bow.

'I have to get home as well.' Maggie jumped up from her seat and moved to the door. 'I'll walk with you; we're going the same way.'

'Actually, I've got my bike.' He stopped, looked Maggie up and down, and smiled. 'But I don't mind pushing it. Where did you say you live again? At the top of the hill?'

'At the doctor's surgery. My father used to be the doctor – Dr Wheaton – but he's retired now.' Maggie knew she'd explained all that before, but she didn't mind too much that he'd forgotten. It saved her having to think of something new and witty to say.

He pushed his bike by the handlebars, and she walked beside him as they strolled back up through the village. Maggie let Andy do most of the talking because her natural self-confidence had deserted her at the door of the clubhouse and she felt unusually tongue tied, but he more than made up for her silence. Andy Blythe talked constantly, and he had a way of looking at her when he was talking that made her just want to grin. For the first time in her life she felt like a grown up – a young woman with a young man looking at her appreciatively.

As they approached the driveway that led to the main part of the house, Maggie stopped. 'Here, this is where I live.'

'Ah, yes, the doctor's house. I suppose that's where we'll go if we're poorly! When we moved here we were given a list of the key points in the village, and this was one of them. Not that there's many. I walked through in ten minutes the first time. Top to bottom and back again in one go.'

As her nerves threatened to get the better of her, Maggie tried her best not to hop from foot to foot. 'It's a nice village though . . . Oh, I nearly forgot. I'm probably having a party next Saturday. Can you come?' The words were out before she could stop them.

He looked at her curiously. 'What sort of party?'

'Just a party with a few friends. I'll be sixteen, so it'll be for that. I just have to make the final arrangements, and I can easily add you to the guest list if you'd like to come . . .' She shrugged as nonchalantly as she could while praying he'd say yes.

'I think my parents have something planned for next Saturday. Again! They're always entertaining, and I usually have to show up and play the role of devoted son, which of course I am, but I may be able to stick my head in at yours for a bit. I'll let you know. Give me your telephone number.'

Maggie dug into her tennis bag and found an exercise book and pencil. She ripped a page out and scribbled the number. 'Do you want to give me your number while I've got the paper here?' she asked.

'Oh, sorry, I don't actually know the number yet. I haven't got round to learning it. Bad, I know, but I will eventually. I'll give it to you when I phone.'

Maggie wondered for a moment if he was lying, but she was pleased that he hadn't said anything to make her feel silly. He hadn't laughed at her having a party, even though he was obviously used to more sophisticated functions. She hoped against hope it was because he liked her. 'I'd better go in . . . When do you go back to school?'

'Didn't you know?' he asked with a grin. 'I'm not going back. I'm finished with school. It's always been accepted that I would go to work with my dad in his business, so staying any longer at school is a waste of time and money. I'll inherit everything one day, so I'm going to start learning how it all works.'

'You're going to live here permanently then? Not just during the holidays?' Maggie asked hopefully.

'No, not really. I'll be living mostly in London – we've got a flat there – but I'll be here most weekends. Ma would never forgive my dad if I didn't come back. I'm still her baby boy.'

'See you around then?' she asked, trying to sound casual.

'Yes. See you around, probably at the club. I'm going to get Dad to replace the record player. It needs livening up there, and I've decided I'm the one to make it a bit more hip, make it the place to be! Anyway, ciao again . . .'

'Don't forget to let me know about the party,' she said, but he didn't answer.

He swung his leg over his bicycle and pedalled quickly away, although he did manage a quick wave of his hand before he disappeared off into the distance.

Maggie turned and walked up the driveway, steeling herself for the telling-off she knew was inevitable after her slamming out of the house earlier.

And then she would try again for a party; there was always a chance Andy might turn up.

Two

After Andy had cycled off home leaving Maggie standing at her gate looking after him, she thought for a few minutes about the party and decided to try a different tack. Shouting hadn't worked, so maybe charm might – if not on her mother, then on her father, so she decided that as soon as she was indoors she would look for one or the other.

From the outside, the Wheaton family home was impressive. Clad in wisteria, it stood at the top of the village high street and was a beautiful landmark for Melton. However, inside it was draughty and damp and in dire need of modernizing and redecorating. Maggie often offered up ideas for making it warmer and brighter, but neither of her parents wanted the upheaval at their ages and especially with George's increasing ill-health.

To make things easier for her ailing husband, Babs had turned what was originally the formal front parlour into a bed-sitting room for George, who now tended to spend most of his time there. It was a light and spacious room with wide windows, and when George retired to bed early, as he often did, Babs would sit in there with him in the evening listening to the wireless or reading until he was completely settled for the night and then she would go upstairs to their old bedroom, which was on the first floor next to Maggie's.

It was an arrangement that worked well, although the strain of constantly helping her husband move in and out of his wheelchair had left Babs with a constantly aching back and knee joints that creaked and crunched at every move. The noisy old stairlift, which had been redundant after George moved downstairs permanently, had recently become her preferred method of getting up and down the stairs, and she had had to accept that she needed a walking stick most of the time. Maggie helped out with much of the running around, but both her parents were loath to ask her to do any more than was absolutely necessary, and Babs Wheaton especially didn't want to give up any of her independence.

But the couple had been happily married for nearly all their adult lives and were still devoted to each other, so even when it was a struggle Babs did everything willingly. She was used to doing it; as a result of childhood polio, George had always been in a wheelchair, but he had led a full and successful life despite it. He had gone to medical school and then been the Melton village GP for most of his adult life, but the time had come when he had had to give it up and retire, and now his health was deteriorating and they were both feeling the effects of getting older.

After many years of childless marriage, which neither of them had wanted but which they had both accepted, baby Maggie had come along just after the war, and they had welcomed her as their very own gift from God.

Margaret Wheaton was the adored daughter neither of them had ever thought they'd have.

Maggie found her mother dusting in her father's bed-sitting room. 'I'm sorry I was rude earlier. I didn't mean it, really, I didn't,' Maggie said, looking sheepishly at her mother.

Babs Wheaton studied her face for a few moments before responding. She was an adoring mother who loved her daughter unconditionally, but she was also very perceptive and realistic.

'Yes, you were rude, and there really was no need to be like it. You know I expect better of you,' she said, still looking intently at Maggie. 'But it seems that at least you realize it. Well, I sincerely hope you do.'

'I do, honestly I do, and I'm really sorry.' Maggie put her arm around her mother's shoulder and hugged her. The hug was genuine enough – they had always been a tactile family – but the underlying motive was to get back into her mother's good books and sway her round to the idea of a real birthday party, a party which someone as sophisticated as Andy would appreciate. 'Where's Dad?' Maggie asked, still trying to decide which one would be the softer touch.

'He's out in the garden. He only got up from his nap a short while ago; he tires so easily nowadays. I'm just having a quick tidy up while I have the chance.' She looked at her daughter and smiled to take the edge off her words. 'So, do you feel better now after your door-slamming tantrum?'

With good grace Maggie shrugged and grimaced apologetically. 'I'm sorry. I know it was really childish. I was sorry as soon as I slammed the door. I only went to the tennis club, like I'd said I would today. I was going to have a practice and see who was there.'

'And? Who was there?'

'None of my friends. I think they must have all gone home after practice. There were some older girls from school, though.' She paused. 'And Andy Blythe, he was there.'

'Andy Blythe?' Babs frowned. 'Blythe? Is he the boy whose parents have recently bought the Manor House? I've always loved that house. I used to promise myself that if we won the football pools we'd buy it, but now we've been beaten to the punch!'

'I'd have liked that,' Maggie said.

'Mr Blythe must be doing really well to afford it; it was ridiculously expensive. I couldn't believe how much it was up for sale for! We were surprised when it sold.'

Maggie saw her opportunity to bring Andy, and the party, into the conversation.

'Andy said Mr Blythe's in the music business, an agent or manager or something. He works in London. He's got an office there; he's even got a flat. Andy's been at boarding school, but now he's going to work with his father. He's got all the latest clothes and records, and they have their own tennis courts, but Andy likes to come to the club.'

'I'm sure he does,' Babs said, smiling. 'It's no good having your own courts if you've got no one to play with. He's an only child, isn't he?'

'Yes, like me. They've got stables as well, but I don't know how many horses. That family must be loaded, but he's a nice boy, everyone likes him, and he's so good at sport. He's not even entering the tournament because he thinks it's unfair. He knows he'll win,' she said.

'Hmmm, sounds a little conceited to me. There are plenty of excellent players at the club. Young Jimmy is a top notch player. And so are you,' Babs said.

'He really is nice,' Maggie continued, desperate to plead Andy's case prior to going back to the topic of a party. 'He's so fashionable and modern, especially compared to the village boys.'

'Of course he is. The family have a lot more money than most of the villagers, so they can afford all those fancy things, but they don't mean everything, you know. The person inside is more important.'

'I know, but he's really nice too.'

Babs carried on pottering around the room with a feather duster in hand as Maggie did her best to lure her mother into gentle conversation. Once her brain had cleared, she had realized that she stood more chance of talking them round if she was all sweetness and light rather than stroppy, but first she had to convince her mother that she was responsible, and then she would turn her attention to her father, who was usually the softer touch.

'Is there anything you want me to do? Take the washing out or something?'

'No, dear, it's all under control, though some help with dinner tonight would be nice. The veg are on the side, ready for preparation.'

'OK, but first I'm going out to see Dad.' She jumped up from the bed. 'I'll make him a cuppa; do you want one as well?'

'I'd love one.' She paused as she looked at her daughter. 'Maggie I'm not silly, and I know where all this going, so please don't go out there to harass your father about this party nonsense. I know what you're up to, and the answer is still no from both of us. He's really not well at all and can do without anything more to worry about.'

Maggie stopped and stared back at her, her expression pleading. 'Oh, please! There'll be just ten of us, we'll be quiet, and it can be after Ruby and all of them have gone. You can have what you want in the afternoon, and then I can have what I want. I promise we'll all behave, but I'll look so stupid if I have to tell everyone I can't have this party. Everyone *else* has them—'

'Now you're really starting to make me cross, Maggie,' Babs

said, interrupting her sharply. 'Please consider your dad in all this. Please? He's not up to these sort of shenanigans, and you know that. He likes peace and quiet with no pressure . . . We're definitely not going to agree this year, so stop it before you upset both of us any more.'

'But Mum . . .!'

'No buts, and no more discussion. The answer is NO, and it's going to stay no, so don't waste your time.'

Maggie looked at her mother, who was shaking her head and pointing her finger at the same time. She looked so cross that Maggie realized that however much she didn't want to, she was going to have to admit defeat.

There wasn't going to be a party of the kind she wanted, with or without Andy Blythe.

Maggie resisted the urge to slam out once again. 'I'll go and make the tea, like I said . . .'

On the following Saturday, the day of the family birthday party, Maggie stood with her arms crossed and a sullen expression on her face as Babs Wheaton watched impatiently out of the window.

'Quick, quick, they're here,' Babs said as a car turned slowly on to the drive. 'Come on, Maggie, let's go out and say hello to them all. Come on, now. Please show willing; they've come a long way to see you.'

She grabbed her daughter's hand and pulled her out of the door enthusiastically, leaving Maggie with little choice but to follow her out to greet the Riordan family, Ruby, Johnnie and their three sons, who were all there to help celebrate Maggie's upcoming sixteenth birthday.

'Ruby, darling, how lovely to see you,' Babs said as Ruby got out of the car. 'We're so glad you could all come. It's been too long since we last saw you.'

'Oh, tut tut, Aunty Babs, of course we came! Have we ever missed the chance to celebrate a family birthday yet?'

Babs smiled and instantly wrapped her arms around the younger woman, hugging her as affectionately as she always did, and as Maggie watched she felt the familiar feelings of jealousy rising up once again. It was always the same when

Ruby Riordan visited or when they visited her; Maggie just couldn't help feeling resentful when her mother acted as if Ruby was the prodigal offspring returning from far-off lands.

Despite having her own family, Ruby had always been seen as a member of the Wheaton family, and Maggie had always known her and loved her as if she was, but as she had got older she sometimes felt irrationally jealous of her in the way of sibling rivalry. As she watched the interaction between the two women she felt once again that Ruby was the favourite daughter, and she suddenly wanted to stamp her feet and tell Ruby what she thought of her. She wanted to tell her she was an intruder on a family occasion and that she didn't want her or her husband and children there.

But of course she didn't.

Instead she stood back with her arms folded defensively, trying her best to avoid eye contact and waiting for the inevitable effusive greeting from Ruby, her perceived older sister.

'And hello to you as well, Maggie. It's so nice to see you again.' Ruby smiled and headed over to her with her arms wide. 'Every time I see you, you look more grown up. Sixteen . . . How did the time fly by so fast?'

Maggie smiled back, but although her mouth smiled her eyes didn't, and at the same time she took another step away, deliberately avoiding the inevitable hug. She felt a twinge of guilt because deep down she knew focusing all her frustrations on to Ruby was unfair, but she wasn't in the mood to play happy families.

All she wanted was to be with Andy Blythe.

Ruby was an attractive woman who didn't look at all like a wife and mother in her thirties. She had thick auburn curls which were trying to escape from the fashionable French pleat at the back of her head, and she was casually dressed in bright-red pedal-pusher trousers and a white sweater that fitted where it touched. She was not dissimilar to Babs in both features and stature, although they weren't related and there were many years between them; both were tall and graceful with curvy waists and hips, and both had wide welcoming smiles for everyone. The two women could have easily passed for mother and daughter.

'I don't really know. How *did* time fly by so fast?' Maggie eventually responded with as much sarcasm as she dared.

As Maggie and Ruby stood opposite each other, almost in a stand-off, Babs Wheaton frowned fleetingly at her daughter, before making a big show of looking back at the Riordans' car, which was parked up on the driveway behind their own.

'And where are those boys?' Babs asked in a long drawn out high pitched voice, peering in the car window. 'I know they're in there somewhere . . .'

'I'm here.' Johnnie Riordan, Ruby's husband, laughed from the other side of the car as he stepped out of the driver's seat.

'Not you, you big silly! I'm looking for the little Riordans. Now, I know they're here somewhere . . .'

A child's head popped out from the car's rear door. 'Boo, Aunty Babs, I'm here!'

Again Babs Wheaton held out her arms, and the youngest boy, Russell, Ruby and Johnnie's five year old son, jumped in for a hug, followed closely by the two older boys, Martin and Paul, Ruby's stepsons, who were a little more formal and restrained in their greetings.

Maggie knew Johnnie Riordan would also make a beeline for her, but she didn't mind. She didn't feel the same sibling jealousy towards him as she did to Ruby; he was just her tall and handsome big brother with a ready smile and a laid-back personality who was always laughing and joking with everyone.

'Mags, me old darling!' he said as he leaned over to kiss her on the cheek. 'You're looking gorgeous as always. How's life been treating you?'

'OK I suppose,' she said with a hint of her first genuine smile that day.

'Good. We can have a chat later and you can tell me all about it. Whatever *it* is, of course.'

He winked and then turned back to the others. Maggie noticed that he then went over to his wife and put his arm around her shoulders and gave her a gentle, almost reassuring, hug. For a moment it looked as if Ruby was about to burst into tears, but instead she sniffed and smiled at him.

'I'm so pleased you're all here,' Babs said. 'George is dying to see you all again. It's just a shame Gracie couldn't make it too.

I haven't seen her or Fay for so long, and now she's likely to be going off abroad and leaving us all.'

Taking yet another step back, Maggie Wheaton rolled her eyes, puffed out her cheeks and sighed loudly. She saw Ruby frown and glance in her direction, but she didn't care; she simply sighed again and turned to walk back to the house.

As she walked ahead she could hear Ruby and her mother talking. She didn't look round, but she slowed her pace slightly and held her breath so she could hear their words.

'Is Maggie alright? She seems a bit . . . I don't know what the word is . . .' Ruby asked.

'Difficult? Rude? Sullen? You choose. She wanted a proper birthday party with friends and boys – one boy in particular, in fact – but we said no. She's sulking a bit and blaming everyone for her ill-fortune, but she'll come round. I'm sure we're doing the right thing. She's a good girl but still too young for boys – especially slightly older, overindulged boys.'

'Maybe . . .' Ruby said quietly. 'But she's growing up, and there's nothing as painful as first love, if that's what it is. It sends us all a bit mad. She'll be fine.'

'I hope so. It's hard for everyone, and I'm sorry she was rude to you. Youngsters today see everything so differently. They think they know everything, and they think they can do whatever they want. I do try to be understanding, but there's a limit.'

'Didn't we all know everything?' Ruby laughed and nudged Babs affectionately with her elbow as they carried on walking. 'I mean, I gave you a fair share of problems when I was her age, remember? More than a fair share, in fact!'

'Yes, I suppose you did, didn't you? I do forget about the different ages and phases. It seems so long ago; so much has happened since then.' Babs Wheaton fell silent for a few moments. 'Maybe I'm being a bit hard on her. She's never been any trouble to us before. It's my digging my heels in that's upset her, I think; I usually give in.'

'She'll get over it, I'm sure, and I'm big enough to take the bullets,' Ruby said with a slight jerk in her voice. 'She's a credit to you, and I don't think you could ever be hard Aunty Babs, even if you wanted to be, not really. Hard isn't in your nature!'

Ruby grinned at the older woman, who laughed and shook her head as they continued walking towards the back door arm in arm.

Maggie pretended not to hear but she seethed silently. She wanted to turn round and tell them exactly what she thought, how she hated the whole fake family thing, but, despite her rising anger, she knew that would be the wrong thing to do because her parents would never forgive her.

Ruby Riordan, formerly Blakeley, had been a part of the Wheaton family for all of Maggie's life and a part of George and Babs' life ever since, as a ten year old, Ruby had been evacuated from East London out to the country at the start of the war. The childless couple had welcomed the little girl with enthusiasm, and she had stayed with them for five years: a time during which a deep bond had been formed. All these years later, they still treated Ruby as one of their own.

As time had gone on they had welcomed Johnnie Riordan, Ruby's husband, and his two children from his previous marriage into the family fold, and when Ruby and Johnnie's son Russell had been born, everyone had been ecstatic and had gone out of their way to emphasize that they were all one big family.

Only, to Maggie's mind they *weren't* family. Sometimes she resented the way George and Babs Wheaton constantly sung their praises, and that particular Saturday was one of those times. She didn't want them there, she didn't want to be there herself, and she was resenting every moment of it already because they were moments she could have spent with Andy Blythe.

As they walked in through the back door which led straight into the large kitchen, the hub of the house, Ruby momentarily seemed miles away. Maggie watched surreptitiously as Ruby looked around and then gently ran her hand along the edge of the well-scrubbed, ageing pine table that dominated the room alongside the vast range where the kettle was simmering and several trays of cakes and scones were cooling. After a few moments she seemed to shake herself back to where she was.

'Now is there anything you want me to do?' Ruby asked. 'I'm here to help.'

Maggie wanted to say, *Yes, I want you to turn around and go home so I can go and see Andy.* But instead, desperate to get away from the gathering, she said to no one in particular, 'I'm going out to get Dad.'

'We'll come with you, Aunty Mags,' Russell shouted as he took hold of her hand leaving her with no choice but to head out into the garden to fetch her father with the three small boys in tow.

'Ruby and her mob are here,' she said as the boys ran over and clambered on him.

'Grandpa George, Grandpa George,' they all shouted at once.

'Hello boys.' He grinned back, but Maggie could see it was a struggle for him with three of them hanging off both his wheelchair and his neck.

'Come on, get off there! You'll break Grandpa's wheelchair if you're not careful,' she said after a few moments. Her tone was sharp, but she managed a smile alongside. 'We're going back inside now, and Grandpa's coming as well, so how about you all run on ahead and tell them we're on our way. You can check they're ready for us in the kitchen; tell Nana Babs to get that kettle boiling.'

The boys ran off, and her father looked at her and smiled. 'That was nice of you, Maggie. I know you're unhappy about all this, and it wasn't what you wanted for this birthday, but sometime we just have to grin and bear it. Your mother loves gathering everyone around her; it's just her way.'

'I know, but it's my birthday! I'm sixteen in a few days, and I should be able to do what I want for it.'

'I know, but you've got plenty more ahead of you when you can do what you like, so let's all enjoy this for what it is. Sometimes we have to put ourselves second on the want list. It's just one day, and it's making your mother happy, so put on your best smile. She's put you first often enough.'

Maggie looked down at her father and realized exactly how poorly he looked. His hair had all but disappeared, and his head was covered in liver spots; his once muscular shoulders were narrow and hunched; and his eyes were rheumy and bloodshot. Tucked up in his wheelchair, with a tartan rug wrapped around his paralysed legs, he looked really old, and it saddened her.

'I'm sorry,' she said. 'I just get so jealous of Ruby being the favourite.'

'I know you think that, but she's not, and deep down you know it too. Your mother has more than enough love to go round, so chin up, my beautiful girl. Get me to the fray right now – I'm in the mood for a party!'

He laughed, and Maggie couldn't help but join in. She loved her mother deeply, but her relationship with her ever kind and gentle father had always been something extra special.

'OK, let's go,' Maggie said as she pushed the wheelchair down the garden path back to the house.

Once everyone was together back in the kitchen, they settled down around the table the way they always had, with George and Babs seated at either end and everyone else grouped around on either side. Laid out were cups of tea and chunks of home-made fruit cake, the traditional starter to Maggie's birthday celebration, and from then on the day progressed exactly as Maggie had anticipated and, for the first time, dreaded, but every so often she would catch her father's eye and he'd wink, reminding her to smile and enjoy the day for what it was.

Babs had arranged her usual open house style party with a buffet laid out in the garden. On one side a trestle table bowed under the weight of the food, while on the other side there was a table with the drinks, which was manned by a rota of adults to keep the youngsters in check.

The weather had been kind, and the sun shone brightly in a clear blue sky. Everything was perfect for a garden party, and at lunchtime the first non-family guests started to arrive, and from then on there was a steady stream of guests, some who were just dropping in and others who were obviously there for the duration and the sherry. Maggie knew every single person who came through the door, and she greeted them all politely as they handed over birthday cards and gifts, but she still resented what she saw as the hijacking of what should have been her day with her friends.

And Andy Blythe.

From the moment Andy had cycled off, Maggie had hung around the house waiting expectantly and had rushed to the hall every time the phone rang, but it was never him. So the day before the party she had written him a short note explaining that the party in the evening had been cancelled because of her father's ill-health. Worried he wouldn't get it in time she'd sought out the Manor House gardener, who also maintained the garden at the surgery, and asked him to hand deliver the carefully sealed envelope, preferably to Andy himself. She'd written her phone number across the top, but still he hadn't rung.

Maggie got through the day as best she could, but still she was distracted; she simply couldn't get the young man out of her mind.

She was hopelessly in love.

Three

Babs Wheaton looked both ways as she carefully turned off the winding country lane which led out of the village of Melton, on to the main road which went directly into Cambridge. It was Monday, Maggie's actual birthday, but she was still sulking about the party. All she'd wanted to do was to forget about it and hang around the tennis club in the hope of seeing Andy, in the hope that he might appear with a birthday card, but her mother had insisted on the day out.

'So have you decided what new clothes you want?' Babs asked. 'Wasn't it good of Ruby and Johnnie to give you money on top of your present? And the watch they gave you is beautiful; why aren't you wearing it?'

'She probably didn't want to risk losing it. The strap is a wee bit too big . . .' George said quickly, his tone conciliatory. 'Actually, we could have got it altered in Cambridge. Very silly of us not to think of it.'

Maggie didn't respond to either of them. Instead, she looked down and tried to avoid eye contact with her mother, who kept glancing at her in the rear-view mirror.

'Come on now, you must have something in mind, Maggie. It's a lot of money, and you could buy some really nice, fashionable clothes – I know you're fed up with me making things for you – or even a nice piece of jewellery to keep. A necklace, maybe . . .'

'Well, I don't have anything in mind, I don't know what I want and I wish you'd stop going on about it. I'll see when we get there. I have got other money to spend, not just Ruby's.' Childishly, she turned her head and stared out of the window, defiantly determined not to get into conversation.

'I know you have, and you got so many lovely presents. I really don't think you should cut off your nose to spite your face, so enjoy the day out and your birthday money. I don't think you realize exactly how lucky you are, young lady,' Babs said, her tone still relatively genial.

When her mother had suggested that they spend her actual birthday in Cambridge, a combination of a family lunch in a restaurant followed by a shopping expedition for her and Babs while George went off to meet an old friend from medical school, Maggie had agreed. But now they were actually on their way she was torn; she had liked the idea of a family day out with her parents to herself, but she also wanted to be wherever Andy Blythe might be, and that wouldn't be Cambridge.

Because of his disability, the result of polio as a child, George couldn't drive. When he had been a practising GP, he'd had a driver to help him on his rounds and drive the family around when necessary, but now he was retired it was Babs who did all the driving. Not that she minded, especially in the new pale-blue Mercedes, her pride and joy, which was big and comfortable with soft leather seats and plenty of room in the boot for George's wheelchair. They'd had great fun when they'd chosen it a couple of months previously; they had all gone together to the showroom, and although Babs and George had decided on the make of car, they had let Maggie choose the colour. It had been a lovely day, but that had been before Andy and Maggie's infatuation with him.

Now the car was of no interest to her at all.

'Come on, Maggie, this is really very ungrateful of you,' Babs said. 'You've got the chance of a shopping spree thanks to Ruby, and all you can do is sulk like a spoilt child. I'm disappointed in you; this should be a lovely day for us all.'

'I said thank you to her. What more do you want?'

'A little gratitude and a lot more good manners is what I want and expect from you. You weren't brought up to behave like this to anyone, let alone your nearest and dearest.'

'But they're not my nearest and dearest, so why should I treat them like they are?' She glared at her mother in the rear-view mirror. 'All hail Queen Ruby of Southend . . .' She mumbled the last words under her breath, but it was just loud enough for her parents in the front to hear.

'We heard that, and that's enough,' George said. 'You're not being fair at all.'

'I don't care.' Maggie slid back down the seat, her arms still wrapped around her chest defiantly.

'I'm getting to the point of turning the car around and going straight back home,' Babs said sharply. 'You're spoiling the day before it's even started. I don't understand why you're being like this!'

'Good. Let's go home then.'

'Oh, do stop it, Maggie, please, you're distracting your mother,' George said mildly, glancing round at his daughter slumped in the back seat.

At the same time Babs looked over her shoulder to remonstrate with her daughter again, but the combination of the new, powerful car and her anger at her daughter's behaviour made her lose her driving concentration for just long enough for the car to veer across the road, clip an oncoming vehicle and then roll into a shallow ditch at the side of the road. The car then bounced and flipped on to its side, smashing the roof against the brick wall of a farmhouse that edged the ditch.

The whole thing happened so quickly that although Maggie was aware of being thrown around inside the car like a rag doll, she was unable to stop herself. Terrified and disorientated, she screamed as she tumbled around. She heard the crunching of metal on stones, the hissing of hot water escaping, and screaming, a lot of screaming, but it all came from far away.

And then came an excruciating pain in her head and neck followed by the silence of blackness.

As she regained consciousness Maggie blinked hard in her confusion and then opened her eyes wide to see a fuzzy image of someone sitting at her bedside; she could also feel them holding her hand tightly.

'Maggie . . .'

Maggie rolled her eyes around in her head trying to focus on the source of the voice.

'Oh, thank God, you're awake. We were so worried about you! We thought we might lose you. Maggie, Maggie . . . Johnnie, call the nurse, tell her she's awake.'

Still confused, Maggie blinked again so that she could see properly and tried to look around to get her bearings. She realized that Ruby was at her bedside; then, as she rolled her eyes again, she saw that Johnnie was on the other side. She couldn't actually turn her head, which she realized was constrained within a neck brace, and she felt as if her arms and legs were weighted down; it was a strange sensation, and she felt as if none of her body parts were connected.

'What happened?' she asked. 'Where am I?' As she spoke, she realized that her tongue felt as if it was far too big for her mouth, and as she moved it around she could feel a strange gap and realized that she was missing some teeth on one side of her mouth.

'My teeth! What happened to my teeth? I've lost my teeth,' she said quietly as tears formed large in the corners of her eyes before rolling slowly down the side of her face. As she blinked them away, her eyes flicked around the room in disorientated panic, and she saw a nurse standing on the foot of the bed holding a clipboard. She started to recollect what had happened, and a sense of impending doom washed over her; she knew something bad was going on. She was lying immobile in a hospital bed, Ruby and Johnnie were at her bedside and there was a nurse in the room, but her parents weren't anywhere to be seen. She scanned round the room as best she could to make sure, but neither of them was there with her. He heart started to pound in her chest, and she knew she was going to be sick.

'You're in hospital, my dear. There was an accident, and you've been hurt. You have to lie still. You have a head and neck injury – we don't think it's serious – but that's why you mustn't move your head at the moment,' the nurse said gently. 'Can you remember what happened?'

Maggie closed her eyes, and as soon as she did so the accident was there, being replayed in front of her, first in snippets and then the scene in slow motion. She remembered it all too well. There had been a terrible car crash on the way to Cambridge. The car had gone off the road, and it was her fault because she had been throwing a tantrum and had distracted her mother and made her lose control of the new, more powerful car.

As she closed her eyes she could again hear the squealing of brakes, the terrible crunching of metal and the screaming from both her parents and herself.

'I'm going to be sick,' she cried.

Ruby pushed a small metal bowl under the side of her face, allowing Maggie to vomit fiercely without sitting up.

'I don't know what's going on,' she sobbed as Ruby wiped her mouth. 'Where are they? Where're Mum and Dad?'

As her voice changed and her speech quickened in panic, she caught the look that the couple exchanged and tried to work out what was happening; she wondered how much trouble she was in and whether either of her parents had told them the accident was her fault.

'How much do you remember, Maggie?' Ruby asked. 'You've been unconscious since yesterday! We were so worried about you. You've got concussion and a broken arm and lots of cuts and bruises, but you're alive, thank God.'

'My teeth? How many teeth have I lost?'

'I'm not sure,' Ruby said shaking her head. 'Maybe three, but that can be easily fixed as soon a dentist sees you. But Uncle George and Aunty Babs . . . your mum and dad . . .' The tears started to fall down Ruby's face.

'Where are they?' Maggie interrupted. 'Why aren't they here? Are they OK? They were both in the car; we were going to Cambridge for the day. I was going to spend my birthday money. We were going out to lunch.'

Feeling disorientated and nauseous, she blinked her eyes rapidly as she threw the words out, and she tried unsuccessfully to sit up. The nurse put her hand on her shoulder and stayed her on the hospital bed.

'Maggie, I'm so sorry, it was a terrible, terrible accident and they didn't survive the crash. They both died in the car,' Ruby sobbed, taking her hand. 'It was instant for them. You were lucky because you were in the back away from the windscreen. The police are going to need to talk to you about it, but we thought it was better if you heard it from us rather than them.'

Maggie said nothing as she closed her eyes and tried to wish herself somewhere else, anywhere else but in the middle of the nightmare that was unfolding.

Her parents were dead, and it was her fault. She remembered exactly what had happened, she remembered every second of it, up until the final spin of the car against the wall when she was knocked out.

'Maggie? Speak to me. I know this is a terrible shock, but you're very lucky that you came out of it without any serious injury.'

But still she said nothing.

'How did it happen?' Johnnie asked. 'Was it a fox or something? Did something run out and your mum try to avoid it?'

'I don't know. I was asleep in the back . . .' she lied.

Ruby stood up and let go of Maggie's hand. 'We'll be back in a minute.' She pulled a handful of tissues from the box on the bedside cabinet and wiped her eyes. 'We're just going to talk to the doctor.'

Maggie kept her eyes squeezed shut. She didn't want to open them and face what had happened.

'Oh God, it was all my fault, my fault,' she murmured as they left the room, but neither Ruby nor Johnnie heard her.

Once the door to the single room clicked shut, Maggie tried hard to get her thoughts into order; she wanted to think the situation through before they came back. A huge wave of guilt and self-hatred enveloped her as she realized the enormity of what she had done. She couldn't blame anyone but herself for the situation she was in because the accident was all her fault.

Her stupid childish behaviour had killed her parents.

She tried to turn over, but it was impossible with the neck brace, so she settled for lying motionless and silent. She didn't want to be awake when Ruby and Johnnie came back into the room. Knowing what she knew, she didn't want to have to face them, and neither did she want to face her own uncertain future.

Maggie Wheaton just wanted to go to sleep and never wake up again.

'She's not cried yet, you know, and she's not said anything about Babs and George. She's just fretting about her teeth,' Ruby said, pacing back and forth in the hospital corridor while Johnnie sat perfectly still on one of the chairs outside the doors to the ward where Maggie was being treated. 'I don't understand . . .'

'Yes, you do; it's just shock and denial. It's easier to focus on the small things than it is to face up to the bloody horror of what's happened. Can you imagine how the poor kid must be feeling? She's lost both parents in a split second, and she's having to mentally adjust to that, as well as having her own injuries to contend with.' Johnnie got up from the chair and stood in front of his wife. He put his hands on her shoulder. 'Bloody hell, Rube, think about it. Of course she's going to concentrate on something small; the whole thing is too much for her. For all her bravado she's still only sixteen, and it all happened on her bloody birthday. She's never going to be able to have a happy birthday again, poor kid.'

'Well, of course I understand all that; do you really think I'm that stupid that I don't know what's going on with her?' Ruby snapped back sharply as she roughly pushed him away. 'I just don't understand why she's not saying anything at all, not asking anything about the accident. It's been nearly a week; if she can't remember then surely she'd want to know what happened? She didn't even react when we told her about the young man in the other car. Poor bugger nearly lost his leg, and she doesn't seem to understand.'

'Of course she doesn't; she's in shock. Give her time to get it together in her own head, and then she'll be able to talk about it. But it may take a long time, and in the meantime . . .' His voice trailed off as she stared again at the doors to the ward.

'Oh, Johnnie, Johnnie, what are we going to do? We have to take her home with us, but then what do we tell her? I just don't know what to do for the best, for her sake, for everyone's sake; there are the boys to think about.'

'Let's play it by ear for the moment. It's early days, and when they say she can go home, when she's recuperated, then we can decide what to do next. We mustn't rush into anything.' Johnnie Riordan took his wife's hand. 'Come on, let's go back in and see if she's awake. We're all she's got now.'

'I still haven't told Gracie,' Ruby said as they walked back to the main doors to the ward. 'I didn't want to spoil her holiday, but I have to let her know before the funeral . . .' She paused, and the tears welled up again. 'How are we going to arrange that? When Leonora died, George and Babs did it all. I don't know what to do.'

'We'll go back to Melton after we leave here and talk to the vicar,' Johnnie said, his tone gentle and reassuring. 'George and Babs were a part of that village and went to the church; we'll ask all about it then. There's plenty of time. Maggie has to be our main concern now.'

Ruby suddenly dissolved into floods of tears. 'I can't believe this has happened. I'm going to miss them so much! They were just like parents to me, they did everything for me, and now they're gone . . .'

Johnnie Riordan put his arms around his wife and hugged her close. 'I know, and you have to mourn them as well as look after Maggie, but we'll manage. We always have.' He pulled his wife close and kissed the top of her head.

'But there's so much to do, both up here and in Southend,' Ruby continued. 'I don't know where to start.'

'We'll start by getting through today . . . Now, let's get back to Maggie. For all her pretence she's a child who's lost her parents. The change in her life is going to be bloody awful.' He paused and looked at his wife. 'It's going to be bloody awful for everyone.'

One of the benefits of living in a small village was that everyone knew everyone else and in times of need they all rallied round. The downside for young Maggie Wheaton was there were people around all the time who meant well but who were always asking questions she didn't want to hear let alone answer. All she wanted was be alone with her sorrow and her guilt.

But it wasn't happening.

When Ruby and Johnnie had brought her home from hospital after ten days, Maggie was still wearing a small neck brace and her arm was immobile in a plaster of Paris cast, but the stitches in her head wound had been removed just before her discharge. Apart from her missing teeth she was physically in one piece and was recovering well, which was a miracle in itself, considering the crash had taken the lives of Babs and George.

However, she was not recovering mentally. She was confused and angry and completely enveloped in guilt. The sights and the sounds of the crash were with her every time she closed her eyes; she had no respite from the nightmares and no respite from her guilt.

The police had formally declared the accident to have been just that, an accident; no one had seen exactly what happened, George and Babs had both perished and Maggie had reiterated that she couldn't remember a thing about it. When the car was found to have no faults and it was proven the road had been clear and dry, the conclusion was that it had been caused by Babs swerving to avoid an animal running out in front of the car and losing control.

It was the obvious conclusion to everyone, as it had happened at a stretch of the road where foxes often darted from one side to the other, oblivious to traffic on the road.

It was a terrible accident, and case closed.

But it wasn't closed for young Maggie Wheaton. It never would be because she knew what had happened and that it was all her fault.

Ruby had moved into the Wheaton home in Melton temporarily to look after her, and to try and deal with the injured and grieving youngster as well as the family affairs, but it was hard because at the same time Johnnie had to go back and forth between Melton and Southend as often as he could.

It was a fine line for Ruby and Johnnie Riordan to tread because, despite their concerns and fears for Maggie, they owned two busy seafront hotels in Southend and the month of May was the start of the busiest season for them. However, Ruby's best friend Gracie Woodfield, who'd been on holiday in Cornwall, was due to arrive back that evening and had promised to help out with the business and the children, freeing them to concentrate on Maggie.

But Maggie didn't want their attention; she didn't want attention from anyone. All she wanted was to be left alone with her misery. Everyone who visited, from close family friends to the milkman, told Maggie how grateful she should be to Ruby and Johnnie, that there was so much to do and arrange that she could never have coped on her own, but it didn't make her feel any differently; Maggie resented what she saw as outsiders taking over everything, including Maggie herself.

Ruby was around every minute of the day, fussing and caring for her, talking to her, preparing her meals, and acting as gatekeeper to the many visitors who wanted to pay their respects. As a priority she had arranged for a dentist to make a temporary denture to fill the gaps where Maggie's teeth had been knocked out, and she had taken control of the everyday things that Maggie, as a sixteen year old, had no idea about. The nurse from the surgery attached to the house kept popping in to check on her wounds and well-being, and the doctor had given her a mild sedative to help her sleep at night. Everything was being done for her by so many people, but there was no one she could confide in about her part in the accident.

She couldn't tell anyone about the guilt that was consuming her.

'Maggie?' Ruby called. 'Where are you? I have to go into town to talk to the solicitor about some odds and ends; there's paperwork to deal with. Do you want to come?' She paused, but there was only silence. 'Maggie?'

When there was still no answer, Ruby went looking and found Maggie curled up in a ball on the bed in her mother's bedroom with a long pale-pink winceyette nightdress hugged close to her. Because it had all been so sudden, everything in the house was the same as when the family had climbed into the Mercedes on Maggie's birthday and headed off to Cambridge.

The nightie was the one Babs had been wearing the night before the accident, and Maggie had found it neatly folded under her pillow. She could still smell the lingering scent of her favourite perfume, Tweed, the newest bottle of which stood central on her dressing table, a gift from George the previous Christmas.

Ruby walked across the room and sat on the bed alongside

Maggie. She sat there a few moments before lying down next to her and putting her arms around her. The young girl fought against her and tried her best to pull away, but Ruby held on to her regardless and soothed her until she felt her relax.

'I'm so sorry, Maggie,' Ruby said as she loosened her hold but still kept her arms around her. 'If there was any way I could change all this, I would. I can't believe it either. Aunty Babs and Uncle George were like parents to me; they treated me as their own and helped me at the worst time in my life. I'm devastated, and I know it's ten times worse for you.'

'You don't know how it is for me! You've no idea how I feel. It was all my fault . . .' As soon as the words were out, Maggie regretted them.

'Of course it wasn't your fault. It was an accident, something that could have happened to anyone. It wasn't anybody's fault. Maybe a squirrel or a fox ran across the road? That's what the police think, and even the poor man in the other car said it could have been something like that.'

'I was being rude to her. I distracted her . . .'

'And not for the first time, I doubt,' Ruby said, smiling sadly. 'You mustn't blame yourself darling, you mustn't.'

'But—'

'No buts. It was an accident, and sadly accidents happen all the time to lots of innocent people.'

Maggie lay there quietly. Her instinct was to push Ruby away, but there was something comforting about being wrapped in her arms. After a few minutes Ruby sat up.

'I'm sorry, Maggie, but I have to go and see the damned solicitor. There's so much to arrange, and I don't know where to start. Are you coming with me?'

'No. I'll stay here. Alison said she'd come round, so I'll be fine,' Maggie lied easily.

'I'll be as quick as I can,' Ruby said. 'There's still some final funeral details we need to go over together before tomorrow. We'll talk about it when I get back.'

'OK.'

Maggie waited until she heard Ruby's car pull away, and then she ran to her room. She pulled on a clean skirt and jumper, ran a brush through her hair and headed on foot out of the village towards the Manor House.

She was determined to see Andy Blythe, and if he wasn't going to visit her – which he patently wasn't – then she was going to try and find him.

Four

Ruby was puffing and panting as she threw open the door to the solicitor's office and went straight up to the vast old desk that dominated the small reception area. She caught her breath as she waited patiently for several seconds before the fierce-looking woman perched on a typing chair behind it looked up from her machine and frowned. Her upright demeanour and formal two-piece tweed suit reminded Ruby of Leonora Wheaton, George's late sister.

'I'm Mrs Ruby Riordan. I've got an appointment with Mr Smethurst. I know I'm a bit late, but I got lost in town. I had the wrong street in mind and then missed your car park. I don't know how it happened.'

'Mr Smethurst is expecting you. If you go through I'll let him know you've arrived at last,' the woman said brusquely, completely ignoring Ruby's apology. 'His office is at the end of the passage. His name is on the door; I'm sure you can't miss that.'

Ruby went out into a small dark corridor and took a few steps to the correct door, but as she reached her hand out to the brass doorknob, the door was opened sharply from the other side.

'Good day, Mrs Riordan – Ruby.' The man held his hand out to her and smiled.

'Good day to you too; you must be Mr Smethurst Senior,' Ruby replied, taking his hand. 'It's nice to meet you in person. I've heard a lot about you over the years, but up until now I've only ever met your son.'

'Bertie is away on holiday in Italy or Switzerland or somewhere in that direction – who knows if he's where he said he was going . . .' The man looked puzzled for a moment. 'But anyway, as a result I'm temporarily shunning my early retirement and hopping back into the saddle, so to speak, to help out. I'm sure you'd sooner have someone who knows the family.'

'I would, thank you; we appreciate it,' Ruby said.

'It's unfortunate that it's under such sad circumstances that we're finally meeting,' the elderly man continued. 'I'm shocked, my dear, truly shocked at such a terrible turn of events. Who would ever have thought it?'

'I know. I still can't believe it. It's awful for all of us, but especially unbearable for Maggie. She's only just turned sixteen, and now she's an orphan.'

'You're right, it's awful, awful, but at least she still has you.' He smiled sympathetically and put his hand on her back to guide her across the room.

Ruby felt relieved that she wouldn't have to go over everything with someone else. Herbert Smethurst had been the Wheatons' solicitor right up to his retirement and had remained a family friend, but Ruby had only ever seen his son, Herbert Junior, who also worked at the family firm. The junior Smethurst had taken the helm a few years previously, although his father still stayed involved on the periphery. The son was tall, sporty and ruggedly good-looking, so it was a shock for Ruby to find that Herbert Senior stood a good head shorter than herself and was as round as he was short, with a narrow edging of crazy grey hair around a shiny bald pate. His tweed jacket, which didn't meet around his rotund middle, had definitely seen better days, and his faded yellow tie was all askew, but he had the same wide smile and kindly eyes as his son, which put Ruby at her ease.

She sat down on the well-worn leather captain's chair that he indicated and waited while he rounded the desk and then shuffled through the papers on his desk.

The room was spacious and airy, but it was filled with bookcases, and there were several chairs around his desk bearing Manila files tied with pink tape. It was a crowded but neat working space that reminded Ruby of how Aunt Leonora's office used to be when she had first gone to live at the hotel.

'The Smethursts aren't best known for tidiness . . . Aha! Here we are,' he said as he pulled a file out from amid the organized chaos. 'This is the relevant one.'

'I can't stay long today,' Ruby said apologetically. 'I've left Maggie at home on her own. She has a friend coming round, and she didn't want to come with me to see you. I did ask her . . .'

'Probably best she didn't. She's too young to hear all the legal mumbo-jumbo from an old man who's not used to the young folk of today. Best coming from someone who knows her and loves her to start with. Someone like you, my dear.' He fumbled around a little longer and then pulled a long envelope from the folder. 'Here we are. The wills. I knew I'd put them somewhere safe in readiness. Now, I'm sure you've seen this already—?'

'No, I haven't. I've brought the locked box file that was in Uncle George's office cabinet . . . I remember them saying that everything was together in case of an emergency, but I never expected this. I couldn't find a key for it, and I didn't want to break into it. It seems so intrusive.' Ruby passed him the large metal box, but he simply put it on the floor.

'I've probably got everything here,' he replied, 'but I think we're going to have to force the box open just to be sure. But not right now. I'm sure that can wait until after the funeral. Now we shall deal with the wills, unless you want a formal reading of them after the funeral?'

'No, no, I can't put Maggie through that! Just tell me. I need to know what I have to do for her and how to do it. I know she wants to stay in that house somehow, but that can't happen. She's too young, and I have so much to try and do before I go back home. It would be different if we didn't have three young boys and two hotels, and I need to know if there were requests for their funerals, and . . .' The words tumbled out as she tried her best not to cry. 'And then there's the—'

'It's OK, my dear, I do understand,' he cut in kindly as her eyes filled. 'I'll keep it informal. We'll go through the contents of the wills, and then I'll give you copies to take away with you. Everything else will take time to get into order. Their passing was unexpected; George always thought he would be the first to go.'

Ruby could feel her throat start to itch, so she swallowed hard to keep the tears from rising again.

'Did they not discuss their wills with you?' he asked.

'Not really; I know provisions were made for Maggie . . .

But, go on,' she said, not trusting herself to say anything else. She just wanted to get it over with so she could go back to Maggie.

'We'll make another appointment for after the funeral, by which time I'll have had time to assess the situation properly and do some sums, but in the meantime these are the last wills and testaments of both George and Barbara Wheaton.' He handed her several pages, and then he went through them with her.

The more he explained, the further her heart sank.

'Oh God, what am I going to do, Mr Smethurst? I can't put all this at her door right now! Can't it wait until she's twenty-one and able to make her own decisions?'

'Not according to the wording here. I know George and Babs weren't anticipating something like this when they drew the documents up – none of us ever think about joint deaths; it's just a precaution – but it's happened, and I have to execute their wills as directed. That means I have to share the contents with all the beneficiaries, yourself and Maggie being the main interested parties. I'm sorry.'

Ruby's worst nightmare was coming true. It was something she knew would happen one day, but now the wording and contents of the wills meant that, however much she didn't want to, Ruby had no choice but to tell Maggie the truth about her life and parentage right away.

A truth that would rip her world apart at the most vulnerable time in her young life.

On the day of the funeral, Maggie was sitting perfectly still on the wide window seat in her bedroom, just watching and waiting. She'd been there for over an hour.

The early summer sky was overcast and cloudy, but the air was as still and quiet as Maggie herself. As she peered out at the scene below, she prayed for rain, a deluge with thunder and lightning, which to her mind would be the only suitable weather for the day on which she was going to have to say her final goodbyes to her parents.

A large number of villagers were already lined up on the pavements outside on both sides of the high street, many of whom had been standing there for longer than Maggie had been sitting at the window. There were people she had known all her life, but there were also some elderly strangers from the outlying villages and farms who George Wheaton had treated in his many years as a GP. They had been chatting among themselves up to that point, but in an instant the street fell eerily silent and Maggie knew the moment had come.

The hearses were making their way to the house, bang on time.

All the male bystanders, young and old, removed their hats, and every single person edging the pavements bowed their head as the shiny black funeral hearses crept up the road almost silently before rolling to a halt outside the house. As they stopped, Maggie stood up and pulled the lace curtains back on the wire so that she had a clear view of the two glass-sided hearses which held two simple coffins.

The coffins which contained the bodies of her parents, George and Barbara Wheaton.

There were family wreaths and tributes already in the vehicles both on top and around the coffins, and there were dozens lined all along both sides of the path from the road to the front door which people had been delivering respectfully all morning.

Maggie felt strangely detached as she watched the undertakers step out of the cars in unison and form a guard of honour on the path where they stood, hands crossed in front of them and heads formally bowed. Then one of them stepped away and walked up to the house to knock formally on the front door, even though everyone had seen the cortège arrive.

It was time for George and Barbara Wheaton to leave their home for the last time.

The church was in the centre of the village, so the decision had been made that the mourners would all walk in procession behind the hearses to the church with Ruby and Maggie leading, Johnnie, Gracie and her husband Edward behind, and the close friends of the family following on, while the mourners lining the road would join the procession at the back.

Everything had been precision arranged by Ruby and the vicar to be as fitting as possible for the couple who had always been such a huge and important part of the village life while also taking into account Maggie's feelings and wishes as chief mourner.

Ruby and Johnnie had been to the chapel of rest in the nearby town to view the bodies for the final time before the coffins were closed, but Maggie had refused point blank to go. She had also refused to have them back to the house overnight; she could imagine nothing worse than having to look at the faces of her beloved parents knowing that she would never see them again and also knowing that it was she who had caused them to be lying there.

But now, as she looked at the matching coffins in identical hearses, she tried to imagine her parents lying inside, but she found she couldn't picture their faces. She simply couldn't imagine what they, her beloved mum and dad, would look like in death, especially after such a horrendous car crash.

As she continued to look out of the window she felt a strange detachment from the situation wash over her; she switched off and just waited for the knock on the door from Ruby or Johnnie to call her down.

She climbed from the window seat, straightened her clothes and slipped her shoes on before glancing at herself in the mirror one last time; her previously slender body, clad from top to toe in black, was now thin and, with her long blonde hair pulled back from her face and topped with a small black hat, she looked older than her sixteen years. But at that moment she didn't really care what she looked like so long as she was, as everyone kept saying, neat and tidy.

'Maggie? Maggie, darling, it's time to go . . .' Ruby was knocking on the door, and Maggie knew she was waiting on the other side, but she needed just a few more moments to compose herself.

'I know,' she answered. 'I was looking out of the window. I'll be down in a minute. I'll see you down there.'

Maggie picked up the black leather handbag that was ready on the bed; it was the last in a long line of Babs Wheaton's famous Sunday bags. Every year, just before Easter, Babs Wheaton would buy a new handbag especially for the Easter Sunday church service.

'I don't have an Easter bonnet any more, but I do have an Easter handbag,' she'd say, laughing, when George went into his ritual of rolling his eyes and saying: 'Not another one . . .'

She would use the handbag every Sunday throughout the year, and then, the following Easter when a new bag was purchased, it would be demoted to everyday use. It was a family ritual that they had always laughed about, so Maggie knew she just *had* to use it that day as a mark of respect and to keep her mother close.

Inside, there was a small lace handkerchief her mother had sprayed with Tweed, a phial of smelling salts, an enamelled powder compact and a Revlon lipstick. In the purse pocket were some coins her mother had already put there for the church collection.

Maggie had kept the bag exactly as she had found it on the top shelf in her mother's wardrobe. She had added nothing of her own and was as ready as she would ever be to carry it to church on her mother's behalf. She held the bag up to her nose and savoured the smell of her mother on the polished leather and opened it once again to check the contents to reassure herself that everything was there. She had initially wanted the bag to go into the coffin with her mother, to keep her company, but at the last minute she knew she couldn't part with it; she had to take it with her.

She opened the bedroom door and calmly made her way down to the lobby where everyone was waiting for her, as chief mourner, to lead the procession down to the village church. As she reached the bottom of the stairs, the waiting vicar grabbed both her hands, murmured a few words and smiled sympathetically, before turning and walking slowly out of the door first.

Ruby then took Maggie's hand in hers and, almost in unison, they both breathed in and out deeply before stepping out of the front door and following the vicar down the path to the road and the waiting hearses.

They stood for a few moments alongside the hearses and bowed their heads in respect before walking to the rear of them. The high street was closed to traffic so that the two hearses could make their way side by side instead of one behind the other, and as soon as the vicar was ready, along with Maggie and Ruby, the vehicles pulled away almost in slow motion. Swelling with mourners along the way, the procession wended its way through the village where George and Babs had lived for so long, the village they had both served and loved so much.

As they walked oh so slowly, Maggie tried to think of other things to stop herself from crying. It seemed as if the walk that they had all done so many times from the surgery down to the church in the centre of the village would never end. Her heart missed a beat when she saw Andy Blythe standing at the side of the road with a group from the tennis club; she wanted to run over and fall into his arms, but she didn't even make eye contact. She knew if she did she would fall apart.

Then after what seemed forever they arrived at the gated archway to the village church and graveyard. It took a while for the mourners to fill the church, leaving many standing outside.

Again detaching herself from the situation, Maggie wondered if those outside were all going to stand around or if they would drift off once the service started inside. There were so many people there, most of whom had closed their shops and business for the procession; she also wondered if Andy would go straight home or if he'd wait for them to come out.

Ruby's grip on her hand tightened, and Maggie knew it was the moment she would have to follow her parents into the familiar church, which suddenly felt frighteningly alien and claustrophobic.

'It'll be OK,' Ruby said as she squeezed Maggie's hand even tighter. 'It'll be OK, I promise. We're all here with you . . .'

The mournful sound of the organ was audible from outside, and then as the vicar moved ahead to lead them in the choir started to hum very quietly.

She didn't want to go in, she wanted to turn and run and keep running, but Maggie Wheaton knew what she had to do out of respect for her parents, so she forced one foot forward and started the second slow walk, doing her best to focus on the music.

She had been an integral part of that same choir for so many years and had sung at numerous weddings and funerals, but she had always been there as a singer. Now she was the principal mourner and her voice was silent.

As they took their places in the front pew, Maggie knew that whatever happened she could never sing in that choir again.

'Dearly beloved, we are gathered here . . .'

The service seemed to go on forever, and Maggie was finding it increasingly hard to keep her attention away from it all. She thought about the choir, the flowers and the number of people who had turned out, including Andy Blythe. Then the service was over and the procession started again, this time to the far corner of the churchyard where the joint graves were ready and waiting for George and Barbara Wheaton.

As the graveside service continued, Maggie was feeling sick and light-headed. She didn't cry, she couldn't, but she had to fight the waves of nausea. She opened the handbag, pulled out the smelling salts and slowly inhaled the released wave of ammonia from the crystals, the way she had seen her mother do so many times in the past.

'It's over now, Mags; the worst of the day is over,' Johnnie said as he took her by the shoulders and turned her away from the adjoining open graves that now contained the coffins. 'Come with me, and I'll get you a cup of tea and a biscuit. You're as white as the plaster on your arm.'

He helped her back across the churchyard and into the church hall, which was already prepared for the funeral reception, and led her to a nearby chair. He turned to his wife. 'Rubes, you and Gracie need to welcome them all in. Maggie's not up to it; it's too much for her. You go, and I'll look after her.'

But no sooner were the words out than Maggie, with the smelling salts still in her hand, leaned forward to put her head on her knees, but instead she carried right on until she hit the floor in a cold faint.

As those nearby grouped around in panic, tending to her, Ruby alone stepped back and looked away; her expression was blank, her grieving mind elsewhere.

As a child, Ruby had been one of the group of evacuees

from a Walthamstow school who had been dropped off in Melton to be billeted with local families. Standing in the same hall on such an emotional day brought it all back to her; once again she could smell the hot chocolate and chunky home-baked biscuits which had been doled out to each child, and she recalled again her meeting with Barbara Wheaton, the woman who was going to be such an integral part of her life.

Ruby looked around, and she was there again; she could clearly see Babs Wheaton standing in front of her smiling encouragingly, and once again she wondered what path her life would have taken if a different person had picked her from the line-up of children of all ages, back in 1940 . . .

'Come along with me dear.' The woman smiled down at the small child whose eyes were focused absolutely on her feet. 'Come on, there's no need to be afraid; you're going to stay with us for a while, just until London is safe again, and then you can go home.' She held her gloved hand out. 'Come along. I don't bite, you know; really, I don't.'

Ten-year-old Ruby Blakeley slowly raised her eyes and, knowing she had no choice, she reluctantly picked up her small suitcase. She let the woman take her by her other hand, and together they walked up Melton High Street to the doctor's surgery at the top of the hill where the woman, Barbara Wheaton, lived with her husband George, the village GP.

Ruby Blakeley had never known such fear; she was petrified to the point of wanting to drop dead then and there to make it all go away. When she had been told she was going to be evacuated, she had cried and shouted and fought against being sent away from the family home in Walthamstow, the only home she'd ever known, but it had all been in vain. Everyone agreed it was best if she was out of London and safely away from the war, which was quickly escalating. She didn't understand why she had to go and her three older brothers were being allowed to stay behind and carry on their lives as normal, but there was no arguing; she didn't have any choice. Ruby Blakeley was to be evacuated.

'Look,' Barbara Wheaton said as they walked along together, 'this is the village church which my husband and I go to every Sunday without fail, and these are the shops. There's everything we need here, but if we want anything else we can go into the next town either on the bus or in the car – petrol permitting, of course.'

Babs Wheaton laughed, and it was such a natural, friendly sound that it comforted Ruby just a little, but still she feared where she was going.

'I know it probably looks a little cramped to you after living in London, but it's a friendly village and it's very safe. There are lots of children around these parts, and you'll meet them all when you go to the school. Some of the other evacuees who came with you will be at the school as well, so you'll have old friends and new ones. I think they're going to adjust the school hours to accommodate you all, so it'll probably be a shorter school day.'

Ruby couldn't think of anything to say. She didn't care about the church and the shops and the local children, and she was horrified at the thought of living in a strange house and going to a strange school. All she wanted was to be back in her own home with her family, even if it meant cramped accommodation, falling bombs and regular blackouts.

But she had been brought up to be polite to adults, so she forced a smile and carried on walking up the hill to the doctor's surgery and adjoining house at the top. She didn't cry, and she didn't say anything out of place; she simply accepted that she was there and had to get on with it until she was sent home again.

Little had Ruby known on that particular day that her life was about to take a route she could never have imagined, that she was going to be living with the Wheatons for five happy years and would be a part of their lives from that day on. Her successful life and future was all a result of the Wheatons choosing her that day.

There had been both highs and lows in her life since that day, but when things were at both their best and their worst George and Babs Wheaton had always been there alongside her.

But now they were gone. She couldn't imagine how she was going to get over losing them, and she also feared the task that still lay ahead of her.

Telling Maggie the truth.

Five

Maggie was sitting on the front wall down by the road when the solicitor, old Mr Smethurst, pulled up outside and parked haphazardly with two wheels on the grass verge. Despite her fears about the meeting, she was moved to a slight smile as she watched him climb out of his car and shake his trouser legs straight. He then reached back in for his jacket and briefcase before shaking his trouser legs all over again.

Somehow the fat little man waddling up to the house, carrying an old leather briefcase with broken straps, didn't match the shiny low-slung convertible Jaguar that he had clambered out of.

He walked over to her. 'Hello, Maggie, we meet again.' He smiled and waited for a response, but all he got was an almost imperceptible nod. 'I'm Herbert Smethurst,' he continued. 'The old Mr Smethurst, as opposed to my son, the young Mr Smethurst! I met you at the funeral, but I'm sure that was just a big blur of faces. My condolences again. Terrible day, terrible events. Well, to be honest, we have met before, but you were just a babe in arms then.' He laughed and again waited for a response, but still Maggie said nothing.

'Oh, I'm sorry, I should have enlarged on that introduction. Just in case, I'm your late parents' solicitor. Now can you point me in the direction of Mr and Mrs Riordan? We've got a meeting arranged. If I'm correct in my thinking, I'm going to have a bit of a chat with them, and then you'll be joining us.'

'They're in there. Go through to the dining room. I'm sure you'll find your way, though I don't know why I can't be there right away, as this is all about *me*,' Maggie said pointedly as she turned her head and looked the other way; furious once again that she wasn't involved in the discussions or arrangements, even though they were about her, she had no intention of showing him the way.

'You will be in on it all in a very short while, my dear. I just have to talk to Mr and Mrs Riordan first, and then I'll have a chat with you and you can ask any questions you like of me. It's what I'm here for.'

He smiled at her sympathetically, but it only made her seethe more. Standing up sharply she marched off across the front lawn in the other direction.

'Patronizing old bugger,' she muttered under her breath as he disappeared into the house. Once he was safely inside and keeping Ruby and Johnnie occupied, she went indoors and phoned the Manor House, hoping against hope that Andy would be there. He was the one person who didn't keep looking at her as if she was poor sick child who had to be treated with kid gloves.

When she'd left the house the day Ruby had first gone to see the solicitor, Maggie had not known exactly what she was going to do; all she'd known was that she desperately wanted to see Andy Blythe because, despite everything that had happened, he was still in her thoughts. She saw him as someone who had nothing to do with any of it; someone who had never met George and Babs, so his sympathy over the accident and its outcome would be for Maggie herself.

Thinking of Andy and fantasizing about their budding relationship instead of the accident and its aftermath had helped her cope in the dark days and even darker nights of despair and guilt. And on that day she'd wanted to see him more than ever.

She'd still felt unwell then, and her arm was still immobilized in a plaster of Paris cast, but mostly she'd felt detached from herself as she walked for over a mile along the country lane, which didn't have a pavement. The sun was shining down and she could feel the perspiration soaking into her fringe and dripping down her back, but she kept going until she came to the familiar dense hedge which was about ten feet high and bordered the classic property she was heading for. She carried on until she came to a gap where the high wrought-iron gates stood behind a huge signpost stating 'The Manor House' in elaborately etched gold script.

As luck would have it, one of the shiny curved gates, which were obviously newly painted, was wide open, so she walked up to the property perimeter and looked around. The tarmac driveway was very black and new and edged with lots of perfectly aligned, identical fir trees which swept regally up to the house. Maggie glanced around, and to the left of the house she could see Andy Blythe banging tennis balls against the wall of the garage, one after the other.

'Andy,' she shouted. 'Andy . . .!' As he looked across, she waved frantically with her good arm.

He peered curiously in her direction for a moment, then put his racket down and walked quickly over to her. 'Maggie! Sorry, the sun was in my eyes. How are you? We heard about your accident; how bloody awful was that? I wanted to ring you, but I didn't want to intrude.'

Maggie shrugged. 'It was as awful as it gets; still is, actually. I feel I'm stuck in a nightmare and can't get out. It's horrible . . .'

'Oh, God, I'm not surprised. And your arm! Is it broken? I bet that hurts.'

'Yes, it does a bit still, but it's OK, really, not much longer till the plaster comes off, and I feel better now the bloody neck-brace has gone for good. I felt like Frankenstein's monster walking around wearing that.' Maggie tried to keep her lips together as she spoke, the way she'd practised in front of the mirror, not wanting him to notice the temporary plate in her mouth in place of her missing teeth. Ruby had arranged for the local dentist to visit Maggie first at the hospital and then again at home, but it was going to be another few days before she was fitted with the proper denture, and she was still mortified at the thought of having false teeth.

'I don't know what I'd do if that happened to me. I mean, to lose both parents at once – I can't imagine it,' Andy continued, and then paused. 'But what brings you here? I mean, it's nice to see you, but I've not seen you out this way before. Did you want me to do something? I mean, I'll help any way I can; you just have to ask.'

'Oh no, it's nothing like that. No, I was just out for a walk to get away from the house for a while. The gate was open and I saw you, so I just stopped to say hello. I'm on my way back now before they send out a search party for the orphan Maggie.'

'Oh, I thought you might have been out here looking for me.'

Maggie was surprised that Andy actually sounded disappointed, and she was glad she'd lied. She didn't want him to think she was chasing him.

'Everyone's talking about the funeral,' he continued, his eyes flitting around looking in every direction except at Maggie. 'It's tomorrow, isn't it? The tennis club are arranging for the members to line the street near the church, and someone said the road is being closed off and the shops are shutting while it's on. I said I'd go. Is that OK? I don't want to sort of, you know, intrude.'

'Oh, not at all, but I know the church is going to be packed, and the hall after, you won't be able to get in.' She paused and looked at him. 'Though you might get into the hall for a sandwich afterwards.' She felt confused by his thoughtful reactions and, because her thoughts were not in any rational order, she wasn't sure what to say. The last thing she wanted was to start crying in front of him, so she changed the subject. 'When do you start working in London?'

'I've got another couple of weeks at home. My mother wanted me to herself for a while before I fly the nest, but I've been going back and forth to the office to learn the ropes. Mum drives me to Cambridge station and I get the train. What about you? What are you going to do? Is your sister going to live with you now or you with her?'

'She's not my sister; she's not a blood relation at all . . .' She stopped. 'Oh, it doesn't matter. I don't know what she's planning, and she's driving me mad hovering around behind me. Johnnie, her husband, is OK. But tomorrow everyone's going to be there. It's going to be so unbearable; I don't want to go.'

He looked at her, genuine sympathy etched on his young face. 'I can't imagine losing my parents; that has to be the worst nightmare ever, and to be there when it happened, to see it . . .'

'I didn't see it; I was asleep in the back,' she said a little too quickly. 'But thank you . . .' she added, feeling her eyes prickle, but then the moment between was sharply interrupted.

'Coo-eee, Andrew,' a female voice wafted from nowhere. 'Coo-eee. Can I interrupt you, darling?'

Andy's head spun round, and Maggie was momentarily irritated, until the owner of the voice appeared in view.

Heading towards them from the direction of the house was an older woman whose age was hard to determine. She walked as gracefully as if she was parading at a fashion show with her shoulders back and her hips forward, and she was dressed and perfectly made up as if for the same. Her flower patterned cotton sun-frock was pulled in tight at her tiny waist by a wide white patent belt which matched her high heels, while her very black hair stood rigid in a backcombed beehive. A huge tortoiseshell comb and a shiny layer of hair lacquer held it all in place.

Maggie stared at her in wonder. She thought she was the most beautiful woman she had ever seen.

'Maggie, this is my mother. Mother, this is Maggie, a friend from the tennis club. You know, the one I told you about, whose mum and dad were killed in that car accident? She's got a broken arm, and the funeral is tomorrow.'

Before she could take a breath to say hello, Maggie was swept up into a bear hug and enveloped in wafts of a very heady perfume.

'Oh, you poor, poor child, what a terrible thing. I said to my Andy here when we heard the news, what a terrible thing to happen. If there's anything we can do, anything at all, you just have to ask. I've arranged to send flowers; they'll be there tomorrow.'

Eunice Blythe held her close for a couple of seconds longer, and then let her go as quickly as she'd grabbed her. 'I'm sorry to interrupt you young things, especially right now, but Andrew, my darling, Daddy wants you to ring him at the office right away. You know what he's like – now means this very second.' The woman shrugged her shoulders and smiled at Maggie. 'The business world always comes first with Daddy, and it's what keeps us in this wonderful house! Now, don't keep Andrew too long, will you, my dear? We have to keep Daddy happy.'

As the woman floated away back to the house, Maggie realized she hadn't even opened her mouth.

'Sorry about that,' Andy said. 'She does get a bit het up over things.'

'She is so beautiful. I wish I looked like that.'

Andy looked surprised. 'Do you think so? I suppose because she's just my mother, I never noticed, although Dad does call her his beauty queen.'

'You'd better go and ring your father,' Maggie said. 'I have to get back. It's the funeral tomorrow . . .'

'That is so horrible for you, Maggie. I'll be there on the pavement sending you support as best I can. Depending, of course, if Dad calls me up to London or if he comes home,' Andy said with a proud edge in his voice. 'Never know with him; he's always so busy running his business. I do what I can to help him out, but it's hard work, and we all have to fit in around him.'

'It's OK, I'll be OK. If you don't go to London, will I see you around sometime afterwards?' she asked him expectantly.

'I'll ring you, I promise. I really want to see you again, but I must run and ring Dad now.'

He leaned forward to kiss Maggie on the cheek just as she turned her face, and he ended up brushing her lips.

'Ooops,' he said with a laugh. 'Sorry about that. Oh well, good luck for tomorrow. Gotta go . . .'

Maggie had felt herself redden as she'd watched him run off in the same direction his mother had just gone, waiting until he was out of sight before she'd leaned against the tall brick gatepost.

He'd kissed her. Andy Blythe had actually kissed her.

Upset that she hadn't been able to talk to Andy on the telephone, Maggie had gone out into the garden. She was sitting on the old moss-covered bench which was tucked away in the curve of the vegetable garden. It had always been her favourite place in the whole garden; it was a hidden corner with a natural canopy of greenery which couldn't be seen from any part of the house. She'd hidden there as a child, and she was there now, although she wasn't hiding as much as taking refuge, waiting for the inevitable summons.

Maggie had long had the ability to distract herself with song; whether she was sad or happy, she would sing. In the bath, in bed, in the garden, even in the church choir . . . it was her escape from reality. This time she wasn't singing aloud, but she had an exercise book on her lap in which she'd written the lyrics to her favourite pop records, and she was trying to remember them all by heart. Every time she got a new record she would play it over and over again, write down and learn the lyrics, and then practice singing the song until she was word and pitch perfect.

'Can you come indoors now, Maggie?'

The song that was going round in her head was interrupted by Ruby calling to her from the back door.

'We're in the dining room, and we have to talk to you before Mr Smethurst leaves . . .'

Desperately not wanting to go and face the inevitable, she carried on staring into the middle distance and mentally reciting lyrics for a few more moments before standing up and heading slowly back to the house.

Maggie Wheaton was an intelligent and well-educated girl with a good general knowledge of the workings of the world; she could hold her own in any adult conversation and had recently become adept at eavesdropping. So even though she didn't want to face it, she knew her future as an orphan was not going to be the one she had anticipated just a few weeks before. She had only caught snippets of conversation, but she knew there was talk of selling the house, and she simply couldn't imagine not living there.

Everything in her life was about to change even more, she knew that, and she also knew it wasn't going to be for the better; she knew the meeting was going to be serious and argumentative, and she had wanted to put it off as long as possible – but now the moment had arrived. All the homely chats with Ruby, Johnnie and Gracie, which had been full of suggestions and questions, meant nothing.

Her future was about to be decided, and she felt sick with apprehension.

Looking down at the ground, Maggie stared at the familiar runner on the floor in the hall as she followed Ruby into the dining room to find Johnnie sitting at the table surrounded by assorted pieces of paper in what looked like orderly piles. Ruby then went straight over and sat beside him and immediately picked up a piece of paper and started fiddling with it. Maggie knew she was meant to sit down at the table also, so she deliberately didn't.

Despite the fact that the couple weren't sitting in either Babs' or George's chairs, they still looked too comfortable at the table for Maggie's liking, and it irked her. She didn't want them sitting at the family dining table, which had only ever been used for special occasions – the table which had been decorated in celebration of every Christmas, Easter and family birthday she had ever known, the table where her birthday cakes had always stood in celebration. It was special, and she hated seeing it used as a makeshift office desk while her parents were lying cold in the ground not a mile down the road. It felt so disrespectful. But she bit her lip and kept quiet.

Determined not to sit with them, she walked across and leaned her back against the familiar sideboard, a family heirloom from George's side of the family, which had always overpowered the room and everything else in it. Maggie had always thought it huge and ugly and she hated it, as did Babs, who had often grumbled that it took up too much room and that the highly carved nooks and drawers were dust collectors, but now she felt the urge to stand by the familiar piece of furniture; she wanted to be able to touch it for reassurance.

What had been a monstrosity now seemed like a comforting constant in her rapidly changing life.

'Come and sit down, Maggie,' Johnnie said gently. 'Please? Come and sit with us.'

'I'd sooner stand. Where's Mr Solicitor? I thought he wanted to talk to me. The old duffer said he did when I saw him outside.'

'He does. As you're a beneficiary, he has to explain the legalities of the wills to you, but we have to talk to you first. He's only gone for a walk down to the shops; he said he needed some tobacco for his smelly old pipe, so I pointed him in the right direction,' Ruby said, still fiddling with the papers on the table. 'He's coming back in a while for the finer details.'

Maggie felt increasingly on alert as she watched the way Ruby and Johnnie kept looking at each other nervously. She knew her life was about to change, that she wouldn't be able to stay in that house alone, but she was hoping against hope that she could at least stay in the village as she'd asked, maybe live with one of her friend's families. She was certain her parents would have left her enough of an inheritance to be able to do that.

As Ruby started to frantically shuffle even more of the papers that were on the table, Johnnie reached over and put a hand on top of hers to still the movements.

'This is really difficult, Maggie, and we know it's going to be a huge shock, but there are things we need to talk to you about, to tell you. Things you don't know,' Johnnie said.

'I know. You've got to tell me what happens next now I'm a poor little *orphan*,' Maggie sneered, 'but Mr Solicitor Man is in charge of that, isn't he? Why isn't he here? Maybe he's going to adopt me, maybe I was left to him; now that'd be a turn up for the books, wouldn't it?' Her tone was defiant and angry, but inside Maggie was scared witless, and she could feel her heart thumping so hard in her chest that it felt as if her whole body was vibrating. She desperately wanted to know what was planned for her, but at the same time she didn't want to know – she wanted to run.

Again, she saw Ruby and Johnnie exchange worried glances.

'There's something we have to tell you, and we all decided it was best if we told you without anyone else here because it's so personal.'

'Why is all of this any of your business? It should be Mr Smethurst talking to me, not you, not either of you.'

'I'm sorry, Maggie, but you see it is our business. George

and Babs left very specific wills. There are arrangements in place for you . . .' She paused and again looked at Johnnie. 'Maggie, darling, you're going to come and live with us in Southend. You're going to be part of our family. It's what they wanted, it's what we want.'

Maggie looked from one to the other and thought for a moment. *Southend?* 'It's not what I want! I'm *not* going to Southend. I'm not going anywhere. I'm staying here; this is my home! I can have a housekeeper, or I can go and stay with friends until I leave school and get a job. I could get a job now; I'm old enough.' Maggie could feel the hysteria rising, but she couldn't stop it. 'Mum and Dad would never have done that to me! They wouldn't make me live with you in bloody Southend. They knew I hate you . . .'

Visibly stunned at the verbal onslaught, Ruby took a deep breath. Johnnie reached his hand out, but she brushed it aside and stood up. She walked over to where Maggie was standing. 'Maggie, I'm sorry. I know you won't like what we have to tell you, but I spoke to the solicitor at length and we discussed George and Babs' wills every which way they could be discussed. Both George and Babs named me and Johnnie as your guardians, until you're twenty-one.'

'What do you mean?' Maggie asked angrily, unable to believe what she was hearing. 'Why would they do that?'

'Because there is no one else to look after you, and also because they knew that was what we would want to do. We had talked about it long ago, but none of us thought for a moment they would both go together. They thought one of them at least would be around to see you well into adulthood.'

As Ruby paused, Maggie saw her exchange another look with Johnnie. Ruby's eyes' were wide as she stared pleadingly at her husband for a few moments before looking back at Maggie.

'Maggie, darling, let's go and sit down. Please?' Ruby said, touching her arm very gently, but Maggie shrugged her off.

'I'd sooner stand. Just get this over with. I'm meant to be somewhere that isn't here with you creeps.' Maggie rolled her eyes to the ceiling in a display of bravado. She tried to cross her arms, but her plaster got in the way. Instead she hooked her good hand into the loop of her skirt defiantly.

'Maggie, there's something you don't know – something we both didn't want you to find out this way, not from us. But your mum and dad's death and the wording of the wills means we have no choice.'

Again the pause followed by a deep intake of breath as Ruby braced herself.

'Just get on with it,' Maggie said.

'Please believe me when I say I didn't want it to be like this . . .' Ruby put an arm around Maggie's shoulder. 'Your mum and dad were just that, your mum and dad, and you know how much they adored you but . . . I'm so sorry, Maggie, there's no easy way to say this . . . You were adopted as a baby. George and Babs weren't your birth parents.'

Maggie stood perfectly still for a few moments. She blinked hard as she tried to understand what Ruby was saying to her, then with no warning she spun round and slapped Ruby full force across her body with her arm that was in the plaster cast. As Ruby yelped in pain at the ferocity of the blow and sunk to her knees, Johnnie jumped up and grabbed Maggie from behind in a bear hug to stop her doing any more damage. His long broad arms easily wrapped around her body, and he held her tight with both her arms in an iron clinch despite her screaming and kicking.

As he held her he whispered to her, 'Ssshhh, ssshhh. Maggie, calm down . . .'

'Get off me,' she screamed and tried to kick backwards at his shins. 'Get off me! You're lying, you're lying, you're bloody well lying because you want everything, that's all you ever wanted . . . Get your hands off me now . . .!'

'When you calm down and promise not to hit anyone else, then I'll let go, but not until then,' Johnnie said, still clasping her tight.

But she carried on screaming and fighting against him until eventually she wore herself out and burst into tears. 'It's not true, it's not true . . .'

'I'm afraid it is, Maggie, my dear. I'm afraid it is true. Barbara and George adopted you just after you were born.' Herbert

Smethurst had quietly come back into the room, and he stood in front of Maggie shaking his head.

Maggie looked at him, and in that instant she knew that what Ruby had told her was true. 'They'd have told me. Mum would have told me . . .' For the first time since she came round after the accident, Maggie started to cry. She sobbed so loud and hard, it sounded as if she was about to stop breathing; the combination of the events of the past weeks hit her in one and took her down.

As Johnnie released his grip, she moved away from the security of the sideboard and sat down as far away from Ruby and Johnnie as she could. Determined to stop crying, she leaned back on the chair, breathed in and out as deeply as she could and closed her eyes, trying her best to regain some sort of composure.

Herbert Smethurst went over and sat beside her. 'Oh Maggie, your parents and I talked about it over the years, and they were going to tell you when they thought the time was right, when you were old enough to understand how it came about. But then this happened and it was too late . . . Now, shall we sit down and talk about this, or do you want me to come back another time?'

Maggie shook herself back to sanity. 'No, let's talk about it. I want to know everything, but I don't want *them* here.'

'Maggie, they have to be here.'

'Well, tough. I want to talk to you, Mr Smethurst, just you. I want you to tell me everything you know.'

'I can't without Mr and Mrs Riordan – Ruby and Johnnie – also being present. Again, I'm sorry, but they are now your legal guardians, and . . .' He looked from Ruby to Johnnie and then back to Maggie, as if he wasn't sure whether or not to continue. Maggie saw Ruby nod.

'But I don't want them here. I want to know about the will, and I want to know why I've got to go to Southend with *them*. I want to talk to you in private.'

Herbert Smethurst's expression was kindly, his tone gentle as he spoke the words which would compound her tragedy and change sixteen-year-old Maggie Wheaton's world forever.

'They have to be here, my dear. I'm sorry to be the one to

tell you this, but I have to.' He paused and took Maggie's hand in both of his. 'Ruby and Johnnie are not only your guardians, but they are also your natural parents – your real mother and father.'

Six

Despite knowing that a happy ending couldn't be possible, and despite being confident she would remain detached, Ruby Blakeley had fallen in love with her baby daughter as soon as she was born. Just looking at her as she lay swaddled in white, with eyes wide open and a knowing frown on her brow, had made Ruby's heart swell with a love she could never have imagined.

Knowing that it would be an impossible task to bring up a baby in her circumstances, she had fought her feelings as best she could from that very first moment, but then when she had to feed her, bathe her, change her and care for her during her time on the maternity ward, it had been impossible not to fall for the little scrap she had given birth to.

Her own family had no idea of her predicament or even where she was, and Ruby had no intentions of letting them find out. Instead she was being supported by Babs and George Wheaton and his sister Leonora, who were all doing their best, but Ruby was worldly-wise enough to know her options were actually limited to just the one: adoption.

In 1946, sixteen-year-old single girls just didn't get to keep their illegitimate babies.

Ruby knew she had been luckier than most pregnant, single young women in that she hadn't been bundled off to one of the dreaded Mother and Baby Homes; instead she had gone to stay with Leonora Wheaton, who owned a small 'ladies only' hotel in Southend on the Essex coast. It was the best solution that could be found to the problem of a pregnant Ruby Blakeley.

She was tall and mature and looked older than her years, so it was feasible for her to be staying at the hotel as a relative of the owner, especially in the guise of a young war widow who had been left alone and pregnant when her service husband had been killed in the war. She saw out her pregnancy working at the hotel, and then, when the time came, Leonora Wheaton drove her to the local hospital to give birth.

Up until that moment Ruby had been focused on getting through her pregnancy and giving birth before moving on and getting her life back as soon as possible. But it hadn't been as easy as she'd anticipated. The baby who had been unseen and unheard was suddenly a living breathing baby girl with the widest eyes and cupid bow lips.

Ruby had lain awake at night on the maternity ward wondering how she was going to survive giving up her baby. She was terrified; she couldn't imagine simply handing her over to strangers who would take her away forever. Not wanting the hospital staff to discover her secret and treat her the same way they were treating her new friend Gracie, another single mother, she kept up the war widow pretext for as long as she could. Then, just as Ruby was about to approach the Hospital Almoner to ask for advice on adoption, the childless Wheatons had offered to take her baby and bring her up as their own back in the house in Melton.

It had been the perfect solution for everyone.

Because it would have been too hard any other way, Ruby then stayed in Southend at the hotel working for Leonora while George and Babs took the baby home with them to Melton. From then on Ruby had stayed involved on the periphery of her daughter's life, but she was no longer her own baby's mother. The Wheatons named her Margaret, immediately shortened to Maggie. They loved her as much as any parents had ever loved their child, and she was brought up thinking of Ruby as an elected big sister. When Ruby had reconciled with Maggie's natural father, Johnnie Riordan, he had been welcomed and treated in the same way.

Everything had worked out as best it possibly could for everyone, with no one really giving any thought to the future and how they'd eventually have to tell Maggie the truth when she was old enough to understand.

But no one could have foreseen where they would find themselves sixteen years on from that time, when the daughter Ruby had loved from afar would have her heart smashed to pieces by the very people who had created her.

Maggie looked from Ruby to Johnnie to Herbert Smethurst several times as she tried to take in what they were telling her.

She was backed up so tightly against the sideboard that she was leaning backwards, and with the three of them crowding so closely around her she was so scared that she couldn't breathe. She started hyperventilating and feeling faint with vertigo; it was all too much for her.

She was adopted? Ruby and Johnnie were her birth parents? The questions were spinning round in her head, but she couldn't think of a way to frame the words. It was all too surreal.

'I didn't want you to find out like this,' Ruby sobbed as she reached out to her. 'It's too much on top of everything else, but the wills stated we had to tell you immediately if anything ever happened to both of them, so that you didn't feel alone. They didn't think it would ever happen, they didn't, it was just a precaution . . .'

Johnnie put one arm around his wife and tried to put the other one around Maggie, but she brushed him away and focused on Herbert Smethurst.

'I was adopted by Mum and Dad from Ruby and Johnnie? Is that what you're trying to tell me?'

'I am, my dear. It was the best thing for everyone at that time. Everyone did what they did for you, only for you . . .'

Maggie shifted her gaze. Her eyes were cold as she stared at Ruby first. 'So you're my mother – you gave birth to me?' She looked at Johnnie. 'And you're my father?'

'Yes, but George and Babs were your mum and dad. They wanted you and loved you,' Ruby said, the words tumbling quickly.

'So you didn't want me . . .'

'No, no, that's not right. It's a long story, and we will tell you everything. It wasn't as simple as that.'

'I don't believe you. This is a trick to get your hands on everything they owned,' she said, but in the back of her mind little bells were starting to ring. Things started to fall into place: her parents' attachment to Ruby, their insistence that she be there for every birthday, their fondness for the boys, especially Russell.

Russell.

'Is Russell my brother?' she asked quietly as the truth of her situation started to sink in.

'Yes, he is, and Martin and Paul are your half brothers. We're all your family, and you're not going to be alone,' Johnnie answered her.

She spun on her heel. 'I hate you, all of you! You're all lying bastards, and you're not my fucking family; you never will be!'

And with that she was gone. She pushed her way past them all forcefully, pulled the door open and went out, slamming it as hard behind her, but they could still hear her shouting abuse back at them.

'Maggie, come back here! Come back . . .' Ruby called.

'Leave her for a while. She has to take all of this in,' Johnnie said, touching his wife's arm gently. 'She needs someone independent to talk to about this. Maybe we should ring one of her friends? Alison?'

'I don't know if she'll want anyone to know . . . Let's just give her half an hour and then we'll go and try and explain some more. God, this is bloody awful,' Ruby said angrily. 'I can't believe George and Babs put us in this position, making us tell her like this . . . We should have ignored their instructions. We should have—'

Johnnie shook his head. 'But Mr Smethurst here couldn't have ignored them. She had to be told. I don't know what's worse – finding yourself an orphan or finding a family you never knew you had.'

Ruby started pacing, a habit she had when things went wrong. Back and forth, while her husband and the solicitor just stood there.

'She doesn't have a clue who she is any more. Everything is upside down . . . I suppose there would never have been a right time to tell her, and she had to know at some time. I just anticipated Babs and George telling her, not us, and not like this.'

Maggie heard Ruby calling after her but she carried on racing as fast as she could down the hall until she reached the front door, where her eyes were drawn to several bottles of expensive sherry left over from the funeral. She paused and stared at the box in the corner of the porch with the unopened bottles neatly lined up and ready to go back to the village off-licence. She only thought for a few seconds before the temptation became too much, and she snatched one of them up by the neck. Running out of the house, she took refuge on the narrow grass strip along the side of the garage where she was out of sight.

The last thing she wanted at that moment was for any of them to find her.

She sat on the grass and tried to think, but her brain refused to work. Her head was spinning, and her arm was hurting like crazy inside the plaster cast after she'd used it as a forceful weapon on Ruby.

Her mother. Ruby Riordan née Blakeley, who she had always thought of as a sibling, was her mother. The ever charming and friendly Johnnie was her father.

It was too much for her to take, so she pulled the top off the bottle and took a swig. Instinctively, she spat it out because it tasted so vile, but then she made herself try again. She didn't want to have to think, and she imagined a few slugs of alcohol would solve that. But instead she got angry, very angry, and drank some more, and the more she drank the more the taste became palatable.

Once everything started to blur, she focused on two things. She really wanted to see Andy, and she wanted a cigarette. She decided that they both went together and determined to go and find Andy. Her legs wobbled as she tried to stand up, and she had to balance herself against the garage wall. But then she climbed through the hedge that edged the house and headed out in the middle of the road in the direction of the Manor House, bottle in hand.

'Maggie?'

Through her stupor she could feel someone pushing and pulling at her, trying to make her sit up, but nothing was working. All she wanted to do was sleep.

'Go 'way,' she mumbled. She reached up to wipe her mouth on the back of her hand, but she missed and ended up with her hand in a pool of vomit.

'Maggie? What's the matter? Are you drunk? Christ, you've been so sick . . . Is this what you've been drinking?'

She did her best to focus, but all she could see was something waving back and forth in front of her face. Another wave of nausea washed over her, and she heaved again, but her stomach was empty. 'I want a ciggy,' she slurred. 'Gimme a ciggy . . .'

'You can't have a cig, your breath'll catch fire. You'll be like a bloody fire-eater spitting flames. I'm going to have to get someone to help.'

'I'm OK.' She tried to form the words carefully. 'I was a bit sick but I'm 'K . . .'

'Come on, get up. You've got to get up,' Andy said forcefully as he grabbed her good arm. 'It's starting to rain. You'll die out here. Just try and stand up, and I'll take you indoors.'

But every time he got her up on her feet, her legs crumpled under her, so in the end he had to leave her lying on the ground while he dashed off at full speed towards the house.

The next thing Maggie knew was waking up and finding herself tucked up in a strange bed wearing an unfamiliar nightdress.

'Ah, you're awake. Good. I was just checking to make sure you were OK; you've been asleep for hours.'

She looked up to see Eunice Blythe looking down at her; mortified, she quickly tried to sit up in the bed, but her pounding head made it impossible.

'Careful now, I think you're going to have the worst headache in the world, young Maggie Wheaton.' Eunice laughed gently. 'Nearly a whole bottle of sherry, I ask you. Sherry. Tut tut! Here you are – try this on your forehead, and when you feel a bit better there's a cup of tea and some dry toast on the tray here.'

She handed Maggie a cold damp flannel, and then perched gracefully on the edge of the bed. 'I spoke to Ruby last night;

Andrew gave me the number. I said I thought you'd be better staying here for the night. She's coming to get you this morning.'

'I don't want her to,' Maggie said as she wiped the soothing cool cloth around her face.

'Well, it's arranged now, and she's bringing you some clean clothes; your others are not a pretty sight. They're probably not *so* bad now – I think Anna's washed them, because they were a little mucky – but they won't be dry yet.' Eunice Blythe stood up and looked out of the window. 'Yes, that looks like your clothes out there on the line. And your shoes – she's even sorted out your shoes! I love Anna. She's the best housekeeper in the world.'

'I'm really sorry,' Maggie said. She put her hand up to her mouth as she was suddenly aware of the gap in her teeth again. She was mortified to realize she must have lost the temporary denture, probably in the garden outside when she was sick. 'I didn't mean to drink all that; I've never even drunk alcohol before. I don't know what happened . . .'

Eunice smiled down at her. 'Well, I do. You've had a bad time, darling girl, and we all understand. Just don't do it again. You scared my poor Andrew half to death; he thought you'd expired on the lawn.'

'I'm sorry . . .' Maggie felt as if her head was going to explode. She leaned over and reached for a piece of toast and tried to remember what had happened the day before, after she'd left home with the bottle of sherry from the porch.

'Don't keep apologizing, honey, we've all done it at one time or another. It's a rite of passage. But a little tip from Aunty Eunice: never ever drink alcohol when you're unhappy. Now, I think you should go and have a bath and wash your hair. Make yourself presentable while I go and tell Andy you're alive. He was so worried about you. He's such a good boy.'

'I'm sorry. I feel really bad.'

'Well, next time you have the urge to raid the sherry, just remember how bad you feel right now. I'm sure it'll put you right off!' Eunice patted her cheek gently, explained where the bathroom was and then left her to it.

Maggie bathed herself in the very luxurious bathroom opposite the guest room and washed her hair as best she could with one arm held up in the air. She put the nightie and dressing gown back on and towelled her hair dry.

As her headache had lessened in the water, so her feeling of embarrassment had grown. She tried desperately to remember what had happened the day before, but although she remembered starting to walk towards the Manor House, she had little recollection of anything after that.

She went back into the bedroom and was shocked to find Ruby sitting on the edge of the chaise longue that was under one of the wide draped windows. Now the curtains were open she could see the room clearly, and despite her bleary hung-over eyes, she did a double take. It was twice the size of her own room at home, filled to overflowing with furniture and decorated in all shades of blue. The swagged flowery curtains matched the quilted bedspread and the stool tucked under the dressing table; the bedside rugs were powder blue, as was the etched fire screen which stood in front of the fireplace; and the four pictures on the walls were all similar sea scenes.

'It's very blue. Do you like it?' Ruby asked with a smile as Maggie looked all around.

'Yes, it's beautiful.'

'Ah. OK. Well, I've brought you some clean clothes and shoes to change into. Do you want me to wait outside while you get dressed?'

'Yes, I want you to wait outside,' Maggie said very slowly and deliberately while staring at her.

Ruby stood up and walked to the door. 'I do understand, you know; I understand why you did it, and I'm sorry, I know it wasn't your fault, it was a reaction. Everything that's happened to you, it's all wrong, all of it, but we can get over this if we try and understand each other.'

Maggie shrugged but didn't answer.

'Mrs Blythe, Eunice, was so understanding, such a nice woman. Just shows you shouldn't believe all you hear in the village gossip circle,' Ruby continued. 'Anyway, she's waiting downstairs to see you before we leave.'

'Why?'

Ruby sighed and shook her head, her exasperation breaking through. 'Probably because, as an uninvited guest, you passed out in her garden and you were sick all over her lawn. She took you in, cleaned you up, changed your clothes and then let you stay in her home despite it. So that's probably why, Maggie. Just maybe she's expecting you to thank her and say goodbye politely.'

Maggie had the grace to feel bad, but she wasn't going to admit it to Ruby. 'I'll get changed.'

As they walked downstairs together, with Maggie keeping a defined space between them, she took in the vastness of the Manor House with its sweeping divided staircase, galleried landing and doors everywhere indicating a large number of rooms over three floors. At the bottom of the stairs was a lobby, which was big enough to double as an extra reception room, and a door, which Maggie guessed led down to the old kitchens and the cellar that her mother, Babs, had told her about when they'd talked about the Manor House.

Andy was sitting in one of the regency striped armchairs by the fireplace reading a newspaper, but he jumped up when Ruby and Maggie walked down the staircase. 'Good morning! How's the head?' he asked with a slight smile.

'It hurts. I'm so sorry, Andy.'

'Oh, after everything that's happened to you, you are entitled. Anyway, I did the same last year at a party, and my friend's dad had to take me home. Mortifying, but no one really minds!'

Ruby smiled at the young man and held her hand out. 'Hello, Andy, it's nice to meet you. I'm Ruby, I'm Maggie's . . . I'm her . . .' She stopped and looked confused.

'You know who Ruby is,' Maggie interrupted quickly. 'My pretendy big sister, only now she's my *guardian*. Wow, I've got a guardian. Aren't I lucky? In fact, I've got two, just to be sure I do as I'm told. Two! Wow.'

'Don't, Maggie, not in public,' Ruby said gently.

'But we're not in public!'

'I said I'd take you both through to Ma once you were

down,' Andy said loudly with a cheery grin. 'Follow me; she's in the orangery with mad Aunt Lily, her batty sister. She likes overindulging in the sherry as well, does our Lily. When you meet her, let her be a lesson to you . . .'

Maggie didn't know whether to laugh or cry. She was desperately in love with Andy, even more so now he was being so sweet, and not so long ago she would have been delighted to be there with him, in his house, meeting his family. But instead she was mortified and wishing herself anywhere but there. She could see she'd blotted her copybook forever with both him and his family, however understanding they appeared to be.

It seemed to take forever for the niceties and repeat apologies to be over, and all the while Maggie just looked down at the floor feeling totally humiliated; she couldn't bring herself to even glance in Andy's direction.

Eunice made a point of telling her how lucky she was that she hadn't collapsed earlier and died alone in a ditch from inhaled vomit and alcohol poisoning. She made it into a joke, and mad Aunt Lily, an older and very much rounder version of Eunice, laughed engagingly, but the underlying message was there for Maggie, which just compounded her feeling of humiliation. But then it was all over, and together they all walked out to Ruby's car and said their goodbyes like old friends; it was as if nothing untoward had happened.

But once they were back at the house it was another story; as Maggie's headache eased and the nausea started to pass, she was left with no option but to think about the day before. Not the alcohol episode, but the information she'd been given by Herbert Smethurst.

She turned it all over in her head, every single word of it, over and over again; she thought about it every which way, but however she tried to work it, she couldn't see a way to deal with it all.

After a sullen interaction with Ruby, she took herself off to her bedroom and closed the door, pushing her chest of drawers across so that no one could get in, and then she curled up on her bed and cried and cried. She cried because she'd lost her parents, her identity and her whole way of life, and she cried because the accident and the destructive aftermath had been all her own fault.

She also cried because she wished she was dead as well.

Or instead.

Seven

'They really think I'm going to let them drag me off to bloody Southend? Well, I'm not going, and they can't make me. Guardians? How could Mum and Dad make them my guardians? It makes me sick just to think about it. Bloody Ruby and Johnnie telling me what I can and can't do? And having to live with those three disgusting brats of theirs as well?'

'Would it really be that bad?' Andy asked cautiously.

'Of course it'd be that bad,' Maggie snapped. 'And worse . . . Andy, I don't want to go, I really don't. Maybe I'll just run away somewhere. I'm old enough to look after myself. I don't need them.'

'Don't think that's a good idea.' Andy pulled a face and shook his head.

'Well, I do!'

Maggie Wheaton was sitting alongside Andy Blythe behind the clubhouse; as she ranted, she strummed her fingers on the decrepit wooden bench they were sitting on and tapped her feet furiously. Her nerves were in shreds. It was only a few weeks since the life-shattering discussion with Ruby and Johnnie, and she simply couldn't accept what she had been told. She couldn't sleep properly, and when she was awake she couldn't sit still for more than a couple of minutes. Her anger was all-consuming.

Because she was going to be leaving her school anyway, she had refused to go back at all; everyone had tried to persuade her it would be for the best if she could get back into a normal routine, even if it was only for a short while, but Maggie already had it in her head that she was not going to cooperate at all.

With any of them!

Instead, she either roamed around the house like a captive animal, snapping and snarling at anyone who approached her, or she hung around the tennis club with, or waiting for, Andy. Despite the traumatic events, she was as besotted with him as ever, and while she was focused on him she could block out some of the misery that was threatening to envelop her and send her careering into a full breakdown.

Because neither Ruby and Johnnie nor the vicar and his wife had had any success in getting Maggie to cooperate, Gracie Woodfield, Ruby's best friend, had been summoned as a last resort to try and reason with her. Maggie had always liked Gracie, but now she put Gracie in the same camp of betrayal as Ruby and Johnnie. Gracie had known about Maggie's history and parentage and had been part of the big secret keeping.

In a strange way, Maggie could see that Ruby was falling over backwards to try and help her, but she was having none of it. She was so convinced in her own mind that they were intent on stealing her inheritance – the same way that Ruby had stolen Aunt Leonora's hotel, Maggie had convinced herself – that she could barely bring herself to talk to them. Her feelings of betrayal and abandonment were so intense, she had no intention of making anything easier for the Riordans. In fact she was determined to make their lives misery.

'Oh Maggie, Maggie, we want you to be part of the arrangements for your future, we want you to have a say and be involved, but if you won't cooperate we have no choice but to go ahead without you. Time is too short. I can't stay here forever, so we have to get on with the arrangements. I'm sorry,' Ruby had said – and that's exactly what had happened; all the arrangements had been made, the time for the big move had nearly arrived and Maggie had done absolutely nothing. She hadn't even sorted her own clothes and personal belongings out.

'I can see what you mean. I suppose it does seem all wrong that you get no say.' Andy frowned as he crossed his legs and leaned back. He had both arms stretched along the back of the bench. 'But what else can you do? I mean, you can't live on your own.'

'I thought fatman the solicitor would cough up for a housekeeper for me, or a companion, or . . . Oh, I don't know . . . But I'm not going with them, I'm not.'

'I suppose they can't drag you off if you don't want to go.

They can't make you go and live with strangers, can they? Though I suppose they're not really strangers.'

'Well, they think they can. They think I'm going with them in two weeks' time. They've even given me the date. Darling Ruby has decided she has to get back to her precious bloody hotels. I mean, even one of them came from my family, from my aunt! She's got a knack of getting into wills has our Ruby.'

Maggie looked away. She felt bad that she hadn't told Andy the whole story, but she simply couldn't bring herself to admit the awful truth to him, or to anyone; she was finding it hard enough to accept herself that her whole life had been a lie.

She wasn't the beloved only daughter of the respected village GP George Wheaton and his wife Barbara; she was actually the illegitimate daughter of an impoverished sixteen-year-old wartime evacuee from the backstreets of London and her secret on/off fancy man.

'Ruby and Johnnie are both named as my guardians; the solicitor said so. What can I do? How can I change it? It's just not fair . . .'

'It doesn't sound fair. I'll ask my dad. He works with lawyers all the time. He might know what you can do.' He shuffled along the bench towards her until their legs were touching, and he took her hand. 'I don't want you to go. I'll miss you, Maggie. I really like you, you know. We sort of click, don't we?'

Maggie blushed as he squeezed her fingers and, unable to think of anything to say, she looked down at the ground and tapped her feet even faster. Andy reached into his pocket and pulled out a packet of ten cigarettes and a matchbook. He lit one, drew deeply on it twice and then automatically passed it to her; she then took a small puff and passed it back to him. It had become a ritual between them to share their cigarettes, and although she didn't really enjoy the actual smoking, which made her chest feel constricted, she loved the act itself. To her, sharing the same cigarette signalled an intimacy with Andy Blythe that she desperately wanted.

After the accident, Maggie found that many of her friends didn't keep in contact the way they had previously, and those who did just didn't want to talk about the accident. Only Andy

Blythe had been a constant, and because of that she loved him more than ever.

'Have they forgiven you for nicking the booze and getting so very pissed?' Andy smiled and shook his head. 'I know I shouldn't say it, but it was so funny, you were falling all around our front lawn.'

Maggie put her hand up to her face. She was still trying to get used to the denture in her mouth, and she was terrified it might fall out mid-conversation. 'Don't! I'm so embarrassed. I'm surprised you don't hate me. I really thought you'd not want to have anything to do with me.'

'That's just daft.' Andy started to laugh. 'We were just worried about you being so ill. And maybe dying on our lawn, of course. We didn't want that either. How were the guardians from the black lagoon when you got home?'

'Bloody furious, but they tried to hide it. Anyway, they can't have a go at me! I'm their golden goose, their route to the Wheaton inheritance. Thieving buggers . . .'

'Not forever, though; they haven't got it forever, and they're only looking after your half of it. If my parents popped off tomorrow they'd never let me loose with the family silver. I'm sure it'd be put well out of my reach. I just hope mad Aunt Lily would be my guardian; she'd let me do whatever I wanted.'

For the first time that day Maggie managed a slight smile before continuing: 'The bitch has got half of everything for herself already, and I'm sure she can do whatever she likes with mine. Her and him and fatman.'

'Oh hey, that's funny.' Andy laughed. 'Her and him and fatman. I love it. Must remember to tell Mum you said that. She rather liked you, you know. She thinks you're a character.'

'Oh, and I liked her. She's so glamorous and beautiful; she's like a beauty queen. And she was so kind to me; she could have just left me there and let her and him deal with it.'

'She wouldn't have done that,' he said seriously. 'She's a good person, my mum.'

'If they make me go, will you keep in touch?' Maggie asked suddenly. 'Will we still see each other?'

'Of course we will. You could come up to London when

I'm working there, and I could come and see you at the seaside.' He paused. 'Have they decided what's going to happen to your house when you go to Southend? Are they going to sell it or what?'

'No, Dr Banbury from the surgery is going to rent it. I think fatman is going to deal with all that. I don't know. I don't care. I've always lived there, and now it won't be my home any more. I'm a bloody homeless orphan . . .'

As her bottom lip wobbled, Andy leaned across, put his arm around her shoulder and pulled her towards him.

And then he kissed her.

At first it was a brushing of lips, but then he moved his hand behind her head, wrapped his fingers gently in her hair and kissed her hard, his tongue pushing between her lips and into her mouth.

After the initial surprise Maggie reciprocated, and when he leaned across and cautiously tried to feel his way up inside her blouse she didn't resist. She was so confused about her life and so much in love with Andy, she would have let him do anything. Her whole body started to tingle as he pushed her bra up and tentatively cupped her breast in his hand.

But the moment was spoiled when she heard someone coming around the corner and jumped away from him like a scalded cat.

It was Suzette, one of the older girls from the tennis club. She walked over and stood in front of them with one hand on her hip and a long tanned leg stretched out in front of her. Her tennis skirt was so short that her frilly white knickers were visible, and Maggie was sure Andy was looking at her in a way he shouldn't have been.

'Andy . . . what are doing out here? Come inside with us. The table tennis table is up, and we really need a fourth.' She pouted straight at him and flicked her hair. 'Pleeeease? We really want you to join us. The winners get a free coke each.'

Andy Blythe did absolutely the wrong thing when he smiled, looked from girl to girl and hesitated.

Maggie was instantly furious, and she could feel an even bigger blush rising up from her chest all the way to her forehead;

biting her lip, she stood up and straightened her clothes. 'See you around . . .'

'Maggie, wait—' he said. 'Wait for me, I'm coming with you.' But as he stood up, she took off at a run round the outside of the tennis courts and straight out of the gates. Without looking back she ran to the high street, only pausing when she reached the corner. But the instinct to get away from the situation sent her running again, and she carried on as fast as she could all the way up the hill to home. The weight of the cast on her arm didn't slow her down but it did tire her out, and by the time she got there she could barely stand, let alone breathe normally.

As she turned into the driveway she was horrified to see Ruby standing out by the car talking to the vicar's wife, Mrs Hobart. They both stopped talking and watched as Maggie carried on running up to the house, puffing and panting and drenched in sweat. Only when she reached the back door did she stop and bend over to try and catch her breath.

'Maggie? What's happened?' Ruby ran over and put her hand on her back. 'Tell me what's happened.'

Maggie caught her breath. The way Mrs Hobart was looking at her told her all she needed to know. They'd been talking about her. 'I've just been running.'

'I can see that, but why? Is someone chasing you? Has someone said something?'

Still breathing heavily, she stood up straight. Mrs Hobart had followed Ruby to the door and was standing just a step behind her.

'What? Apart from you?' Maggie shook her head to release her hair, which was stuck tight to her head with sweat. 'I can see from her face you've been telling her my business, which'll be all over the village before you can sing a hymn.'

Ruby's jaw dropped. 'Don't you dare be so disrespectful,' she said, glaring at Maggie. 'Mrs Hobart was kindly asking how you were.'

Maggie looked from one woman to the other and laughed humourlessly. 'Don't you mean gathering gossip for the flower arrangers to spread?'

'Stop it,' Ruby said.

'Oh, just bugger off, Ruby,' Maggie sneered.

Mrs Hobart had been the vicar's wife since before Maggie was born, and there was nothing that went on in the village that she didn't know about. She was kind and caring and performed her duties with gusto, but she was also a natural gossip, and Maggie knew that whatever was said to her inevitably made its way out into the public domain eventually. That was the biggest downside of village life.

'Now stop this. I know you're upset – we all are – but it's not Mrs Hobart's fault.' Ruby said as Maggie stared her down with lips pursed and eyes full of loathing. 'Losing George and Babs was hard for me as well. We're all grieving, but rudeness like this just can't go on.'

As she looked at the two women, Ruby and Mrs Hobart, standing side by side, Maggie felt as if there was a fire burning inside her, and it was growing fiercer and fiercer. She could feel an anger enveloping her which was threatening to explode. 'Grieving? You've managed to get your hands on half of everything that should be mine! It's mine – this is *my* home, not yours. You were nothing to them, just a bloody evacuee, and now you're a bloody thief, that's what you are, and I hate you! Get out of my house, get out, get out get out . . .'

Maggie watched Ruby Riordan trying not to cry as she absorbed the hatred that was emanating out of her. It gave her a certain satisfaction, but there was also a tiny twinge of guilt at seeing Ruby so distressed. For a moment she wanted to physically attack her, to hit her and hit her until she felt the same pain she herself was feeling, but then she backed off. Not because she had second thoughts, but because over the shoulders of the two women she saw Andy Blythe appear, looking nearly as puffed out as she was.

He looked at her for a moment, staring straight into her eyes, before smiling and gently shaking his head. She slowed her breathing, and as the overwhelming anger started to subside she knew that Andy had saved her from herself once again.

She walked round the silent Ruby and Mrs Hobart and went to meet him, relieved that he had nailed his colours to the mast by coming after her.

'Do you want to come in?' she asked.

'Will that be alright? I don't want to make things worse for you.'

'Things can't get any worse now. We could go into the sitting room and play records?'

'OK . . .'

Andy smiled confidently at Ruby as they both started to walk past her into the kitchen. 'Hello, Mrs Riordan.'

Ruby smiled, and Andy paused, but Maggie carried on walking.

'Hello, Andy, it's nice to see you again. How are you? And your mother?'

'We're all very well, thank you. Mum and Aunt Lily have gone to see my grandparents today – they live near Northampton. And then they're bringing them back to stay with us for a while.'

'That'll be nice for you, Andy, having them with you.'

'I don't think I'll see much of them. Dad has got a lot for me to do in London, so I'll be spending more time there.'

Ruby said, 'That'll be exciting for you, working in . . .' She paused. 'I think Maggie's waiting for you to join her.'

'Come on . . . why did you talk to her?' Maggie asked as they walked down the hall side by side.

'Because I'm a nice polite boy, according to my mother. Manners cost nothing.'

'Is that a dig at me?'

'God, no. But it's your battle, not mine. It's not my place to be rude to your . . . to your . . . to Ruby,' he stuttered.

As they went into the small sitting room where the record player was, Maggie went straight over and put a random selection of forty-fives on to the turntable and turned to volume up, so if Ruby did try and listen it would be hard.

Andy closed the door and pulled her into him. 'Shall we carry on where we left off?'

Maggie slipped her good arm around his neck. And then, just as quickly, stepped away again. All she could see was the expression on Mrs Hobart's face when she'd run into the driveway. It hadn't occurred to her that anyone else would know, but suddenly it hit her like a bolt between the eyes.

Other people in the village had to have known at the time. They had to.

'In a minute. Andy, there's something I have to tell you first. You might not want to carry on when you know the truth about me, but I have to tell you this before you find out from someone else.'

'The truth?'

'Yes, the truth. I'm not who you think I am . . . I'm not even who I thought I was. Nobody knows me . . .'

Eight

Maggie had watched the day dawn from the window seat where she had been all night, silently seething that Ruby and Johnnie and Gracie and Edward were asleep just down along the landing of her house, her home. All four of them had been shifting and shuffling furniture and boxes into an order. There were the things that were staying as part of the rental; the things to be stored in the attic for Maggie to make decisions about in the future; her parents' belongings, which the vicar and his wife were going to rehome; and then everything that was going with Maggie to Southend.

'Isn't it lucky our house is so big?' Ruby had said with false jollity. 'You'll have your own bedroom, which is the big one up on the top floor with lots of cupboards. And you'll be able to make as much noise as you like with your music up there. Johnnie has done his best to make it homely for you. I know it's going to be hard, but you'll settle, I know you will.'

Maggie had looked away. No matter how hard they tried, she was determined not to interact. She didn't want them to think she was coming round to the idea, because she wasn't. She was dreading it more than she had dreaded anything, even the funeral of her beloved mum and dad.

Now the moving day had arrived, and everything was packed and ready to go in the afternoon after the final meeting with Herbert Smethurst. Not that she had any intention of being at the meeting; she knew now that her thoughts on it all were irrelevant and nothing she said would change the way her future life had been organized for her, so she had instead arranged to go and meet Andy at the Manor House to say goodbye.

She was dreading the day ahead – not only the thought of leaving the house and village, but also of being away from Andy, the love of her life, who was the only person she could talk to. When she had told him she'd expected horror and disdain, but he'd taken the news of her complicated history with a queried look and a bit of a shrug.

'Nothing wrong with being adopted, and at least you know where you came from. My mother was adopted. You should talk to her. She and Aunt Lily aren't real sisters, they were both adopted separately, but everyone gets on with everyone . . .' He paused. 'Talk to her. She's good like that, my mum.'

They'd sat side by side on the small sofa and listened to the music. The moment for romance had passed, but Maggie had been happy to just sit there with Andy's arm around her shoulder. Her relief at his reaction had been overwhelming.

'My plaster's coming off tomorrow,' she'd suddenly said, breaking the comfortable silence.

'That'll be good. I bet you're looking forward to it.'

'I am. That'll be it then. No collar, no plaster, no stitches. Everything about the accident will be gone.'

As the car pulled slowly away from the house in Melton later that day, a few of the villagers were there to see them off.

Maggie was in the front seat alongside Ruby, and the personal belongings that comprised her whole life were stacked on the back seat. Following behind in a borrowed van were Johnnie and Gracie's husband, Edward, who'd been doing the main shifting and clearing and preparing the house for rental. Behind them was Gracie in her own car. It was almost a procession, heading away from the village of Melton in Cambridgeshire down to Southend-on-Sea on the Essex coast.

On her last look around her home, Maggie had felt as if the heart of the house had been ripped out. All the identifying items of the Wheatons' everyday life had been stripped from every room, leaving only the furniture, some top-layer bedding and the best of the kitchen utensils. From now on someone else would be living in the only home she'd ever known, and it felt so wrong. Her home, the one she'd shared with her parents all her life, had been transformed into an empty shell with no personality, and she was now being dumped into a new house with a new family, neither of which she wanted.

Now she was silent and expressionless, but her body language said it all. She sat as far away from Ruby as she could, hunched against the door with her eyes closed tight and her knees turned away forced tight up against the door; she was as near to turning her back on Ruby as possible in the front seat of a car.

She just couldn't believe that the day had come and that they had all ridden roughshod over her wishes. But worse than that; she couldn't believe that they'd lied to her all her life and sullied her memories of her beloved parents.

'Look, there's Andy and his mother. Oh, that's nice of them . . .' Ruby said as they approached the Manor House.

Maggie didn't answer and didn't move, although she turned her eyes sideways to see them. Her unhappiness was so overwhelming, she didn't wave back.

'Oh darling, I'm so sorry. If there was another way . . .' Ruby stretched her hand across the wide leather car seats and touched her arm, but when Maggie batted her off and tucked herself away even further she put her hand back on the steering wheel. 'I wish there was some other way, I truly do – we all do – but we can't come and live here. There are five of us, and we have commitments of our own—'

'Just shut up!' Maggie cut in. 'You're enjoying all this: telling me what to do, pretending to care about me. Well, I know you don't or you wouldn't have dumped me when I was born. You're nobody to me. I hate you, all of you.'

Since the dreadful day when Ruby and Johnnie had had to break the news to her about her true parentage, she had barely spoken to Ruby other than to hurl insults, and she had played no part in the packing up of the house. Johnnie had offered to take her down to Southend the week before so she could miss the final packing and leaving, but she had been determined to sit it out to the very last moment in the hope that they may just change their minds.

But they hadn't, and now they were on their way.

Ruby and Johnnie had decided to let the house instead of selling it, after the doctor had expressed interest; it had seemed a good compromise, because that way it left the door open for Maggie to go back to the village, when she was older and able to support herself, if she wanted to.

But Maggie didn't see it that way.

At sixteen, Maggie had had to accept that she really didn't have a choice in her own future in the short term, but although she had accepted it she didn't like it, and she was even more determined not to cooperate at all with any of them. The utter betrayal she felt ate away at her every minute of every day, and she promised herself she would make their life as miserable as she could until they no longer wanted her there.

'We're not pretending to care about you! It's not like that, Maggie, it isn't. We're all devastated about losing your parents, and we're especially devastated for you . . . but nothing can change the situation we're all in. I know how lost you must feel.'

'Oh, stop telling me all that rubbish. You don't know! Your mother is still alive and you have your own family, even if you preferred *Aunty Babs*.' Maggie injected as much poison into the two words as she could. 'So how do you know how I feel?' Maggie screamed at Ruby, but she still wouldn't look at her.

'I know how I felt when I was sixteen and all alone and betrayed. It was Aunty Babs and Uncle George who saved me. I owe them everything, so yes, I do understand how you feel, Maggie.'

'Shut up, you cow.'

Ruby blinked hard and pretended she was concentrating on the driving, but in fact she was back to her sixteen-year-old self . . .

'Here you are, young lady. This is to be your room for the time being until . . .' Leonora Wheaton paused. 'Well, until things have happened and you can go back to wherever it is you want to go. You can put your suitcase in and unpack it later.'

She opened the door and stood back so that Ruby could see inside. The room was a basic but comfortable guest room with everything she would need. It didn't have the frills and extras that her room at the Wheatons' house had, but it also wasn't as bad as she had been anticipating.

'During your time here I expect you to obey my rules, the rules of the hotel, and you must respect the cover story we have prepared for you,' Leonora continued. 'You are eighteen years old. You are a war widow, a distant relation of mine, and I'm looking after you. If

any of my visiting ladies ask you questions, then that's all the information you give them. I don't want to be encouraging any more lies and deceit than is necessary.'

'Yes, Aunt Leonora,' Ruby responded meekly, addressing the woman the way she had been briefed. The last place she wanted to be was tucked away in a genteel, ladies only hotel on the seafront in Southend, but she could see that as a pregnant and unmarried sixteen year old her options were limited if she wanted to avoid the shame of anyone knowing.

'Now, don't you be too hard on her,' Babs Wheaton said to her sister-in-law while at the same time smiling encouragingly at Ruby. 'She's a good girl who's done something silly and regrets it. We're going to leave her here in your capable hands, but we'll be back to visit and we'll keep in touch by telephone. I know you'll look after her.'

'I'm expecting her to pull her weight, you know. I've not got any room for slackers in my hotel or my flat.'

'As I said, Leonora, Ruby is a good girl, and we know she'll do whatever you ask her to.' Babs smiled encouragingly at the woman who was going to look after Ruby, and then passed them each an envelope. 'Here's the money for her keep for the month, and Ruby, this is your spending money for the month. I know you'll be sensible with it, and when we see you next month we'll—'

'I don't need it,' Ruby interrupted. 'I'm going to work here to earn my keep.'

'I know, dear, but just in case. Now, George is waiting downstairs so I have to love you and leave you, but we'll see you really soon. You stay here because I need a quiet word with Aunt Leonora before we leave. Be good and take care of yourself.'

Babs Wheaton gave the still bewildered girl a brief but warm hug, and then disappeared down the stairs with Leonora before there was time for tears or protestations.

There really was no other choice for young Ruby Blakeley; she was going to have to stay where she was.

Leonora Wheaton was a middle-aged spinster who looked, and sometimes acted, like the stereotypical old dragon. As she was George Wheaton's sister, Ruby had met her a couple of times during her evacuation; she had taken little notice then, but now it was different. Not only did Ruby have no choice but to take notice of the woman, she was actually going to live with her and work for her for the duration.

However, despite dreading the changes she knew were about to happen in her life, she had no choice but to agree.

Momentarily left alone in the flat on the top floor of the hotel which Leonora herself owned and ran almost single-handed, Ruby was all too aware that there was no place for any self-pity, so she deliberately blinked away the tears and stamped down her bubbling emotions. Unsure what she was supposed to do at that point, she walked over to the centre of the dated sitting room and looked around, taking in everything around her before going over to the full-length French windows that opened on to a small balcony.

The windows were already ajar, so she slid through and looked over the wrought iron railings at the vista that was Southend seafront on an autumnal Sunday. There were families walking along the promenade and children walking along on the edge of the water, which was lapping the high tide mark. There was also an array of small vessels bobbing about on the estuary, and the sight soothed her a little. If she was going to have to live somewhere strange then Southend itself looked OK, even if life with a spinster aunt might be daunting.

She looked down and saw the Wheatons' car pulling away from the pavement outside. They didn't look up, but she waved nonetheless.

Another chapter in her short life was about to begin.

For most of the drive down to Southend Ruby felt as if she was talking to herself. She tried hard to engage with Maggie, but after her initial outburst the girl had retreated back into silence, and Ruby was at a loss. It took all her willpower not to scream and cry herself, but she knew she had to remain calm because amid it all she was constantly aware that she was the adult and it wasn't Maggie's fault. She absolutely understood her daughter's confusion and anger, but still she found it hard when she was under constant emotional assault. Every poisonous verbal blow which Maggie threw hurt her almost physically and battered her down even more.

From the moment ten-day-old Maggie had been taken to Melton by the Wheatons, while she herself stayed in Southend with Leonora, Ruby had been sure that one day her daughter would know who she was. It was the one single thought that had made the adoption bearable, and then when she had eventually got together properly with Johnnie Riordan, Maggie's father, it had become a fantasy she used to play over and over in her mind in the middle of the night. That one day they would visit the Wheatons and Maggie would know they were more than just family friends.

Then when Johnnie's two sons from his previous marriage had moved in with them and their son Russell had been born, Ruby's maternal feelings had intensified. It hurt her that Maggie had a full-blood brother she didn't know as a brother, and it hurt that she couldn't tell Russell about his older sister. But then the day had come, and instead of them all being one big happy family Maggie hated them all with a passion.

'Here we are,' Ruby said as cheerily as she could muster as they pulled up outside the Riordan family home in Thorpe Bay. It was a large detached house in a side road just off the seafront, and although Maggie had visited it with her parents in the past she was now looking at it with new eyes. She was going to live there.

Visually, it wasn't unlike the house in Melton, and Maggie wondered fleetingly if that's why Ruby had chosen it. 'You do know I'm not going to look after your bloody kids while you're at the hotel. I'm not going to be the cheap live-in nanny.'

'Wherever did you get that idea?' Ruby asked.

'Alison. She said I'd end up as your skivvy.'

'Well, I don't care what she said, that's nonsense; you're going back to school.'

'I'm bloody well not. Oh no. I told you, I'm not going to school ever again, not unless it's back at my own school. I'll go back to school if I go back to Melton.'

Ruby knew that standing on the pavement outside the house wasn't the right place for the conversation, so she took a leaf out of her daughter's book and simply shrugged.

'I'm not!' Maggie continued.

'I heard you.' Ruby said a silent prayer as the other two cars pulled up. 'Time to start the unpacking,' she said as she climbed out of the car and opened the boot.

'Bugger off, bitch,' Maggie said. She then jumped out of the car herself and walked off in the direction of the seafront.

It was three hours later, once everyone was starting to panic, when she marched in. 'Where's my room? I'm going to bed.'

That night, Ruby realized that task ahead of them was going to be harder than anything she and Johnnie had ever been through before.

Nine

Six months later

Maggie Wheaton hopped from foot to foot to keep warm as she waited impatiently on the platform at Southend station for the next train to arrive. Three had already been and gone since the time Andy had said he would be there, and she was starting to panic that he wasn't going to turn up despite his promise. She was just about to turn and go home when the next train pulled in, and he jumped off and loped down the platform towards her with a cheery wave.

'Mag, wotcha!' he shouted from a distance. 'Sorry I'm late. The bloody underground in the rush hour was like sardines in a can!'

As he smiled, all the feelings she already had for him instantly increased, especially when she saw other girls on the platform eyeing him up and down appreciatively. There was no getting away from the fact that he was a very handsome young man. His hair was longer than when she last saw him and now flopped attractively across his forehead. He also looked considerably taller and much older; so much so that she was quite taken aback. The collar on his fashionable three quarter length coat was turned up, and his hands were tucked deep in his pockets, the familiar navy blue duffel bag slung over his shoulder.

Maggie had kept her hair in rollers the night before and then taken ages in the morning brushing her long blonde hair to a shine, backcombing it around the crown and flicking it up around her shoulders the way she'd seen in the magazines. She just wanted to look sophisticated and trendy for Andy. She took the same approach with her make-up and clothes; she'd carefully applied her make-up to make it look subtle and had tried her best to choose an outfit that was dressy without looking as if she'd dressed up especially for him. After trying on nearly every item of clothing she possessed, she'd settled on a black straight skirt which was very tight over the hips and just touched her knees, low pointed heels and a black roll-neck sweater which made her hair look even blonder. She topped it with a cream swing coat which she left casually unbuttoned, but she still felt young and gawky in front of him.

She didn't notice that while the girls who had come off the train were watching Andy, the young men were looking at her appreciatively.

'Hi, Andy. I thought for a minute there that you weren't going to turn up,' she said almost shyly.

As he got up close he put his arm around her waist and pulled her in to him before kissing her on the cheek. 'I wouldn't stand you up, baby.' He stood back and looked at her. 'Wow, you're looking cool, really cool. I love the new hairstyle.'

Maggie was surprised at his ready use of Americanisms but quickly decided it was because he worked in the music business. 'Where do you want to go? We could go to the coffee bar down the high street?' she asked quickly to hide the strange shyness she felt rising up.

'I want to see the famous seafront – I haven't been to Southend since I was a kid – and I want to see your new home. Oh, and the hotel. Life by the sea as lived by Miss Maggie Wheaton.' He laughed out loud.

'Are you taking the mick?' she asked defensively. 'This isn't funny.'

He stopped laughing. 'Of course I'm not; don't be so touchy. I've brought records for you, does that help?' He pulled the bag off his shoulder and showed her what was inside. 'Look, I come bearing gifts for the most beautiful girl in town.'

'Oh, thanks, Andy,' she said, her irritation quickly forgotten. 'I wanted some more, but my pocket money has been cut to try and make me behave! How can they cut your pocket money when it's your money in the first place?'

'Dunno, but I do know I spoke to Dad about the guardianship and everything. I'll fill you in on the details later,' he said. 'So, how about going to yours?'

'There's nothing there.'

'Oh, come on, I just want to be able to picture where you are when I think about you. A coffee bar is hardly right . . .'

Maggie really didn't want to take him back to the house, but in the time it took to walk out of the station she had given in to his charm offensive. 'OK, OK, but I don't want to stop there. I want to show you round the parts here where I go, the parts that aren't all day-trippers with hankies on their heads eating toffee apples. Yuk.' She shivered dramatically for effect. 'Not that there are many around this time of year. They're not as hardy as some of the locals who think it's clever to take a dip every day.'

When Andy took hold of her hand as they walked out of the station and down to the bus stop, she savoured the feeling of togetherness, of being close to someone again. She missed the close and tactile relationship she had always had with her parents. She missed her mother sweeping her in for a hug just for the sake of it, and she missed her father gently telling her she was the brightest and prettiest girl in the village. 'My beautiful daughter,' he'd say. 'If you reach for the stars you'll be able to touch them. Easy-peasy.'

The parents who weren't her parents, the parents who had lied to her all her life, the parents she had single-handedly killed.

Maggie had, from a very young age, been self-assured and confident, because she had been brought up to believe she could achieve anything she wanted, but most importantly she had always felt loved and respected.

Now all of that had been taken away from her. She didn't know who she was any more, and she had no one neutral she could talk to. Even Alison, her best friend in Melton, had pulled away and stopped keeping in touch, and it hurt. It seemed to Maggie as if everyone was on Ruby's side.

Apart from her beloved Andy.

On the phone and in letters he had become her confidant, and she found herself becoming more and more dependent on him. It helped her feel less emotionally isolated, but nothing was the same as it had been in Melton with her mother and father, her school friends and the camaraderie of village life.

'It's not that bad here, is it? I was expecting some kind of seaside hovel with sticky floors and candy floss stuck to the windows, the way you talked about it.' Andy Blythe grinned as he stood on the bottom stair and glanced around the big old house in Thorpe Bay, which was just around the corner from the Thamesview Hotel.

'You're joking, aren't you? I hate it. It's bad enough with Ruby and Johnnie pretending to be Mummy and Daddy, but then there's the three brats. And Gracie and Edward are forever on the doorstep with their kid. It's like a bloody orphanage. Martin and Paul aren't Ruby's, Fay isn't Edward's, and I'm . . .' She paused as she struggled to keep her composure. 'Well, me, I'm just nobody. There are aunts and uncles and cousins and even grandmothers I know nothing about and, as far as I know, they know nothing about me. I'm just the bastard Ruby swapped for a hotel.'

'Haven't you been to meet your real family yet, then?' Andy looked genuinely shocked by her latest admission. 'If they're your family, you should. I mean, they are family, aren't they? Even if you didn't know it before.'

'Not a chance. They won't want to meet me, and I sure as hell don't want to meet any of them. I'm not one of them. I'm a Wheaton! And, anyway, they mostly live in London.'

'Well, that's not far away, is it? Look at me; I'm here from London, and I'm going back this afternoon,' he said with a laugh. 'Have you thought about a family tree? It might help you make sense of it.'

Maggie felt the tears threatening. 'That is such a nice thing to say.'

Andy wandered around the house with Maggie behind him, looking in rooms and out of windows.

The house, which was about the same size as the Melton house, had been tastefully furnished and decorated, but it was still homely – although much more crowded. Because she worked at the hotel, Ruby had employed a daily help, Isobel, who did anything that needed doing and was there most days. Maggie didn't mind the woman, who was always jolly and willing, but she had crossed her fingers that she would be out shopping on the Broadway as she usually was at that time of day, and she was right. The house was empty. She didn't want

Ruby and Johnnie knowing about Andy's visit. In fact, she didn't want them knowing anything about her at all. Maggie was just biding her time in purgatory until she could get away from them and never see them again. Her resentment of them was eating away at her constantly.

'It's not a bad house,' Andy said. 'And it's big enough for you to keep out of their way. And you've got the seafront just around the corner. I bet it's a really interesting place to be, especially in the summer; better than boring old Melton with the same old happenings every sodding day.' He peered out of the French windows into the garden. 'God, I hate that bloody place. I'd have hung myself by now if I didn't get to spend half my time in London. Melton's all so . . . I don't know. Incestuous, Mum calls it. Cousins marrying each other and all that other weird village stuff like—'

'That's such rubbish! I love Melton,' Maggie interrupted him defensively. 'I was brought up there, all my friends are there and it was my home until I was dragged to this dump.'

'You can't love it. There's nothing to love because there's nothing to do, and I'm only there at weekends! You're just being all nostalgic because you don't want to be here. You can make new friends here if you want to. That's what I had to do in Melton.'

'You're so horrible sometimes. It was easy for you; everyone wanted to be your friend because you'd moved into the Manor House. I'm just the local bastard,' she said, shaking her head at him.

'That's silly. No one knows anything here, and you don't have to tell them if you don't want to.'

'Horrible . . .'

'And you're horrible back. I'm just telling the truth, and you know it. You can't change what's happened, so why not make the best of it? My parents have moved so many times . . .'

'Yes, but you moved as a family. This is just me and a house full of people I don't even really know.'

Maggie could feel the tears welling up once again. So many different things would trigger the tears, and no one seemed to understand how depressed she felt. How much she just didn't want to be around; she didn't even want to live most of the time. Sometimes when she lay awake in the middle of the night thinking about everything that had happened, she just wanted to go to sleep and never wake up again. She would lie in her bed and plot how she would end the nightmare that her life had become. Nothing could shake her out of her personal hell, not even Andy Blythe.

It was all there, all the time.

'Are you going to go to school yet? That'll help . . .' Andy settled down in an armchair in the sitting room and motioned for her to do the same, but she didn't. She just wanted to get out of there.

'Of course I'm not, and they can't make me. How could I explain who I am? I don't even know that, not really. No, I just want to get a job and earn some money. Ruby keeps offering me work in the hotel, stupid cow. As if I'd work with her.'

'I'm working in the family business. It has its benefits.'

'Working in your dad's music agency in London isn't the same as making bloody beds in a crummy seaside hotel.'

'OK, OK, enough said. God, you're being touchy today, even for you.' Andy shrugged and pulled a face. 'Shall we go for a walk, then? I didn't drag myself down here just because I fancied a boring old train journey from London and back. And I had to really work hard to persuade Dad to let me have the day off in the middle of the week. No mean feat, that!'

Maggie looked at Andy and felt guilty; she tried to get herself together. 'I'm sorry. I'm being an old moaner, aren't I? I won't go on about it any more. Come on, let's go back to town and have a look round!'

Although they had stayed in touch with each other after she had been forced to move to Southend six months previously, Maggie had only met up with Andy once before, and that had been when Ruby went back to Melton to meet with Mr Smethurst, the solicitor. By arrangement, she had dropped Maggie off at the Manor House on the way.

But it hadn't been a roaring success. Maggie hadn't wanted to go into the village and see everything she was missing, and Andy hadn't wanted to stay in as his father was there also, so they'd ended up hiding out in the summer house in the grounds for three hours until Ruby came back to collect her. It had been nice to sit and talk with him again, but she'd sensed he was on edge and aware that his father might appear any minute, so even though she'd spent time with Andy, Maggie really wished she'd never gone. She'd wanted to cry on the way home, but instead had closed her eyes immediately and pretended to be asleep.

Walking back to the bus stop, Maggie pointed out the Thamesview hotel but, despite Andy's pleadings, she refused point blank to take him in. Ruby and Johnnie had no idea he was visiting, and she wanted to keep it that way. She didn't want them knowing anything about her life outside of the house.

In the past she'd loved the Thamesview. It was such fun for an outgoing little girl like Maggie had been, and she had always been the star of the hotel whenever the Wheatons took her to visit with them. The staff and guests would dote on her and feed her treats, and inevitably someone would take her over the road to the beach to look for sand crabs and shells. The visits to Southend had been some of her favourite memories until recently. Now she hated Thamesview and everything it represented to her.

The hotel had also changed from how she remembered it as a child. It had expanded to three times its original size and was more like a proper hotel than a guest house, and she saw it, along with the house around the corner, as just another symbol of Ruby and Johnnie's deceit. She was also mortified at the thought of everyone knowing who she really was, so she stayed away. Ruby had assured her that hardly anyone knew at the time, and that those who did had long passed on, but she simply didn't believe her. She didn't believe anything Ruby or Johnnie told her now.

The intervening months had been traumatic, and she was still a seething mass of anger, upset and guilt. So much had happened in her life, but her crush on Andy Blythe was as strong as ever, and she'd been thrilled when he'd said he was coming down to see her in Southend.

'Southend's only an hour away from town on the train,' Andy continued, interrupting her brooding. 'No wonder it's so popular with Londoners. Quick train-hop and you're at the seaside.'

'Come on, I'll show you around. There's a terrific coffee bar, where I've got to know a few people. There's a juke box . . .'

'Sounds great. How's the singing going?'

'I don't do any now. It's childish. Can you see me in a choir still? I don't even go to church here.'

'But you said you loved singing, and if you want to get away from here then maybe you could get a job as a singer. Dad sees girls and boys all the time who want to be the next big pop star; solo girl singers are so popular now.'

'And you think that's me?' She looked at him and laughed.

'Could be. I heard you sing. You're good and you're in tune with a strong voice, not like some of the ones we hear.'

She laughed. 'What? You heard me in the choir? That's not real singing.'

'I also caught you out singing in your bedroom. I heard from halfway down the drive. I stood there for ages listening as you sang along to your records. I told Dad then.' Andy pretended to be in front of a microphone and started singing: '*Walking back to happiness, whoop pa . . .*'

'Shut up, you're taking the mick again!' She elbowed him gently in the ribs, but she couldn't help laughing.

'I'm not, I mean it, and you look the part as well. You're just right for the pop business. Dad says it's going to be huge.'

'Quick, here's a bus—' Maggie grabbed his hand and pulled him along the road, waving frantically for the bus to stop.

'You can't change the subject that easily, you know. You really should sing. I mean it.'

They climbed the stairs to the top deck of the nearly empty bus and made their way to the front seat, but it was only a couple of stops before they had to climb down again and jump off.

'So this is the famous Southend seafront . . .' He looked around as they walked to the top of Pier Hill, the steep slope which led from the pier to the high street.

'Yes, but we're not going to do the stupid pier and ice cream thing. That's all Ruby and Gracie talk about; they sound like a couple of kids, going on and on and on . . . *Oooh, do you remember when we did this . . .? Oooh, remember that day we went here, we went there . . . Oooh, shall we have a ninety-nine and eat it on the beach . . .? Oooh, remember when we went on the roller coaster . . .?* Boring load of old crapola.'

'But that's what old people do,' Andy replied. 'My mother does it as well. She talks about Scotland like that all the time. They just like to remember the times when they were young and daft. Like we are now! But never mind them; where do we go now?'

'To the Capri coffee bar. You'll love it.'

'Hey, look.' Andy stopped and pointed across the road. 'That's one of those booths where you can make a record. I've seen them in London.'

'Yeah, I know. The day trippers line up to make stupid messages to take home. Imagine singing "Happy Birthday" out of tune and sending it your grandma.' Again Maggie pulled a face and turned her nose up. 'Ugh . . . vile and common, like everything along here.'

'Ooh, snob,' he said, laughing. 'But they can be used for something else, you know; I've seen it. You could make a demo. Tell you what, let's get in there. You can sing a few lines of Helen Shapiro like I heard you doing before, and I'll give it to my dad to listen to . . . Go on. Let's make a record! It'll be fun.'

'Don't be daft. Come on, coffee bar time. We might be able to go to three.'

'Only if we come back here afterwards.'

'OK. Maybe . . .' Maggie hesitated.

Andy stopped in his tracks; standing with his feet apart, his arms crossed and his head on one side, he frowned.

'OK, definitely.' Maggie smiled and gave in. She loved him so much it hurt, and she knew she'd do anything for him. 'Two coffee bars, so you can see where I go, and then back to the booth before they lock it up. Now, let's go to the Capri first. I hope there's someone in there; it might be a bit early in the day.'

But to Maggie's embarrassment, Andy wasn't impressed.

'The London ones are better. Sorry, baby, but it's true. You'll have to come up one day, and I'll show you the real showbiz life. There's one just over the road to the flat – you'll love it. It's always really crowded, and sometimes there are even famous people in there, but because they know my dad and what he does I can always get in and get a seat at the counter. And I get free cokes. Everyone wants to meet Dad.'

Maggie quickly changed her mind about moving on to the next coffee bar as she'd intended; she didn't want to chance another place that wasn't up to Andy's standards. Instead they wandered back down the high street to the recording booth.

It was called a recording booth, but it was really just a square box with a sliding door and not much room inside. They both managed to squeeze in to read the instructions. Andy read them out loud, while Maggie concentrated.

'I haven't got any more money on me,' Maggie said.

He dug in his pocket. 'That's OK, you paid for the coffees. Here you are – two and six, it says. Now, I'll stand outside and you just sing your heart out . . . No one can hear you. Sing, baby, sing!'

After a little more persuading, Maggie pulled the door across tight behind her. She took a deep breath, focused on the red light in front of her and then, eyes closed, started singing. She knew the words inside out – she'd written them down and learned them by heart as she had all the others songs in the Hit Parade – so she concentrated on her tone. She knew she had just one chance to get it right, and it had to be right if someone else was going to listen to it. Especially Andy's father.

'That sounded great from out here; I had my ear to the door! Here, give it to me and I'll take it back to the office,' Andy said as she turned the finished disc over in her hand. 'Dad can listen to it tomorrow, and I'll let you know what he says.'

'But I want to hear it first.'

'Well, make another one. Then we'll have one each. But you have to try and make it the same,' he said, pulling some more coins out of his pocket. 'Go on, quick, before someone else wants a go.'

Maggie went back in and went through the process again,

and this time she found herself enjoying it despite the brevity of the time allowed. She hoped it was good enough. For the first time since the accident she could feel a flicker of enthusiasm for what might just happen.

She hoped Andy's father, the show-business agent Jack Blythe, would like it.

Maybe, just maybe . . . she told herself as she waited for the machinery to stamp out the second disc.

For a few moments, standing in the record booth, she had allowed herself to dream.

Ten

Ruby Riordan was sitting on the sea wall looking out across the dark mud of the Thames Estuary bed. The tide was just starting to come in, and innocent-looking pools of murky water were forming in the mud; in reality they were dangerous, and could be deceptively deep. They had fooled many an unsuspecting holidaymaker into thinking they could just paddle through them. But there were no holidaymakers paddling anywhere in the water on that dull November day, just some hardy dog walkers and a few couples well wrapped against the chill wind as they took the sea air.

Since her very first day living in Southend all those years before when she was just sixteen, it had been her favourite place to sit and contemplate. Happy or sad, summer or winter, she'd walk along the promenade to her favourite spot and then sit quietly staring out across the water and wondering at the Thames Estuary flowing out to sea. She'd look and think about what Aunt Leonora, the expert on ships, had said about setting sail from Southend and being able to carry on sailing through all the seas of the world.

It fascinated Ruby, but today she wasn't thinking about sailing around the world. Her mind was focused elsewhere because she had just about reached rock bottom emotionally, and nothing anyone said could pull her out from under the black cloud hanging over her – the black cloud that was her sixteen-year-old daughter. The daughter who was intent on making her whole family's life a misery – and succeeding.

It was over six months since Maggie Wheaton had grudgingly moved to Southend to live with Ruby and her family, and it had been six long months of hell, because her daughter was getting increasingly out of control.

When it had been agreed that Maggie would live with them, Ruby hadn't expected it to be easy, and allowances had been made for the girl over everything, but she still hadn't expected it to be quite as difficult. The harder she tried the worse Maggie seemed to get, and it seemed as if there was no end in sight.

She still loved her daughter as much and as unconditionally as she always had, and all she wanted was for her to understand a little of what it had been like for her in 1946 when she had made the decision to give her baby up, to realize how hard it had been to hand her over to the Wheatons and step away into a new life. But Maggie would have none of it.

There were no shades of grey; she simply saw her betrayal by them all as unforgivable. All Ruby and Johnnie, Maggie's birth father, could do was watch helplessly as she spiralled out of control.

'Coo-eee . . . Thought I'd find you somewhere along here doing a Lady Leonora and gazing out to sea. Where shall we go today? The Far East? Australia?'

Ruby didn't have to look round to know that it was her friend Gracie. The only person who fully understood what had happened back then when Ruby had handed her daughter over to the Wheatons. Gracie understood because she'd been through it too. Except that while Ruby was to be able see her daughter regularly, Gracie's baby was adopted through the system of the time and she would never see him again or know anything about him.

The day Gracie's baby was handed over he was gone forever.

Gracie wrapped her coat tight around her body and sat down beside Ruby. She didn't say anything more; she simply sat close and waited patiently for Ruby to respond.

'I haven't decided yet. Far away would be nice!' Ruby said, still looking ahead. 'Does the tide come in quicker now than it used to? It looks like it does, but it probably doesn't.'

'Shouldn't think so. It's probably just looks like it because we're getting older.' Gracie put her arm around her friend's shoulder. 'How many times have we sat here in total despair? Both of us, at one time or another. Bloody Hell, Rubes, we've been through the wringer one way and another, the pair of us. And yet it's always all come out in the wash. We've got through it all, and you'll get through this . . .'

They sat side by side and looked ahead.

'I try and tell myself that over and over again, but this time I think I'm really lost. I'm worried for Maggie and her own safety. She's doing such stupid things. Imagine if something happened to her because of all we've put her through?' Fearfully, Ruby shook her head. 'But I'm also scared witless for the boys. She's making their lives a misery with her constant tantrums and her spiteful tongue. Martin and Paul have had enough upset in their lives as it is with losing their mother, and poor Russell doesn't understand why she's especially horrible to him.'

With tears building, Ruby opened her eyes wide and carried on staring out to sea, almost as if she thought the answer might be out there. 'She's disrupting everything. I know she's still in shock; I know she's grieving and trying to understand about the adoption. I know all that, I do, but . . .'

'I know. Johnnie told Edward it's getting worse instead of better. Do you want me to try and talk to her again? I know I'm another villain in her eyes but at least she's not quite as defiant with me. I didn't do the deed. Or what about Jeanette? My little sis could charm the devil out of his lair, you know what she's like, and Maggie can't claim *she* was in on the cover-up.'

'I don't know. I feel like I'm down in a pit and I just can't get out. I can't even see the daylight at the top any more, just a pit of blackness, with Maggie at the top laughing as she hurls bricks at me.'

Gracie touched her friend's hand. 'How about we go for an ice cream? I know it's cold, but let's go and get a double ninety-nine each and pretend for an hour or so this isn't happening. You can tell me I shouldn't be scared of flying all the way to West Africa in a big metal tube, and then you can assure me that I'll love it once I'm actually there. But I'm dreading it. And then I can tell you what a fabulous business-woman you are. Amazing Ruby!'

'Ha ha, very funny.' Ruby managed a slight grin. She always tried to put on a brave face when Gracie talked about her impending move to Nigeria with Edward and Fay, but it was almost unbearable to imagine not seeing her best friend for several years.

'We're going to miss our annual meet-up at the Kursaal once

I've gone, so let's do a bit of it and accept that we've done bloody well for ourselves considering everything.'

'Double back-patting time. Yes. Let's walk. Edward and Johnnie can keep each other company for a couple of hours over at Thamesview; we could walk to the pier and back.'

'Are the boys still over in Walthamstow with Betty?' Gracie asked as they walked along in step with their arms linked.

'Yes, I packed them all off for the weekend. They get on with their cousins, and Betty loves having them all there together. She spoils them all rotten, just like she always did her baby brother. They can do no wrong!'

'That's nice. I feel bad taking Fay away from my mum and dad – she's all they've got, really, what with all that stuff with the mad bad sister – but we'll all write to each other.' Gracie paused. 'Where's Maggie now?'

'Not a clue. I'd hoped to spend some time with her, but she's off out again. She spends all her time and money in the coffee bars in town, smoking and getting up to I don't know what. God knows who she's mixing with.'

'Bit like me and you at sixteen, then . . . Hanging around the gypsy boys on the rides in the Kursaal and the bad boys on a day trip to the seaside from wherever. Do you remember those spivs that followed us home? Lady Leonora soon sorted them out.'

'Oh, don't remind me. I said similar to Babs on that Saturday, that last Saturday, when she said Maggie wanted a proper birthday party because she wanted to ask a boy! Babs thought she was far too young, but you and I both know about young love . . .' Her voice trailed away as once again she could feel the tears starting to well.

'This is all just so sad . . . for all of you. I don't know how you bear it. Babs and George were such a big part of your life, but you've not been able to grieve for them for yourself, only for Maggie.' Gracie said.

'Thanks. It's hard, but . . .' Ruby pulled the belt to her coat tighter as the wind picked up. 'I don't think Aunty Babs realized Maggie was grown up enough to be in love with a boy, especially one who wasn't from the village; an outsider, as they say.'

'Did anything come of that Andy boy? He wasn't a bad kid, you said. Maybe he's worth encouraging a bit to keep her out of trouble. Or would that make it worse, do you think?'

Ruby shrugged as she thought about it. Her instincts told her that he was OK, but her instincts had been wrong before, so she was wary. 'I'm not sure. He seemed alright when I met him, but I don't know about him now. She tells us nothing. His mother and aunt were brilliant with Maggie when she got drunk and chucked up all over the perfectly manicured lawn at the Manor House, no less! Oh God, that was mortifying. I had to go and collect her!'

'Maybe you could invite him down for the day or something? He may be a distraction.'

'Not sure . . . I don't want to push them together, though. She's so vulnerable at the moment that she'd be easy prey.'

'Better the devil you know?' Gracie asked.

'You're right; I'll try and ask her about him. Hah, as if she'll listen, let alone answer.'

The two women walked along together, comfortable in each other's company. They'd met in the maternity hospital when they were both young, unmarried mothers, and they had remained close friends during the intervening sixteen years. So much had happened to both of them, happiness and heartache in equal measures, but life had turned out well for both of them in the end . . . until the day of the fatal car-crash, which had changed everything.

'Have you got your leaving date yet?' Ruby asked Gracie as they walked along. 'It's going to be weird without you around. I'm going to miss you so much. You're as much a part of Thamesview as me and Aunt Leonora. It won't be the same!'

Gracie looked at her friend and smiled affectionately. 'No, not a fixed date, but Edward thinks it'll be just after Christmas. He's chomping at the bit now; he's hated having to work in the London office. Says it's like a prison sentence after the freedom of Africa.'

'And the malaria?' Ruby asked. 'He was so ill.'

'Touch wood it's all OK. He's been passed as fit again and can't wait to get our confirmed leaving date. I'm more cautious;

excited but cautious. I can't imagine living in Africa. Me, little old Gracie McCabe, ex chambermaid at the Palace Hotel!'

They looked up in unison at the hotel, which stood at the top of the hill that led up from Southend Pier to the high street. It was a landmark building for the town, and Gracie had worked there before she went to work at the Thamesview Hotel with Ruby.

'You deserve it. You've worked so hard, and Edward is such a nice man. You're the perfect match. And look, that's where you met.' Ruby pointed across to a point on the beach.

'Who'd have thought it, eh? Me marrying a decent bloke who's a bit of a country gent with a few bob. And now swanning off to Africa . . . Mum thinks I'm mad even considering it, but Dad's all for it.'

'You'll love it, I just know you will! Aunt Leonora would have been so envious of you. She always wanted to travel. And she'd have been proud; she had a bit of a soft spot for you.'

'Oh, I loved her. And I still miss her. Every so often I remember her standing upright and stern in front of me having a go about something or other. Dragon Lady!'

'Funny how things change but also stay the same. Who'd have thought all those years ago we'd end up like this?'

'We've done fine, *both* of us, and this dark moment will pass for you, as have all the others.'

Ruby linked arms with her friend. 'God, I hope so, Gracie Grace. Christmas is going to be the next big challenge, but we have to make it good as it'll be your last before you fly up, up and away!'

'Don't remind me! There's still so much to do, but Edward is the organizer. He's an experienced traveller, and to him it feels like going home. All our belongings are going off by sea next week, and we've arranged a farewell visit to his family. That makes it all so real; we really are going!'

After the trauma of Gracie's disastrous first marriage and premature birth of her daughter, Ruby knew her friend deserved a break, but she couldn't imagine how she was going to manage without her around. For sixteen years they'd always been there for each other, and Gracie had always been Ruby's main motivator, her emotional support and her right-hand man when it came to running the hotel.

They had been as close as sisters from the moment they had met and bonded all those years back, and they had worked and lived together for many of the intervening years, but now all that was about to change.

There were going to be 3000 miles between them, and their friendship would be maintained via letters only for three years.

'You're going to have such an adventure, and how wonderful for Fay to experience all of this so young.'

With their arms still linked, Ruby started to walk a bit faster, pulling Gracie along with her. She didn't want to spoil her friend's moment by bursting into tears. She was so close to falling apart that everything seemed to set her off lately.

'Actually, I've decided on two things,' Ruby said as they neared the town. 'First, I know I'm turning into an old fogey, but it's too cold for ice cream. I need a nice strong coffee. Second, maybe you and Jeanette could have one last try with Maggie before you go, appeal to her better nature. I know she has one; it's just been buried lately under all her vile behaviour.'

'Done. Coffee, and then we'll decide what to do with Maggie. Any idea where she might be today? Could we find her?'

'Now, there's a question! She could be anywhere, but I do know she's not at home where she should be. I'm just praying she comes out of it enough not to mess up Christmas for the boys. I know it's going to be absolutely dreadful for her, the first one without Babs and George, but I have to think about the boys as well. It's like walking a tightrope.'

'It'll be OK. Not perfect, but OK. She's a good girl at heart. She's just in pain and lashing out at everyone . . .'

'I know.' Ruby sighed. 'But knowing why doesn't make it any easier.'

After waving Andy off at the station, Maggie sunk back into her depression. It had been such a good day, and it was the first time she had laughed in a long time; he had been attentive and kind, and she had loved every moment spent with him. His enthusiasm for her singing and his support for her situation had given her so much to think about. She hoped against hope that his father would like her singing, both for her own sake and for his. Andy seemed to place so much store on his father's approval and she could see that he would mortified if the man didn't agree with him, so she had her fingers crossed for them both.

Instead of going straight home, she wandered around town aimlessly for a while hoping to find someone, anyone to talk to, before eventually walking the long way back, clutching her copy of her precious record in her hand. It was a secret that she was savouring.

She stood outside the front door for a few moments, dreading going back into the house that she saw as an unwelcoming prison rather than home. It seemed so much worse after such a good day, but after a few breaths she put her key in the lock and carefully opened the door before creeping indoors as quietly as she could. She tiptoed upstairs to her room, and before even taking her coat off, she put the record on the turntable to play and sat on the edge of her bed to listen to it. It was scratchy and short and the quality was poor, but even Maggie could hear that it was actually quite good. She was in tune, her voice was strong and she was word perfect.

She let it replay as she got changed into more casual clothes, before leaning back on her bed and listening to it over and over again – until a banging on the door interrupted her.

'Maggie, are you in there? Maggie? Answer me.' Johnnie Riordan's voice was angry.

'Yes . . .' she answered, while at the same time snatching the arm off the record and closing the lid of the player.

'Why didn't you tell us you were in?' he shouted through the door. 'We wondered where you were. Your dinner's in the oven if you want it. Don't make a noise when you come down; the boys are going to bed.'

Maggie didn't bother to respond because she heard Johnnie's footsteps going back downstairs immediately. Recently, he had been the one who was the most snappy and disagreeable with her, with rarely a nice word to say. Whereas Ruby was constantly trying to make peace with her, while at the same time keeping the peace with the rest of the family, Johnnie had hardened towards her.

When she had first gone to live with them he'd been friendly and had tried his best to jolly her along, but now he didn't bother; in her eyes all he cared about was not upsetting the boys, and that hurt her. Although she would shrug and pretend she didn't care when there was a confrontation, she cared that he seemed to actively dislike her and want her out of the family.

She didn't bother to go down for her dinner. Instead she lay back on her bed again and started thinking over everything Andy had said, especially his father's comments on her situation.

He had told her what his father had said about the guardianship and the estate of her parents and how it was perfectly legal for Ruby and the solicitor to have control. She brooded and got angry before she went to sleep.

The next day Maggie started to think about something specific Andy had said about her inheritance and his reference to her as an heiress. It made her wonder for the first time exactly how much she, and also Ruby, were worth via the estate of George and Babs Wheaton.

At the time Maggie had laughed at the suggestion, but then she started to think about it properly – especially as Andy's dad had suggested, because it was worth so much, that she keep an eye on her inheritance, even if it meant contacting Mr Smethurst herself.

'What does he mean by "so much"?' Maggie had asked, but Andy had just shrugged.

'Only you know that,' he'd said.

But when she thought about it, she realized she didn't. She didn't have a clue about anything, except that she and Ruby were to share everything.

After brooding over her breakfast, she waited until everyone had gone out, and then she went through into the small office Ruby and Johnnie had had built on to the back of the garage. Assuming it was for the hotel business, she had never been interested in going in there before, but now her curiosity was roused and she was determined to start digging around. Because of the design there were two doors which led into the room, one directly from the kitchen and another from the back of the garage; Maggie decided to go in through the kitchen door and then leave the one from the garage open for a quick exit if need be.

The room was square and sparse, and although there was a window at the garden end of the room, a huge old cherry tree blocked most of the natural light. Maggie had no choice but to put the light on to look around. There was a utility metal desk with a portable typewriter and an adding machine side by side, along with a stack of both typing and carbon paper. Shelves lined one wall, and there was also an armchair and footstool in the corner by the window, a wireless on a side table and a large Chinese-style carpet on the floor. There was a large framed print of a beach scene on the wall which she guessed was Ruby's touch. It was much more homely in there than Maggie had imagined, and she guessed it was probably where Johnnie escaped to when he wanted some peace.

Slowly and carefully she opened the drawers first, and then pulled down the flap on the bureau that was behind the door, but there was nothing of interest. In fact, to Maggie's disappointment, there was little of anything apart from an old chocolate box with a selection of change in it and several ten-shilling and one-pound notes.

She picked up one of the notes and smiled as she slipped it in her pocket, telling herself it was her money anyway.

Because the office extension was new, the drawers were still half empty, as were the shelves above it, apart from several books and two empty folders. She quickly flicked through everything and was just about to give up when she spotted the familiar metal filing box from home on the floor in the corner, the same one she had seen Ruby leave the house with on the day she had gone to the solicitors. For a few moments she just looked at it, wondering what to do, but as soon as she realized that the lock was broken she picked it up and stood it on the desk.

Despite her ongoing anger and defiance, she hesitated about going through it, but then she convinced herself that it was her parents' box, not Ruby and Johnnie's, and as such she was entitled to look at anything inside it. Everything that had belonged to George and Babs Wheaton was hers, whatever anyone else said.

Despite knowing exactly what was in her parents joint wills, she couldn't resist reading through them again. Seeing the words in black and white brought back the feelings of unfairness that had so overwhelmed her at the time, and seeing the information laid out on her birth and adoption certificates compounded her sense of isolation and lack of identity. She held them both for a while and debated taking them but decided against it. Much as she hated Ruby and Johnnie, she knew the documents were safe with them. She pushed her feelings away as she carefully put the papers back and forced herself to move on to look through everything else.

She flicked through the sections one by one until she found exactly what she was looking for – the letters from Herbert Smethurst listing all the Wheaton assets and their values. Maggie read and reread the accounts slowly, taking in the figures involved.

The Blythes had been absolutely correct in their assessment. One day, in the not too distant future, Maggie would be a wealthy young woman, despite having to share everything fifty-fifty with Ruby. She was elated, but her excitement at finding what she wanted was tempered by the fact that Ruby was worth similar, plus everything she already had courtesy of Leonora Wheaton.

All Maggie could see was that Ruby and Johnnie Riordan had become a very wealthy couple off the back of Ruby handing their daughter over to the Wheatons all those years before.

Her first instinct was to rush off to the Thamesview and confront Ruby and Johnnie with the information she now had, but then she thought it through and decided she would save it until the time was right. She grabbed a pencil off the desk and an empty envelope out of the bin and wrote down the figures as briefly as she could, stuffed the envelope in her pocket and put everything back as it had been.

She was just about to leave the room when she had a second

thought; she went back to the desk and gleefully filled her pockets with several pounds' worth of coins before switching the light off, closing the doors and running up to her bedroom to think about the information she had and to count the money she had taken. She took a book down from the shelf over her bed, put the envelope in-between the pages ready to show Andy the next time she saw him, and then stretched out her bed to think.

She was upset and angry about what she had discovered, but at the same time it cheered her to know she'd put one over on Ruby and Johnnie, even if she was bound to get into trouble for it at some point.

Eleven

'Well, someone's been in there; I know they have. The money from the cash box was in the drawer in the old biscuit tin from the hotel. I didn't have time to count it, so I just dumped it in the tin and brought it home.' Johnnie Riordan's face reddened with anger as his voice started to get louder. 'I bloody well know there was a lot more in the tin than there is now. It must have been Maggie! It had to be her; it can't have been anyone else,' he shouted, making no attempt to hide his rising frustration.

Although Ruby knew he was probably right, she just couldn't bring herself to openly condemn her daughter out of hand without talking to her first. She carried on wiping the table as if it was the most important job in the world. She stared down at the surface and rubbed away at an invisible mark. 'Maybe you made a mistake?' she said, without looking up. 'And, anyway, it can only be a couple of pounds. We don't keep much indoors. Is it really that important?'

'It's no mistake, and it's quite a few quid that's missing. Anyway, it's the principle not the money itself. It's the only room in the house that's a no-go zone for the kids. All of them. I know the boys wouldn't have gone in there and stolen money; in fact, I can't think of anyone who would . . . except Maggie.'

'Stolen is a strong word, and I don't think we should straight away blame her for everything,' Ruby said, trying to be reasonable. 'I know she's being difficult, but so have the boys lately, and—'

Johnnie interrupted Ruby mid-sentence. 'Difficult nothing, and don't you try blaming the boys. If they're difficult, it's because of her. The Wheatons spoilt her rotten since the minute she was born. They let her think she was a bloody princess who could have whatever she wanted and do anything she took a fancy to – dancing lessons, tennis lessons, everything she asked for – and now you're doing the same. Seems she can wreak havoc in this family and you'll still stick up for her. You're so focused on her, you ignore everyone else.'

Johnnie was furious and pacing the floor, and although she could understand his anger up to a point, it still hurt Ruby that he couldn't be more understanding of their daughter; more understanding of the fact that, with the best of intentions, they had been the cause of Maggie's grief and anger.

'That's not true, and you know it,' Ruby responded. 'I try my best to be fair to everyone, including Maggie . . .' She paused and then looked at him. 'And you, even though you're an adult.'

'Like it or lump it, Rubes, I'm right. You only ever consider Maggie nowadays. She's taking us for idiots, and the boys are suffering because we're always bloody arguing about her. Well, it's going to stop.'

Ruby stared at her husband in disbelief. She understood that he was frustrated – angry, even; they both were – but she couldn't believe that he was talking like that about his daughter, who had been through so much in the past few months. 'Oh, listen to yourself, Johnnie. You go on about the boys as if they're somehow separate from her. Maggie is *our* daughter. Absolutely ours, both of us, and whatever has happened to her is because of us. No one else. We're just lucky to still have her in our lives.'

'Not sure I agree with that,' Johnnie snapped back. 'She's ours by birth, but we didn't bring her up and, let's face it, it's becoming unbearable here. She might be happier somewhere else – maybe back in Melton at the vicarage. Mrs Hobart did say she'd think about it.'

Ruby had tried her best to keep calm, but she could feel herself reaching breaking point; deep down she knew that Johnnie was right, that Maggie had most likely been behaving badly again and stolen the money from the office, but her maternal defence mechanism was suddenly working at full speed and she couldn't believe what she was hearing. 'You're kidding me, Johnnie. You've spoken to them? You've actually bloody phoned and spoken to them behind my back? You want to throw the towel in on our daughter? How could you!'

'I had to. I needed to know if there was an alternative. I have to consider the boys . . .'

'The boys, the boys, you keep saying that . . . Do you think I've forgotten we have them? Well, I haven't, there are three, and they are our sons, but in exactly the same way Maggie is our daughter. We can't just give up on her, especially when it's OUR FAULT. The whole bloody mess is our fault. Not Maggie's. It's not that heartbroken sixteen year old's fault her life is a mess; we did this to her,' Ruby shrieked. She could feel the red mist of anger rising. She couldn't believe that her husband, Maggie's father, would go behind her back to find a way to get his own flesh and blood out of the house.

'Rubes, listen to me. It's for her sake as well,' Johnnie reasoned as he started to pace faster and gesticulate with his hands. 'She's so unhappy; can't you see that? She didn't want to leave Melton in the first place, but we made her. We dragged her away from everything she knew because we thought we knew best. But we didn't. Can't you see we did the wrong thing? It wouldn't mean we were abandoning her if we sent her back; she could come here whenever she wanted, and we could go there.'

'Well, of course it would. You're not stupid. You know it means exactly that, and that's how she'll see it. It's not going to happen; we're not sending her away.' Ruby had turned to the kitchen sink and had started to wash the cup and saucers, but she spun round to stare at her husband, who was alongside her leaning against the draining board. 'I can't take much more, Johnnie. It's bad enough trying to deal with it all as it is, but without you on my side? That's just crazy – how can you think like that? Well, I'm sorry, but if she has to go then I'll go with her. You can write her off, but I can't.'

Johnnie looked back at his wife, and for a few moments they locked eyes, but then without another word he walked across the kitchen and opened the door to the office. Ruby closed her eyes as the door slammed shut and the key turned in the lock. She knew it was the end of the conversation as far as he concerned.

Both of them had taken a rare day off together, a day off when the boys were at school. They knew Maggie wouldn't be around – she never was during the day – and they wanted to try and spend some time together. Their life had been one long round of crises since the day they'd received the phone call about the accident; it seemed to be just one thing after another, with someone or other upset by Maggie, and Ruby had been about to blow even before the latest revelations.

She dumped the tea towel on the draining board and went through into the front sitting room and walked over to the overly ornate wood and glass cocktail cabinet, which she hated but which had come with the house. She looked at it for a few moments before opening the glass doors and reaching in to pour herself a large neat brandy.

She took a sip and shivered at the first taste before, glass in hand, she walked across to the windows that overlooked the front garden and stared off into space.

She had tried so hard with Maggie, but she could see no light at the end of the tunnel; in fact, it was getting darker by the day.

The happy family they had carefully built was crumbling before her eyes.

The two older boys, Martin and Paul, who were Ruby's stepsons, were starting to play up for attention, and Russell was permanently on edge. He was only five and desperately wanted his big sister Maggie's approval and friendship, but her resentment of him was so great that she ignored him as much as possible.

Ruby hated seeing her son so upset, but at the same time she understood how Maggie could see Russell as her main rival. He was the biological brother who had always been Russell Riordan, who had always lived with both birth parents, and who would never be anyone else. Unlike his sister.

She also had an ongoing dread of Maggie finding out about Martin and Paul's mother Sadie, who had committed suicide several years before. They had simply told her that Sadie had died. With the way Maggie had been behaving lately, she could imagine her using it as weapon against them without thinking through the consequences.

Staring silently out of the window of the family home, Ruby felt the tears building at the back of her eyes, and her bottom lip wobbled as if it had a life of its own. She was at a complete loss. Her daughter was totally out of control, and Ruby herself was about to fall apart. It had been hard enough when she and Johnnie had been on the same side, but they were at each other's throats and the happy family home she had always wanted, that she'd had such high expectations of, was now a war zone.

Ruby sat down in the armchair by the window and sipped the neat brandy slowly, savouring the feel of it as it burned the back of her throat before hitting her empty stomach. The struggle of managing a growing business, of looking after all the children and the family home had been a manageable struggle until Maggie came to live with them. Now every day was a challenge and a worry. She never stopped worrying about all her children, but especially Maggie, because she was sure something terrible was going to happen to her if they couldn't find a way to get through.

'What are you doing in here in the dark?'

She looked up to see the outline of her husband in the doorway. 'Thinking,' she said.

'Look, Rubes, I'm sorry. I was horrible, and I'm sorry,' he said. 'I'm not sorry I phoned Mrs Hobart, but I'm sorry I didn't discuss it with you first. Don't you think it would be a solution? Not forever, but just until she gets over her hatred of us all. Mrs Hobart and the vicar could deal with her, she could go back to her old school, go to the tennis club, see her old friends, including that Andy . . .' He paused and walked over to the table lamp and turned it on. 'I did it for her. We dragged her away from everything she knew at a terrible time.'

Ruby didn't answer. In a way it seemed as if it might be a solution, especially as Maggie had never wanted to leave Melton anyway. 'Don't tell me you did it for her, Johnnie Riordan. You did it for you, because you're throwing in the towel on your own daughter. Are we seriously going to tell her she hasn't come up to scratch so we're sending her back?'

When her husband didn't answer, Ruby emptied her glass and stood up. 'Well, I'm not doing that, and if you don't like it you can lump it.'

'OK.' Johnnie raised his voice as she started to walk away. 'Just answer me. Do you know where she is right now? And yesterday? She's not at school, and she sure as hell isn't working. And now she's stealing? I'm worried sick about her every minute of the day, don't you know that?'

'No, I don't know where she is, where she was or where she is going to be, but I'll find out, and I'll certainly talk to her before I start calling her a thief.'

'Hello, Maggie. Bet you didn't expect to see us here, did you?'

Maggie looked up and blinked at the two women standing by the bench-table where she was sitting; because she had been miles away listening to a tune on the jukebox and trying to memorize the words, it took her a moment to realize it was Gracie Woodfield, Ruby's best friend, and her younger sister Jeanette. 'Are you following me?' Maggie asked.

'You're joking, aren't you? I haven't got time to even think at the moment, let alone track you around town!' Gracie laughed. 'No, we were just passing and saw you through the window, so thought we'd join you. That's OK, isn't it?'

'Free country . . .' She shrugged with a slight smile.

'What would you like? Take your pick, it's my treat . . .' Gracie said as she took off her coat and dumped it on the plastic covered seat.

'Frothy coffee for me, please, sis, and a cake, or maybe even two cakes if you're paying, bugger the waistline.' Jeanette laughed as she plonked herself down next to Maggie. 'What about you? Same again? Do you want anything to eat? Go on, if Gracie's buying you should make the most of it. She's buggering off to Africa soon, and there won't be much to spend her money on there!'

'Just a coffee, thanks,' Maggie said, looking down. She wasn't used to hearing adults swear, and it had actually made her blush.

'I know you know Gracie really well, but I'm sure you don't really remember me. I'm Jeanette, Gracie's baby sister. Everyone calls me Jeannie. I've got a twin called Jennifer, but she's the black sheep of the family so we don't talk about her.'

Maggie looked at the two sisters and after some thought decided they probably *had* just been passing by; the large windows fronted on to the main high street, so she would have been easily seen.

'So, this is the Sorrento, eh?' Jeanette said as her sister placed the order. 'I've walked past it often enough, but I haven't been in here before. Is it *the* place to go now? Seems really modern and sort of American.'

'It's OK,' Maggie replied. 'It's better than the seaside cafes on the front, and the music is really good. It's a bit quiet at the moment cos everyone's at work or school, but sometimes it's full to bursting.'

'I'm probably too old to be in here, really, but who cares? I can go home and say I've been in a coffee bar for the first time. The other nurses will think I am so cool and with it!'

As Jeanette pushed her shoulders back and pulled a silly face, Maggie couldn't help but laugh. She didn't really know Jeanette, having only met her once before that she could remember, but she liked her instantly; there was something about her easy-going manner that made her feel at ease. It was a nice feeling, after being constantly on edge for so long.

Jeanette McCabe was several years younger than Gracie and Ruby, but whereas they were both slender and graceful, Jeanette was loud, blonde and round in a shapely hourglass way. She reminded Maggie of Diana Dors, all hair and hips and tight clothes.

'So, what have you been up to today, Maggie? Are you waiting for someone or just killing time? We don't want to cramp your style if there's someone about to appear,' Jeanette said cheerily.

'Just hanging around. Anything to be out of the house and out of the way . . .'

'Blimey, as bad as that, is it? Nothing worse than things going wrong at home. I once moved in with big sis over there to get away from annoying parents. Ended up having to put up with a bossy annoying older sister instead! And at one point all three of us were in the flat at the top of Thamesview. Gracie, me and Ruby! Now I live near the hospital at Rochford with a couple of bossy nurses . . . did you know I'm a nurse?'

'No, I didn't know. Aren't you married then?' Maggie asked.

'No. Think I'm destined to be the old spinster woman; nothing ever works out for me. I keep picking wrong'uns; I'm really good at that.' Jeanette laughed loudly. 'What about you?

I mean, I know you're not married, blimey, not at your age, but have you got a boyfriend? Bet you have, gorgeous girl like you. I bet they're queuing round the block to go steady.'

Maggie laughed but didn't get a chance to answer as Gracie came back to the table.

'Sure you're not hungry, Mags?' she asked as she sat down opposite them.

'No, I'm really not, but thank you.' Maggie leant back in her seat for a moment. She was embarrassed that the two women had found her sitting in there on her own, and she really hoped they wouldn't tell Ruby and Johnnie, although she knew Gracie probably would. Gracie and Ruby seemed to share everything.

Jeanette picked up Maggie's magazine which was on the table and flicked through it. '*New Musical Express*. You into music, then? I used to go out with a bloke who sang in the pub up the road. Last I heard he was doing something up in London, reckoned he was going to be a star.'

'Yes, I love music and singing, and I've got loads of records. I'd like to be a singer, but . . .' She hesitated.

'But what? You're already gorgeous looking. If you can sing as well, then why not try?'

Suddenly, Gracie, who had been distractedly looking through her handbag, jumped up from her seat. 'Oh, bugger, just remembered I was supposed to pick Edward's shoes up before the cobblers round the corner closes. Be right back; don't drink my drink, and don't talk about me while I'm gone.'

'That's Gracie for you! Couldn't sit still if you paid her. She's like a flea on a wet flannel,' Jeanette said after Gracie had disappeared from sight. 'Anyway, singing. Go on . . .'

Maggie thought about it. She'd hated not having anyone to confide in, and although Jeanette was older than her in years she seemed to be on Maggie's wavelength. 'I made a record . . . well, not quite made a record, but I had a go in the record booth by the pier. Andy, the boy I know from Melton, is going to play it to his dad, who's in the music business in London.'

'Wow, that's so exciting.' Jeanette looked really interested, which encouraged Maggie.

'But you mustn't tell anyone. I shouldn't have said! No one knows.'

'My lips are sealed. We're all entitled to our secrets. I hope it works for you. You will let me know, won't you? And I'd love to hear it. I may have to pop round so you can let me listen.'

'It sounds really strange. I've never heard my own voice before, but at least I'm in tune!'

'You give it a go. Follow your dream, my darling.'

For a few minutes, sitting at the table chatting about everyday things, Maggie felt almost normal, and by the time Gracie came back with the shoes Maggie felt as if she had found a confidante, someone who seemed to be interested in her as a person rather than as a child with a tragic background.

Twelve

'Maggie, I have to talk to you,' Ruby said. 'Can you come into the kitchen? Please?'

Maggie knew what it was going to be about, and she'd already decided exactly what she was going to say when they asked her about the missing money. She was fired up and ready to fight.

'Johnnie is really upset. There's some money missing from his office, so we're talking to all of you to try and figure out what's happened.'

'You don't have to ask the others. I took it! It was me, guv; it was me what dunnit.' Maggie held her hands up over her head and smiled. She watched Ruby's face, trying to read her expression.

'What do you mean? Are you telling me you took it? Just like that?' Ruby asked.

'Just like that. It was me. I took it.' She stared at Ruby defiantly.

'Maggie, that's stealing; it's dishonest. Do you realize I was about to question Isobel about it? Imagine that. I stuck up for you, I said—'

'Yes, it was dishonest. I mean, who would steal money from someone else?' Maggie interrupted her quickly. 'Oh, I forgot. Like you've stolen from me, you mean?'

'Now you're being silly.'

'It's silly to steal someone's inheritance, is it? That's not dishonest? But a couple of quid from the drawer and you want to hang me?' Maggie let her hands drop and rolled her eyes at Ruby before looking away.

'Maggie, that's not true.'

'Yes, it is. I've seen all the papers, and I've read fatman's letters.' Maggie smiled smugly when she saw the look of horror on Ruby's face as it dawned on her exactly what Maggie had done.

'You went through our personal papers? In the office?'

'No, I never looked at any of your personal papers. I went through *Mum and Dad's* papers, and as they're dead they're now *my* papers.'

'That's so deceitful.'

'No, what's deceitful is you never told me how much money I've got. Or how much you got from them. And you can have your share, I can't. Not even giving me any pocket money when you're sitting on a bloody fortune of my money?' As her voice got louder, she started to gesticulate wildly. 'My money, mine, *Wheaton* money, just like the hotel should have been Wheaton money. You must think I'm stupid.'

'Maggie, I've explained this to you over and over – we all have. You can't have your inheritance until you're twenty-one. It's the law, and as we're your guardians we have to implement it. Johnnie and I have no choice in this.'

'So you've got your share but I can't have mine? I can't even buy a packet of fags.'

'Maggie, most of your inheritance is in the Melton house and surgery.'

'Liar!'

Ruby looked at her so sadly, that for a moment Maggie felt a twinge of guilt.

'I'm going to have to tell Johnnie, before he talks to Isobel and the boys.'

'Ah, I wondered how long it would be before the precious boys got another mention. Well, if you think I'm hanging around waiting for Mr *You Do As I Say*, then you're mistaken. I hate him even more than I hate you.'

'Don't talk about him like that, please. He's your father.'

'He isn't my bloody father, he's not! He's nothing like my real father, who was a good, kind man, who loved me!' she shrieked at the top of her voice. 'And you're not my mother, so just shut up and go and look after your precious boys, who happily call you Mummy. I never will!'

'Maggie, you can't steal—'

'I didn't steal anything. I took what was mine. I counted it; it came to six pounds eight and six. Take it out of the thousands of mine you've got your hands on, Miss Evacuee . . .'

As Maggie spat the words, Ruby reached across and slapped her daughter clean across the face. It shocked both of them, but whereas Maggie just looked stunned as she put her hand up to her reddening cheek, Ruby became even more furious.

'Get up to your room now, and if you dare leave the house I'll get on to Mr Smethurst and you'll be a ward of court before you know what it means. There's a limit to how much I'll put with from you, and you've gone past it.'

'That's where I was going, anyway!' Maggie shrugged and sauntered out of the room. She made it to the turn of the stairs before she cried.

Maggie was lying on her bed listening to her records when there was a knock on her door.

'Maggie, can I come in and talk to you? It's Gracie. I have tea and sandwiches.'

'Has Ruby summoned the troops?' she shouted back without moving. She waited for a few seconds. 'It's OK, you can come in.'

Gracie opened the door and stepped into the room with a tray in her hands; Maggie was lying on the bed on her side with her head on one hand and a pencil in the other. She carried on writing furiously in an exercise book.

'It's nothing like that; I wasn't summoned. I just called in on my way home from picking Fay up from a friend's house. Ruby was so upset, and I made her tell me what was wrong.'

Maggie shrugged. 'Good. She hit me. The cow hit me!'

'She told me, and she's sorry, really sorry . . .' Gracie put the tray on the end of the bed. 'Look, do you mind turning the music down a bit? I just want to talk to you for a minute.'

Ruby leaned across and lifted the record player arm off the record. 'Done.' She lay back down and picked up her pencil.

'Do you mind if I sit down? I've been on my feet all day, and I'm knackered. This getting ready to move lark is more tiring than going out to work every day.'

'Help yourself . . .'

Gracie grabbed the chair from under the dressing table and pulled it over beside the bed. It was low, so it meant she wasn't sitting higher than Maggie was on the bed.

'That's better.' She sighed and stretched her legs. 'Look, I can't pretend to know what it's like to have to go through your ordeal, but I can imagine, and I'd hate it. I'd probably behave as you have. I don't know what I'd do, but I can understand how Ruby feels.'

Maggie didn't look up as she spoke, but she didn't interrupt her either. After her meeting with Gracie and Jeanette in town, she had felt a little more kindly towards the sisters, so she was prepared to give Gracie a chance, even though she had no real intention of taking any notice of her. She was well aware that Gracie and Ruby were as thick as thieves and each would always support the other.

But she listened.

'You know Ruby and I have been friends for a long time . . . Do you know how we met?'

'Not really; no one's ever told me. Not that I ever asked,' Maggie said as she carried on writing.

'It was on the maternity ward at Rochford Hospital. Ruby had just had you, and I . . .' She paused for a moment. 'Well, I had just had my son Joseph.'

Maggie looked up, her interest caught. 'Joseph?'

'Well, that's what I called him. My firstborn, but I wasn't married, his father had disappeared off into the great unknown, so I had no choice. My parents sent me off to the mother and baby home, St Angela's, and when he was born he was taken off and adopted.'

'Where did he go?'

'That's the thing, Maggie; I have no idea. I don't know anything about him, not even his name, because I know they would have changed that. I don't know if he knows he was adopted or if it was kept a secret; I don't even know if he's alive. Anything could have happened to him. That's how it is with adoptions.'

'You don't know anything at all?' Maggie asked. She guessed where the conversation was going, but she was too interested in the story to cut Gracie off with one of her usual curt responses.

'Nope. Not a thing. Nothing. I only know his birthday because they couldn't change that even if they wanted to. I have a lock of hair and a piece of paper, his birth certificate, to prove he existed, but that's all. I could pass him in the street and not know. I probably have, if he was adopted locally.'

'That's sad,' Maggie said. 'I knew a girl at school who'd been adopted. We used to feel a bit sorry for her, but I didn't know then that I was adopted as well.'

'Most children weren't told. They still aren't, and St Angela's is still going strong! So you see you are connected to me whether you like it or not. I saw you when you were born, and I enjoyed seeing you and being a part of your life with Babs and George because I hoped desperately that my baby was as lucky as you.'

'How was I lucky? Everyone lied.'

'That's how it was, but you think about it, Maggie . . .' she said. 'Giving up your baby is the hardest thing you can do. It's not the easy choice that lots of people who've never been in that situation think. I saw what Ruby went through, the way her real family were to her. She couldn't tell them, and she had no choice over adoption, same as me. Babs and George had loved Ruby as their own, and she knew they would do the same for you.'

'If it was such a wonderful thing to do, then why didn't anybody tell me? Why was it a secret?' Maggie asked.

'Because you were their daughter, and they were waiting until they thought you were old enough to understand. But the accident changed all that, and that was nobody's fault.'

'It was my fault. The accident was my fault! I distracted Mum. I made her crash the car. If I hadn't been a cow to her she wouldn't have looked round and gone off the road . . .' The words were out before she could stop them.

'No! You can't blame yourself, Maggie. It was a terrible accident which spawned everything that followed, but you're not to blame for the accident, and Ruby and Johnnie are not to blame for the rest of it, so you have to stop tearing them apart.'

Maggie looked at Gracie and shook her head. 'I don't know why they're so bothered by what I do. Ruby has everything and I have nothing. They've even stopped my pocket money. It's not fair.'

'Is it fair that you refuse to go to school? Refuse to work? They're trying to do their best for you. They want to motivate you. They want the best for you, and let's be fair here, they've let you get away with murder . . .'

'They don't care about me; they only care about the boys. Johnnie is forever saying it.'

Gracie laughed gently. 'He's a man. They're not good at saying the right thing! You know deep down inside that it's not true, and saying it over and over won't make it so. Look, how about you come down with me and we work out a compromise? I'll be piggy in the middle and be referee.' Gracie laughed. 'God, the way my family used to fight, I'm good at it.'

'I don't want to.'

'I know you don't, but just give it a try. If it doesn't work then we'll think of something else. You have to try, Maggie my love, for your own sake.'

Maggie stood up. 'OK.'

'Good. Let's go.'

'Maggie? There's a telephone call for you . . .'

As she heard Johnnie call up the stairs, she knew instantly who it was. Andy. She hadn't heard from him as quickly as she'd expected, and she never dared ring him in London in case his father answered the phone. Andy always talked proudly of his father, but she sensed that Jack Blythe was the ruling force of the family and she didn't want to get on his wrong side for Andy's sake.

And also because of the demo disc he had that she was pinning all her hopes on.

Since the confrontation with Ruby, followed by the talk with Gracie, there had been an uneasy truce in the house. Maggie had agreed to help in the hotel behind the reception desk when they were short-staffed and had also let them all think she was seriously considering the idea of going to secretarial college in London. In return for her cooperation, her pocket money was reinstated and increased, and she was also going to be paid for working. The issue of her going through the papers in the office and taking the money would be forgiven but probably not forgotten, as Maggie now had the information.

She knew they were trying to keep track of her, but she was happy to let them think what they liked while she plotted what she was really going to do.

'Maggie? Maggie, it's the phone,' Johnnie called again.

She ran downstairs to the hall, where Johnnie was standing with the phone in his hand.

'It's Andy Blythe for you.'

'Thanks.' She smiled as best she could. She was trying her hardest to be amenable, but it was difficult. She felt as if they were thinking they'd won. 'Hello?' she said cautiously into the phone.

'I've got good news for you . . . Dad wants to meet you and hear you sing properly. Can you come up to London?'

Maggie looked around and saw that the kitchen door was still ajar, which meant Johnnie was listening in.

'I'm fine,' she said cautiously. 'How are you?'

'Did you hear what I said?'

'Yes, I did. I'm fine.'

'Ah. Someone is listening?' he said.

'Yes. It's cold here too.'

'Get the train to London on Monday. I'll meet you at Liverpool Street Station, and we'll get the underground to the office. OK? Monday, eleven o'clock at Liverpool Street Station.'

'Oh, yes. I'm looking forward to Christmas as well.'

'Is that a yes?' he asked.

'Yes.'

They spoke in coded terms for a little longer, and when Maggie put the phone down she went into the kitchen to find Johnnie looking out of the window. He had so obviously been eavesdropping on her phone call, but she wasn't going to say anything. She'd promised herself she'd remain calm. Until she didn't have to any more. 'I'm going into town,' she said.

'Did Andy want anything in particular?'

'No, just saying hello. I haven't talked to him for ages.'

'Maggie, I want to talk to you while your mum, Ruby, isn't here.'

'I haven't done anything wrong!'

'I know, but I know you're unhappy. Look, I won't beat about the bush. Do you want to go back to Melton? I'm sure we could arrange something for you, somewhere to stay. You could go back to school, pick up where you left off . . .'

Instantly, Maggie was alert. She knew Ruby desperately wanted everything to be fine between them, but Johnnie was a different kettle of fish. She had always liked him when he was just a brotherly figure in her life. He was always up for a laugh and would stick up for her to her mum and dad. But where he used to be fun as an occasional brother, now his role had changed, and so had he; where Ruby was desperately trying to get close to her, Johnnie seemed to be constantly pushing her away.

'Are you trying to get rid of me?' she asked him calmly.

'No, I'm not. You're my daughter, our daughter, but we want to do what's best for you. More than anything we want *you* to be happy, and I know you're not.' He went over and put his arm around her shoulder, but whereas previously she had felt comfortable with Johnnie, now she had to force herself not to recoil.

'So what do you want to do with me? Apart from throw me out, that is.'

'I thought you could go back to Melton for term time and then come back here in the holidays. We could find somewhere for you to stay.'

'Like where? When I wanted to do that, you told me it was impossible.'

'Maybe at the vicarage with the Hobarts?'

'I thought we'd agreed that I'd to go to secretarial college.'

'No, you didn't agree, Maggie. You can't kid a kidder, and I know you have no intention of doing that . . .' Johnnie smiled at her. 'But it's just something for you to consider. Think about it, and remember, we love you. We all do, even if you don't want to believe it.'

Maggie smiled and said nothing.

The uneasy truce instantly became uneasier on her behalf, but she didn't want anything to stop her going to London on Monday. There was just the weekend to get through . . .

When he heard the front door click shut and he knew Maggie had gone out, Johnnie Riordan made himself a cup of tea and went through to his new office. His den, the one place where he had time to himself.

He sat in the chair under the window, put his feet up and closed his eyes as he tried to think straight.

He loved Maggie as the father he was, but he couldn't bear to see how she was ripping his previously happy family apart. He understood her and her feelings of estrangement from everything, but he was becoming fed up with forever treading the fine line that kept the peace in the household. It was also affecting Ruby at work and by default everyone else at the hotel, because she was short and snappy with the staff. She was also making silly mistakes because she was forever worrying about Maggie, wondering where was and what she was doing.

But mostly he hated the way Maggie's behaviour was having an impact on the three boys and making them unsettled. After Martin and Paul's mother had died in awful circumstances, they had lived with Johnnie's sister Betty in Walthamstow, and he had fought for so long to have them living with him and Ruby.

Now, albeit unknowingly, Maggie was about to sabotage all that, because the boys had told their Aunty Betty just how unhappy they were with Maggie around the place.

Johnnie hadn't told Ruby. Instead, he had decided it was up to him to try and find a resolution that suited all of them. Including Maggie. Whatever Ruby and Maggie thought, he did want what was best for his daughter.

When Ruby had given birth to their daughter, Johnnie Riordan had known nothing about it; he hadn't even known she was pregnant. All he knew was that she had disappeared from Walthamstow into thin air. He assumed she had run away from her family and had tried to find her, but eventually he had moved on and married his first wife Sadie, and they had two sons.

It had been several years later when fate had finally brought the two of them back together, but by then Maggie was a formally adopted Wheaton, she had a new family and a new home, so all they could do was keep in touch as family friends, visit occasionally and hope that one day she would know she was their daughter.

Johnnie loved his daughter, as he always had, but he also had a more rational, almost unemotional, view of their daughter than Ruby. Unlike his wife, he had accepted that although he and Ruby were her birth parents, she would always be a Wheaton. It was they who had adopted her and raised her as their own. He knew that she would never be able to accept them as mum and dad because they weren't, and much as he hated to admit it, he really didn't feel the same about her as he did about the boys. The best he hoped for was a familial bond one day.

But while Johnnie was being realistic about their daughter, Ruby was absolutely enveloped in her own guilt and determined to make up for everything one way or another. She believed in happy ever after and was determined that they would all be a family sooner rather than later.

He picked up the telephone extension in the study and listened carefully for a few seconds to make sure no one else was on the line, then he dialled the number for the vicarage.

'Mrs Hobart? Johnnie Riordan here again. I'd like to come up to Melton and see you, to talk face to face. I think Maggie needs to be back in Melton with her friends . . .'

Thirteen

Maggie had been to London several times with Babs Wheaton on days out and shopping trips, but she had never been there on her own before, and she felt increasingly nervous as the train rattled through the stations en route. She prayed fiercely that Andy would be there as he'd said, because she didn't even have the actual address of where she was going let alone know how to get there.

But when she got off at Liverpool Street Station and looked through the crowds she could see him standing at the end of the platform near the gate. He waved as he saw her, and when she got near she could see he was actually excited. He pulled her in tight and kissed her on the lips, as if they were a real couple.

'I'm so pleased you're here. Couldn't talk to you properly on the phone, but Dad really loves the demo,' he said as he hugged her. 'And, guess what? I showed him a photo of you as well . . . one of those I took at the tennis club before you left. He really wants to meet you and hear you sing in person. He thinks you've got just the right look.'

'Sing in person? What, stand up and sing in front of him? I can't do that. It was bad enough in the booth on my own.' Just the thought of it made Maggie jump from foot to foot nervously. Apart from the choir, she'd only ever sung to herself in the mirror, and the thought of singing by herself, actually in front of someone, was a terrifying prospect.

'Don't be daft, of course you can. That's why you're here. Dad's agreed to see you. He's going to see you personally, and that's really something! He's really impressed that I got you to make that demo; he said I'd shown initiative. I hope he likes you . . .'

Maggie registered once again how deferential Andy was whenever he talked about his father; he idolized him and was in awe of his business success. She found it strange, because although she had always loved and admired her own father, George, she had never been in awe of him.

Although he was a very attractive young man, Maggie had been drawn to Andy when she first met him because he was supremely self-confident, almost arrogant, and she'd never met anyone like that before; he was still very sure of himself, and yet whenever he talked about his father he sounded quite childish in his puppy-like adoration. She found it quite unnerving, but at the same time she was looking forward to meeting the very important businessman she had heard so much about: Jack Blythe. Musical and Theatrical Agent.

They got off the underground at Tottenham Court Road Station and walked hand in hand through side streets and alleyways behind Oxford Street; she had no idea where they were, but he pointed out certain landmarks and told her they were taking the short cuts to their destination, the building which housed the Blythe business and London accommodation.

'This way,' he kept saying as he pulled her by her hand down yet another alleyway.

It was a crisp day, and Maggie was wearing a camel coat with a tie belt which had belonged to her mother, over the same skirt and jumper and heels she'd worn when she'd made the demo disc, the outfit Andy had said he thought was cool. She just hoped that she wouldn't look too young and unfashionable in front of Jack Blythe and that she wouldn't make a fool of herself in front of Andy. She sensed it was as important to him that his father liked her as it was to her.

'Here we are; this is it. The Blythe family business,' Andy said proudly as he stopped by some steps and pointed his arm at the building. 'The public office is on the ground floor, then there are other offices, bedsits and things, and we have the penthouse flat on the top floor.' He pointed upwards. 'That's where I live during the week when I'm working. It's fab being in the centre of London. There's so much going on. Look around! Everything is here. You must have been to Oxford Street? It's only a little way over there.'

Andy's enthusiasm was catching, and Maggie looked around

eagerly. The building they were outside was more ordinary than she had expected after the glamour of The Manor House in Melton. It was in the middle of a terrace of identical old properties which fronted a quiet cobbled side street, the majority of which had a shop or cafe on the ground floor and flats and offices above. The plaque on the wall alongside the door they were standing outside stated: *Jack Blythe and Associates. Music and Theatre Agency.*

'Who are the associates? What does that mean?' Maggie asked curiously. 'Are you one of them?'

'Not really, but I will be soon. At the moment I'm still learning.' He smiled at her enthusiastically. 'If you turn out to be a star, then Dad'll have to make me one, and one day, when he retires, it'll be Andy Blythe and Associates, and I'll get to pick my own associates! Come on, let's go in.'

They went up a few stone steps to the entrance, and Andy pulled the glass door and held it open for her to go in first. Several people waiting in the reception area looked up expectantly as he walked past them up to the desk, and then they looked down again at their magazines and newspapers.

'Monica, this is Maggie Wheaton. She's got an appointment with Dad?'

The receptionist smiled as Andy greeted her. 'Oh yes, but you might have to kill an hour or so first, Andy. Mr Blythe has just this minute popped out.'

'Oh, he didn't tell me he was going out today. He knew Maggie was coming,' Andy said, his disappointment obvious. 'Where's he gone?'

'He said he had a meeting near Harley Street. He won't be long, no doubt. Shall I ask Sally to make you a drink?'

'Yes, please. We'll be upstairs. Can you tell Dad when he gets back?' He walked around the desk and opened what looked like a cupboard door in the corner. 'This way, Maggie.'

He led her along a narrow unlit corridor to a wooden staircase which doubled back on itself up to the first floor. When they reached the first floor landing, Andy turned and led Maggie into a large and airy room with several high sash-windows and a large neglected fireplace. It was sparsely furnished with just four upright chairs, an old piano stacked high with music sheets, a record player on a wonky drop-leaf table and a microphone on a stand which was next to a battered old amplifier. As they walked across the room it echoed with emptiness.

Andy pointed to a mark on the floor near the microphone. 'This is where you'll stand to sing, and Dad will sit over there. He has the same routine with everyone. But sometimes I do the first interview . . . It's mostly singers in here, but some comedians and even actors. Everyone wants Jack Blythe to represent them; sometimes it's standing room only downstairs with people waiting to see him. Did you see them all downstairs? They all want to be taken on by Dad.'

'Where's your office?' Maggie asked as she looked around and took in her surroundings, which didn't fit in with the mental picture she'd had. The room looked as if it hadn't been decorated in years. The walls and ceiling had the brown tinge of tobacco, and the bare floorboards were shabby and worn.

'I don't have an actual office of my own. I move around, and I'm often out. Dad trusts me to do a lot of stuff he doesn't want the others to do. I go and see people and deliver urgent documents that mustn't go by post.'

'Andrew!' a voice bellowed from behind.

Ruby and Andy turned and looked towards the door.

'Dad!' Andy said, his smile wide. 'This is Maggie Wheaton. You said you wanted to meet her, so here she is.'

Maggie smiled and held her hand out. She stood straight and confident, but she had never felt so overawed in her life. Standing way over six feet tall, he was a charismatic giant of a man, whose athletic frame filled the doorway. He had a thatch of very dark hair which was flecked with grey and perfectly groomed, and as she looked at him she noticed his piercing blue eyes looking back at her curiously.

'Ah, yes. Maggie. You're the girl from the village. I'm sorry about your parents. Such a tragedy. We never know what fate has in store for us, do we?'

'Thank you, Mr Blythe.'

'I've got a couple of phone calls to make, but if you want to warm up, then be my guest. I'll be back to hear you shortly.'

As quickly as he'd arrived he was gone, through another door on the opposite wall.

Maggie and Andy had been in the room alone for nearly an hour before he came back. Because Maggie had refused the chance to warm up, it had been an uncomfortable hour of stilted conversation interspersed with several long silences and thumb twiddling before the man appeared again.

'Andy, there's an envelope on my desk to be hand delivered. You do that while I talk to young Maggie here.' His tone was dismissive as he pointed in the direction he had just come from.

'But . . .'

'No buts. You know that, son. Now, off you go, chop chop.'

Without another word, Andy scuttled through the door, and after a few moments he appeared with a large envelope in his hand. 'I'll be straight back,' he said to Maggie. 'Good luck.'

As Andy left the room, Jack Blythe unbuttoned his suit jacket, loosened his tie and sat down on one of the chairs. He leaned back so far that the front two legs of the chair were off the floor, and Maggie wondered for a moment if he was going to topple backwards. Still balancing, he crossed his arms and legs at the same time and looked her up and down critically before putting his head on one side and staring into her eyes. His focus on her was disconcerting, but she stood her ground and met his gaze.

'Come on then, young lady. My boy was right about one thing, you certainly look the part. Now sing for me, show me what you're made of. X marks the spot, off you go.'

Caught off-guard, Maggie didn't know what to do without Andy there to guide her, it was nothing like she had anticipated, but she knew it was going to be her only chance so she went over to the spot on the floor that had been marked with a splodge of black paint.

'Take your coat off. I need to see how you move. It's not just your voice; it's your performance. You have to persuade me you're different; pretty little singers are two a penny nowadays.' Jack Blythe's booming voice echoed around the empty room making her feel even more nervous. 'The mike isn't working, but I want you to pretend it is. Use it properly and sing into it.'

She took her coat off and dropped it on a nearby stool along with her handbag. Before she moved back to the mark she self-consciously straightened her clothes and tugged at her hair as best she could without a mirror. There was nothing else she could do apart from get on with it.

She moved back, took a deep breath and, with no backing, started to sing. As she did so she swayed a little and tried to imagine herself up on stage singing to an audience; she also tried to ignore the man sitting across the room staring at her.

'OK, that wasn't bad. Have you got another song, or are you a one-trick pony?' he asked as she stood silently at the end of the song.

'I know lots.'

'Have you brought a list?'

'No, sorry, I didn't think . . .'

Jack Blythe sighed loudly as he lifted his arms up and crossed them behind his head. 'Pick another one from your mental list then.'

Maggie was halfway through her third song when Andy slid quietly into the room and sat beside his father. She had started to relax a little and get into the songs, but now she suddenly felt nervous all over again. She carried on until the end, though, and then stood silently on the same spot, unsure of what to do next.

Jack Blythe stood up and, without a word, walked through into his office.

'He didn't like me,' Maggie said as she walked across the room and sat down beside Andy on the seat his father had vacated. 'Now I feel stupid for doing it. Come on, let's go. This was a daft idea . . .'

'No, no,' Andy said quickly. 'We can't go until Dad says. We'll just sit here, and he'll soon come out again. It's what he does. He needs to go off and think on his own. If he likes you then he'll talk to you in his office.'

Maggie didn't want to stop there a second longer. Her face was scarlet with embarrassment, and she could feel the walls closing in on the room. She had made a fool of both herself and Andy. 'Will he be cross with you if I wasn't good enough? It was hard standing there in front of your dad like that . . . He made me feel so nervous.'

'Why would he be cross with me? I only gave him the record to listen to; it was his choice to see you after he heard you sing on the record. He did that, not me, so no, he can't blame me.' Andy smiled encouragingly, but Maggie could sense his nerves also, and again she wondered at it.

Andy was normally so confident and proud of his role as heir to the Blythe business, yet in the presence of his father he seemed almost tongue-tied and nervous to the point of being scared.

The door opened. 'Come in now, young Maggie. You too, Andrew, as she's your lucky find.'

They went in together to a smaller room where Jack Blythe was seated behind his carved wooden desk. It was obviously his office, but it was also warm and nicely furnished, with a couch and coffee table on the other side of the room and framed photos all over the walls. While Maggie sat on one of the chairs opposite Jack, Andy went round and stood behind the desk next to where his father was sitting.

'How old are you, Maggie?' Jack Blythe asked her.

'Sixteen.'

'That could be the sticking point, then. Your parents or guardians will have to sign an agreement giving you permission to perform. Will they do that?'

'My parents are dead . . .'

'Guardians then . . . I know you have them. I know the story, remember?' He smiled and winked at her. 'I don't want to get into the emotional hoo-ha about what happened with your inheritance, but Andy here said you're living with guardians and that they have control of the whole kit and caboodle. I'm sure they'll sign if you can persuade them that this is a reputable agency. Most parents love the idea of their kids earning them a fortune.' He laughed loudly. 'And this is, of course, a reputable agency, in case you're wondering.'

Maggie felt extremely uncomfortable but forced herself to smile and be adult about the situation. It would soon be over.

As he was talking, she studied the man surreptitiously. She

could see the family resemblance between father and son, but where Andy's features had been softened by his mother's more gentle genes, Jack Blythe had sharp, handsome features. He was tall and broad shouldered but not too muscular, which allowed him to wear his clothes well. Despite her young age, Maggie was perceptive about people, and she could sense a powerful and ruthless streak in him that could probably be very hard.

As she was thinking about similarities between Andy and his parents, her mind wandered, and she started to think about the photos she'd studied recently of Ruby and Johnnie and her own genes. Much as she didn't want to admit it, she could see something of both of them in her own appearance.

'Are you listening to me, young lady?' Jack Blythe snapped at her when she didn't answer immediately.

'Of course. I'm sure that'll be OK with them. But what are they agreeing to? I need to know so that I can discuss it with them. What am I going to be doing?'

'I don't know yet. I'm going to need to see you again, maybe with some added vocals and a mike, see what you're really capable of.' Again he stared at Maggie, and then after a few moments he let his eyes wander slowly up and down her body then back to her face. 'You've got a good voice, a great figure. I could maybe use you as a backing singer for one of my acts, get you some experience. I don't know. I'll have to give it some thought first.'

'Thank you, Mr Blythe. I'll talk to them when I get home.'

'Oh, thanks, Dad.' Andy grinned and put his hand on his father's shoulder.

'Don't do that, son. It's not businesslike.'

Jack Blythe quickly swatted him away in irritation, his frown telling Maggie all she needed to know. She felt a wave of sympathy for Andy, so she pretended to rub away at an imaginary mark on her stocking.

'Sorry,' Andy said sheepishly. 'Shall I see Maggie back to the station now?'

'Yes. Give her the forms she needs to take home, but go through them with her, and then you can take the rest of the day off . . . I've got appointments in here this afternoon, and I need privacy to make decisions.' Jack Blythe pulled open a drawer of his desk and proffered something to his son. 'Here's some luncheon vouchers. Go and treat yourselves down the road.'

'Can we go upstairs first? I'd like to show Maggie the view . . .'

The man shook his head and laughed. 'You do that, son, but no hanky-panky. Your mother'll have my guts for garters if you get in trouble up there.'

As Jack winked at her, Maggie blushed and looked down, and when she looked up again he had already picked up a folder, opened it and started scanning the pages.

She knew they had been dismissed.

'Is that all there is to it?' she asked Andy once they were out of the office with the door closed behind them. 'But I don't know about the permission. Ruby and Johnnie will go ape at this idea; they want me to go to secretarial college. Or back to live in the vicarage in Melton.'

'You never told me about that.'

'It doesn't matter. It's just another of Johnnie's ideas to get me away from being a bad influence on their precious boys. I'm not going.'

'OK.' Andy looked bemused but didn't pursue it. 'What do you think about asking them? If you do and they say no, they'll be on the alert . . .' He paused. 'Unless, of course, you want to forge it. That'll be easy enough; others have done it. Dad doesn't mind so long as he doesn't know about it.'

'I don't want to ask them and have them say no or, even worse, have them interfere. It'd be her, him and fatman all over again. I'll have to think about the best way to get round it.' She paused and frowned. 'And they're bound to find out what I'm doing . . . Oh, I don't know. Maybe I might just run away. I don't think they'd mind; they'd probably be grateful to see the back of me. Their perfect lives could be perfect all over again. They probably wouldn't even bother to look for me.'

'Find something with their signatures on, then, but don't you dare tell anyone that's what I said if you get caught. I'll find the papers for you later. First, let's go up, and I'll show you the flat.'

It wasn't a large apartment, but it was at the top of the

building. There was a small balcony at the back with a view out over fire escapes and chimney pots. It was nothing exceptional and certainly nothing like the picture Andy had painted of it, except for the fact it was right in the centre of London. As Andy showed her around, Maggie couldn't help but notice that there were very few feminine touches in the flat. In fact, it was almost utilitarian.

'Does your mother stay here as well?' she asked.

'God no, she hates it. She's happiest being Lady of the Manor in Melton. No this is Dad's place. And mine.'

'It's nice,' Maggie said. 'I'd love to live in London.'

'Perhaps you can if you get your singing going . . . Maybe you could stay here. I'll ask Dad.'

'There's not enough room though.'

'We've got rooms downstairs that Dad lets out. You could have one of them. Dad doesn't spend many nights here, anyway; he's always out with his friends. They all like gambling and drinking and staying up late, all the things Mum hates. We have a cleaner for the flat, which means I don't have to do anything.'

'Her, him and fatman would never let me.' Maggie frowned and shook her head.

'Don't tell them. Don't forget, when you get your inheritance you can do whatever you like. Until then duck and dive, go back and forth, pretend you're working in John Lewis or something . . .'

'My inheritance is years away – five years away, in fact. Well, four and a half years . . .' Maggie said after a few seconds' thought. She had been about to show him the piece of paper with all her financial details on, the information she'd got from the filing box, but something stopped her.

'Come on then,' Andy said. 'Let's go and make the most of these vouchers. Dad doesn't usually hand them out willingly. We can decide when you're going to come to live in London, at least for part of the time, like I do!'

'I'm not sure, Andy. They're bound to try and find me.'

'Just get the papers signed somehow, and we can take it from there. It'll be such fun . . . We can go out in London.' Andy laughed and pulled her in close and, as they fell back on to the sofa, he kissed her, and she responded hungrily. Over the past months she had felt so deprived of affection, the real affection her mum and dad had shown her. It was as if the floodgates were suddenly opened, and she clung to him. She was alone with Andy Blythe, the boy she was in love with, he liked her, his father liked her singing, and she was being offered somewhere to live that wasn't with the Riordans. It was as if a light had been switched on after the months of misery she had suffered since the terrible accident. Suddenly, she could see ahead in her life; she could see a light at the end of the tunnel for the first time since her life had been turned upside down so dramatically.

'Come on,' Andy suddenly said. 'We'd better go before Dad comes in and catches us.'

Maggie smiled to herself as she straightened her clothes. She had been wondering how she could stop things going further than she intended without hurting Andy's feelings, and then he'd done it for her. She decided she would give Andy the paper with her financial details, after all.

On the train home Maggie closed her eyes and thought about everything that had happened and wondered if it was just possible she could escape the Riordans and Southend and have a new life in London.

With Andy Blythe.

Fourteen

Maggie was a clever girl, so it hadn't been hard for her to get both Ruby and Johnnie's signatures just right. She had simply hung around at the hotel and snooped in the office until she found something recent with them on, and then she'd sat up into the night in her bedroom practising over and over. As soon as she thought it was good enough to at least look genuine and adequate enough for Jack Blythe to accept, she had signed the actual agreement.

It wasn't as perfect as she'd have liked, but he would have nothing to compare the signatures to, and Andy had told her he would have no interest in verifying them. He wouldn't care if they were genuine or not; he just needed the signed piece of paper on file to cover himself.

The next day she'd posted the signed papers back to Andy so that he could give them to his father, and then she'd crossed her fingers and waited.

Soon, she hoped, she wouldn't have to suffer being the outsider in the Riordan household any longer, she would be able to escape and do what she wanted to do, but in the meantime she spent hours in her room singing along with the records Andy had given her and writing down every lyric.

When she really thought about it, Maggie knew she was sometimes unfair in her behaviour, especially to the boys, but she couldn't help but keep brooding on what Ruby and Johnnie had done to her.

Her worst time was always in the middle of the night when she couldn't sleep and her life ran back and forth in front of her eyes like a film in the cinema. Her life in Melton with Babs and George had been so right, but now, since that fateful day, it was all wrong, all of it, and the nightmare of that accident, the accident that was her fault, was with her every moment. Sometimes, when she tossed and turned, she wished she could just go to sleep and stay asleep forever; then the nightmares would stop.

She would lie awake and pick over all the details of her previous life with her mum and dad, trying to find any clues she might have missed, anything that might make sense of it all. It was so overwhelming, and it seemed as if no one except Andy Blythe gave a damn about her.

'So when can I have my money?' she asked Ruby casually over breakfast. It had been another bad night with recurring nightmares; with everything closing in on her, Maggie was feeling twitchy and irritable and spoiling for another confrontation.

'What do you mean?' Ruby asked distractedly as she tried to coordinate three young boys for breakfast before school. 'You've had your pocket money *and* your wages, if I remember rightly.'

'No, I mean all my money. My inheritance . . . I mean, if you send me back to Melton like Johnnie wants, you'll have to give it to me, won't you? If you're not going to look after me, I should get the lot, shouldn't I?'

Ruby sighed and shook her head. 'Maggie, I don't know what you're talking about. No one's sending you anywhere. Whatever gave you that idea?'

'Johnnie told me.' Maggie stared at Ruby waiting for a reaction. 'Off to the vicarage it is for me, he said. Then probably next stop will be a handy convent.'

'You must have misunderstood him, because that isn't going to happen; now, I have to get the boys ready for school and myself to work.'

Ruby's tone was measured, but Maggie could sense an underlying anger in her voice and realized she might have hit a nerve. It made her feel minimally better to know that maybe Ruby didn't share Johnnie's views on sending her away but she still couldn't stop herself from sniping, 'That's not what Johnnie said. In fact, he said—'

'Oh, do stop it!' Ruby interrupted her wearily. 'Look, if you want an adult discussion about all of this then that's fine, but we'll have it at the hotel in private. You're doing a shift today, aren't you?'

Maggie shrugged. 'Supposed to be, but I don't know why. There's nothing to do, and there's no one there. It's so boring . . .'

'Out of season is always a difficult time for hotels,' Ruby said as she carried on clearing the breakfast table. 'It usually means more work for the rest of us when the seasonal workers aren't around and the decorators are in making a mess. Come to the office around eleven, and we can talk properly. I'd say we could use the flat, but Gracie and Edward are staying there until they leave for Africa. I don't know if they're in or out today.'

'Yes, Mrs Riordan, ma'am. Eleven o'clock in your office, ma'am. Anything you say, ma'am.' Maggie clicked her heels and saluted.

'Instead of being so childish you could help me with clearing the table,' Ruby said calmly.

'I've got to get ready for work myself, ma'am.'

The boys, who were all at the table having breakfast, sniggered in unison.

Maggie bowed theatrically in front of Ruby, before backing out of the kitchen tugging at her forelock. Feeling a little guilty, she paused at the bottom of the stairs for a moment and wondered about going back in, but instead she went up to her bedroom to get ready for work at the hotel.

In a detached way, Maggie had grown to quite like the boys. It continued to irk her that they were all related and she had never known, but there was a certain innocence in their acceptance of the situation that she rather liked. They all simply accepted that she was their sister, just another member of the family, and she wished she could do likewise instead of picking on them, especially Russell, her brother by blood. She always felt mean when she upset him, but she just couldn't help it. Her resentment was too great, and the words were always out before she could stop them.

As she went up the stairs she could still hear their giggling, and she promised herself she would try not to be mean to them any more. As Andy had sensibly said, none of it was their fault either. However, even though Maggie could feel herself mellowing slightly towards the boys, she couldn't do the same with Ruby and Johnnie; she just couldn't rise above their betrayal of her. She also hated the hotel with a passion because it was a constant reminder that Ruby and Johnnie had everything while she had nothing. As she saw it, because Ruby had effectively sold her to the Wheatons, Ruby now had the hotel which had belonged to Leonora Wheaton and half of the inheritance that should all have been Maggie's.

She'd lost her parents, her old life and her future in a split second in time, and no one except Andy understood. It rankled constantly, especially when he reminded her she was an heiress living like a pauper in a strange family and being treated like a naughty schoolgirl. But although Maggie had confided her thoughts and fears to him, she had left something crucial out. When he sympathized and told her he understood how she felt, she wondered if he'd be that understanding if he knew the accident was all her fault.

Once she was ready, she went downstairs and slipped quietly out of the back door, trying to bypass everyone, including Isobel who was ready to take the boys to school; instead of waiting to go with Ruby, she walked round to the hotel on her own. She paused as she passed the phone box and thought for a moment about ringing Andy, but she decided against it. She'd posted the signed forms back; she would have to wait until he contacted her again.

At eleven o'clock on the dot, Maggie knocked loudly on the office door and waited, despite the fact that the door was open and she could easily see Ruby sitting behind the desk, which faced the door.

'You know you don't have to knock if the door's open,' Ruby said, resisting the urge to sigh in frustration. 'Come in and let's talk. Do you want a drink or a sandwich? Or we could walk along to the cafe and see if it's open? It's a nice day.'

'No, thanks, and anyway, it's not open. It's not open again until after Christmas.' Maggie folded her arms and feigned looking out of the window.

'That's a shame. Well, close the door and let's talk. I've sorted out our work so we can sit here all day if we want. No one will come in, and if they do knock I'll ignore them.' Ruby smiled as she stood up and went round to the other side of the desk and sat on one of the upright chairs in the room.

'I'm pleased you came to talk to me, Maggie. I wasn't sure if you would.'

Since the previously tiny office had been extended, there was more room to move around, but it was still a compact space on the ground floor at the front of the hotel with a view out over the promenade and the sea. Johnnie had suggested moving it to the back of the hotel, but Ruby had been adamant. It had been Leonora Wheaton's office in the original Thamesview Hotel, and she wanted it to stay that way.

Although the hotel had been expanded from one building to three, which were all interconnected, the heart of the building remained at the original Thamesview. Ruby and Johnnie had turned the property from a small ladies only establishment, which appealed to a niche market, into a family hotel, although the original rooms remained 'ladies only' to cater for the long-standing regulars.

The fact that Ruby loved it so much made Maggie hate it even more.

With her back upright and her arms still folded in the way Ruby had come to recognize and expect, Maggie perched on the very edge of the chair that was furthest from her, deliberately avoiding any contact. 'I'm here, but I don't want to talk all day. I just want my money, then I can go and get on with my life and you can go back to how you were before you were lumbered with me.'

'We're not lumbered with you, we want you. But hypothetically, if you had the money, where would you go?' Ruby reasoned, deliberately keeping her tone even. 'You're clever and beautiful, but you've never had to fend for yourself. How would you do that?'

'Easily, if you hand over my bloody money. For a start, you could chuck the doctor out of my house and I could live there.'

'But you've just said you don't want to go back to Melton, and you'd still have to earn a living as a sixteen year old with no qualifications.'

'No, I didn't say I didn't want to go back to Melton. I said I didn't want to be sent back in disgrace to live like an orphan in the vicarage!'

Ruby looked sideways at her daughter and, as had happened

so often over the previous few months, did her best not to react. She understood Maggie, the girl who was her flesh and blood. She understood her anger, and she ached for her, but she didn't know how to get through the safety barrier that Maggie had constructed around herself. It seemed that whatever she said or did was wrong. 'We've explained it to you so many times, Maggie. That can't happen because of the law. The wills were specific, everything is as they wanted, and it's impossible to change any of it. They're legal documents—'

'Oh, it's always the wills,' Maggie interrupted rudely. 'But you said yourself that Mum and Dad didn't really mean it. They were being careful, just in case.'

'Yes, but *just in case* happened, and that's how it is. We can talk till the cows come home, and it won't change. But as I've said over and over, if there's anything you need, you're our daughter. I know you can't accept it, and I can see why, but we have to deal with everything as it is, not how we wish it was.'

As Maggie shook her head and looked down, Ruby could feel the same old helplessness washing over her. She wanted to do the right thing, she wanted help her daughter, but Maggie was as unyielding as a brick wall.

'OK, you can tell me why you think Johnnie wants to send you away, because I find it hard to believe that he'd say that.'

'Are you saying I'm lying?' Maggie asked.

'No, of course I'm not, but I do know you're so het up that you could have got the wrong end of the stick.'

'I haven't got the wrong end of the stick, and I know because he said so to my face . . . I told you, he wants me to go and live in the vicarage like a homeless orphan. Probably only one step up from Edgar the tramp, who the Hobarts give their leftovers to.'

'I have to admit that it was an option which was talked about because we were desperately trying to find a way of making you happy. You had wanted to stay in Melton, but we thought it'd be best for you to be here with your family . . . No, don't interrupt,' she said quickly as Maggie opened her mouth. 'We couldn't all go and live there with you, so it was just an idea. We thought *you* might want to go back, but it's not what *I* want. We are your family, and we always will be, whether you like us or not. I want you here, and so does Johnnie, but we also want you to be happy – and you're not, are you?'

'Well, I wouldn't be, would I? What did you expect? If Johnnie didn't want me to go to the Hobarts, then how come I know about it? He told me all about it.'

'I didn't expect anything. I never even thought about a situation like this, so we're all as confused as each other. But as Johnnie and I are the adults in the eyes of the law, we had to do what the law says and abide by Babs' and George's wills.' Ruby paused and looked at her daughter. 'I'm sorry. All I want is for you to be happy, and for us all to get along together, I really do.'

Maggie didn't answer. She simply looked across to the window feigning uninterest, but Ruby knew she was fighting tears. She knew exactly what it was like to be an angry and frustrated sixteen year old in a difficult situation with no way out in sight.

'Maggie, when I was your age I was as unhappy as you are now, so I know how you're feeling and I'd do anything to make that better, but I can't turn the clock back and do things differently. I just can't . . .' Ruby resisted the urge to reach out and hug her daughter to her. Instead, she lightly touched her arm and waited, giving Maggie time to hold back her tears and be able to speak.

'You should have told me, they should have told me,' she said angrily. 'I'm not me any more, and it's not bloody fair.'

'I've got a suggestion for you. Don't answer now. Think about it and let me know. I'd like you to come over to Walthamstow with me and meet my mother, your grandmother. I know you said no before, and you were right, it was too soon, but now? You could also meet Betty, Johnnie's sister. She's the one in Hornchurch where the boys go and stay sometimes; she used to live just down the road to my family home. It's where Johnnie lived also.'

'Not a chance! They don't even know I exist.'

'They didn't at the time, of course they didn't, but as we told you, they do now. Think about it. My brothers and their children are best left out of it for the moment; they'd be a bit too much all at once, but just those two. Please?'

'I'll think about it, but it'll still be no,' Maggie said as she stood up. 'I'm going back to work; you and Johnnie can have another conflab about me and my money.'

As she walked out, Ruby went over to the window and looked out as she always did when she wanted to think. She thought she may have got through to Maggie just a little, she hoped she had, but she was all too aware that it was going to be a long hard slog for them to get anywhere near the normality they'd all had before the accident.

After several minutes' thought, Ruby went out into the hotel lobby. 'Is Mr Riordan around?' she asked the decorator, who was stood atop a ladder carefully painting the elaborate coving that stretched through the original areas of the hotel on all floors.

'I saw him out in the garden earlier. He was giving Ed a right old telling off for leaving his ladders and things on the flower bed.'

'I'll go and find him. If anyone needs me I've gone that way, and Ed had better hope the ladders are gone from my precious beds before I get there!' Ruby laughed.

The painting was a huge job, and it all had to be done when the hotel was empty of guests, so they had closed the original hotel off completely from the two extensions for the winter.

Ruby and Johnnie had stretched themselves to their financial limit when they had bought the third adjoining property the previous year, and the house where they all lived was fully mortgaged, but the business was doing well and they were looking to the future rather than the present. Ruby was determined not to use anything that the Wheatons had left her until the day Maggie could access hers, which was another bone of contention between her and Johnnie. He wanted her to invest it in the hotel, but she couldn't bring herself to do it – not while things were as they were with Maggie. Ruby was starting to think that life was once again conspiring against her.

She walked out through the main building to the garden and found Johnnie standing with his hands on his hips, looking through the arch in the wall that led to another part of the garden.

'Hello darling,' she said as she walked up behind him and put her hands on his waist. 'I hear you've been having a go at Ed . . . Poor bloke, he's a good painter, but not that sharp. I hope you weren't too hard on him.'

'Nope. I just told him you'd have his guts for garters if you caught him so much as looking at the flower beds the wrong way!'

'Quite right too.' She paused. 'I've just been having a chat with our Maggie. I think I may be getting somewhere at last. She came to see me, and she didn't rant and rave quite as much.'

'Any resolutions?'

'Not really. I tried to persuade her to come with me to meet my ma and your Betty.'

'Is that a good idea if she's going back to Melton?'

'She's not going back to Melton, Johnnie, how many times? Not, not, not!'

'Isn't that for us all to decide?'

'No, it's not, because it's not an option. We are not going to send her off to the vicarage, and that's it.'

'But I've spoken to Mrs Hobart again . . .'

'Well, then you can unspeak to her. She's not going, and that's that. We're going to get through this as a family – no buts, no Hobarts, no nothing.'

Fifteen

'Maggie . . . Maggie? Can you hear me? Andy's on the phone.'

Maggie jumped up from her bed when she heard Johnnie bellowing. She switched her wireless off and, barefoot, ran out of her bedroom across the landing and down to the ground floor, pushing past Johnnie who was still standing halfway up by the turn of the stairs.

'Blimey, you must be keen to move that quick.' Johnnie smiled, but Maggie didn't look at him and unusually didn't bother with a smart response; it had been so long since she'd heard from Andy that she'd started to think he had dumped her and, equally as important, that her budding singing career was over before it had even begun.

She snatched the phone up. 'Hello?' she said cautiously, aware as always that Johnnie was listening to her. She was just grateful he hadn't been down in the office and able to listen in on the extension.

'Maggie, I've got good news. Can you talk?'

'Sort of, but not really . . .' she replied in a whisper, looking up the stairs and seeing Johnnie's legs still on the same stair he had been standing on when she'd run past him. 'I was wondering when you'd ring. I thought you'd forgotten me.' She stretched the cord of the telephone as far as it would go across the hall from the telephone table and turned to face the corner of the entrance hall on the opposite side to the stairs. It was as far away as she could get from Johnnie.

'It's just been so busy,' Andy continued, speaking quickly. 'Dad has such a lot going on, and I'm really having to work the hours to help him out. But I don't mind because he always works so hard. I have to do the same. We've got a lot of new acts. And now I've got to get back to Melton because Mum's got a party tonight. It's all so busy in this industry. Oh, and I've got a car. Dad bought it for me, but it's going to stay in Melton. I don't need it in town.'

Maggie didn't really want to hear any more about how hard he was working or how wonderful his dad was; she wanted to know about herself. 'Any other news? Anything about you know what?' Maggie asked cautiously when Andy paused for breath.

'Yes, but I need to talk to you properly in private when you can talk back! I tell you what, get yourself to a phone box and ring me at the Manor House tonight. Reverse the charges. Eight o'clock. I'll be back by then.'

'OK, but I'm . . .' She tried to respond to tell him she wasn't sure what time she could get out of the house as she'd promised to stay in for dinner, but the tone coming down the line told her he'd already put the receiver down.

'Everything alright, Mags?' Johnnie asked as he got to the bottom of the stairs.

'Yes.'

'You weren't on the phone long . . .'

'He's working. It was just a quick call.'

'It's impressive that he works so hard at his age.' Johnnie smiled. 'How about you invite him down here for dinner on Sunday? Or maybe sometime over Christmas. Any time, doesn't have to be formal. I'd like to get to know him. Ruby liked him, and she got on well with his mother. What do you think?'

Maggie thought for a moment, unsure if Johnnie was leading her into a trap. Whenever she thought about it in depth, which she tried very hard not to do, she was always surprised that it was Johnnie who was proving to be the most hostile towards her. He had always been the jovial big brother whose company she enjoyed, but now it felt as if he was constantly behind her, trying to catch her out.

Maggie surreptitiously looked at him through her long, mascara-coated eyelashes; Johnnie Riordan was tall and broad and, as he leaned casually against the banister, she still found it hard to reconcile that the good-looking young man was actually her birth father and that she was really his daughter, the daughter he didn't want around.

It was obvious he loved all three of his sons unconditionally, she could see that whenever he was with them, and he was a really good father to them, but he just didn't treat her in the same way. She felt she was the outsider; neither his sister nor his daughter, just an intruder into the neat Riordan family, the disruptive cuckoo in the already settled nest.

'I don't know,' she said after a few moments. 'I'll ask him, but he's always working. His father runs this big business in London, a show-business agency, and Andy has to be there nearly all the time, especially as he's going to take it all over one day. He's the only child, so he gets the lot.' She was about to add 'unlike me', but for once she kept her counsel.

'Ah yes. The great Jack Blythe, Lord of the Manor; I've heard a lot about him, not all of it good, I might add. Seems he's a bit of a wheeler-dealer is our Jack,' Johnnie said with a slight frown.

The critical undertone in his voice put Maggie on alert, and she immediately wondered what he meant, if maybe Jeanette had said something about the record she'd made in the booth. Suddenly, she was scratching around in her head to try and remember what she'd said to Jeanette. 'What do you mean? He's a respectable businessman. He's really rich, and he's got a huge place in London as well as the Manor House,' she said defensively.

'I didn't know you'd met him.' Johnnie looked at her quizzically. 'I thought you'd only met the fabulous mother and mad aunt.'

'I don't have to meet him to know he's alright. Andy's told me all about him. He really looks up to his dad, everyone does.'

Johnnie opened his mouth as if to say something more, and then stopped.

'Go on, tell me what you mean, what have you heard?' Maggie asked, trying her best not to be too confrontational.

'Oh, it doesn't matter, you know what village gossip is like. Even the Pope would have to prove himself ten times over to be accepted in Melton. You ask Andy if he wants to come to visit and meet us properly. He can come to dinner one Sunday while we're still in the quiet season and we're not rushing round like idiots.'

Again he smiled, and again she wondered why Johnnie Riordan was being so nice all of a sudden. She hoped it wasn't because he was thinking of trying to send her to the Manor House instead of the vicarage.

'OK, I'll think about it; it'll depend if he's got time.' Maggie shrugged, feigning uninterest, while at the same time desperately wanting to ask Johnnie what he meant.

That evening she sneaked out of the house while Ruby was playing monopoly with the boys and Johnnie was safely ensconced in his office hideaway and ran across to the phone box on the opposite side of the road. She didn't want questions, and she didn't want them seeing her going to the phone box when there a phone indoors.

Andy answered the phone almost immediately. 'Guess what? Dad's got a job for you as a backing singer, after Christmas he said, and he said you can have one of the bedsits downstairs rent free until you earn enough to pay for it. I told you he was the best, didn't I? You can get away from Southend forever, this is your big chance, so long as you don't actually let on to him that the guardians don't know about it. He can only turn a blind eye if he doesn't know for sure you signed it yourself!'

For a few moments Maggie didn't know what to say. It was everything she wanted, all she had thought about since the moment Andy had taken her record off to London with him, and she could feel her excitement levels rising, but along with it came apprehension. The idea of running off to London and living in a bedsit was very scary for a sixteen year old who had led a very closeted life up until just a few months before.

'Do you know anything else about it? Backing who? And where? Is it in London?'

'I haven't got all the details, but it's a good start, and Dad thinks you might be good enough to make a proper record. He just wants to see how you perform live first. It'll be fab, Maggie, really fab. After Christmas, OK?'

'OK . . .' Maggie said, trying to sound enthusiastic despite the feeling of fear which suddenly enveloped her. 'Which day?'

'I don't know yet. I'll be in Melton over Christmas, so I'll let you know when I'm going to be back in London. Now, what else has been happening with you?' Andy asked, but before she could answer he simply carried on telling her all about himself and his father. As he always did.

'How's Melton?' she asked, when there was a gap in the conversation.

'Oh, Christ, it's as boring as ever. You're lucky to be out of here. I hate the place. If it wasn't for Mum I'd never come here. Compared to life in London it's all so childish. I mean, who has a tennis clubhouse as the centre of entertainment?'

Maggie made the right noises, but all she could think was how much she used to love the tennis club – before she met Andy Blythe, before the accident and before the bombshell.

Just the thought of it made her feel so homesick she wanted to cry.

'I'm going to have to go. They don't know I'm out.'

'Just think, once you live in London on your own you'll be able to do whatever you like, especially if you can get your hands on your inheritance first!' He paused. 'You are still trying to get access to it, aren't you? Dad says you need a solicitor.'

'Of course I'm trying, but no luck so far. I may have to have a conversation with fatman.'

'I think you should; it's not right. Even Dad says it's not right. It's your house in Melton, and that fatman is obviously in on it with them.'

'I don't know. I just want to get away. The inheritance can wait! I mean, I'll get it eventually . . .'

'Only if they haven't spent the lot by then.'

By the time she got back to the house, Maggie's brain was in a whirl of confusion, but amid it all she wished she hadn't told Andy the information she'd found out about the inheritance and how much it was actually worth.

'You know, there's something bugging me,' Johnnie said when he and Ruby were alone in the sitting room later that evening. 'I was listening to Maggie on the phone earlier, and it was an odd conversation, even though I only heard one side. Something dodgy's going on with that Blythe family and Maggie, and I can't put my finger on it.'

'They seem nice enough, and Maggie's going to be guarded if she's talking to Andy and knows you're listening in; you shouldn't do that, you know . . .' Ruby said without looking up from her book. She was curled up in one of the pair of old leather wingback chairs they'd brought back from the hotel when it was refurbished. They were old-fashioned but comfortable, and the boys always fought over them with Martin, the strongest, usually winning the battle to sit in one on his own with Paul and Russell having to share the other. Now the boys were in bed, so Ruby and Johnnie had got them to themselves.

'I wasn't hiding. She knew I was there. I answered the phone and called her down!' He laughed. 'But seriously, there's this niggle in the back of my brain that something is going on that we don't know about. I know dodgy when I see it, I've done dodgy and beyond in my time, and I can smell trouble a mile off. Something's not right in the Blythe family. We need to get the Blythe boy down here so I can find out. I suggested Maggie invite him.'

'And did you tell her that if he comes you're going to lock him in the cellar and interrogate him?' Ruby sighed and rolled her eyes.

This time she looked up, and Johnnie could see he'd got her full attention at last. 'Not quite, but I don't fall for all this Blythe entrepreneur stuff. It's a con, I bet. I've done similar myself – I was an *entrepreneur*, if you remember – and you can't pull the wool over my eyes with big houses and fancy London offices. Something isn't right, and I can see Maggie getting sucked in. She falls for all the guff that boy tells her about his father, and she thinks the mother was sent down from heaven—'

'Well, they did buy the Manor House in Melton,' Ruby interrupted. 'That must have cost a pretty penny, and Eunice always looks a million dollars. Her clothes certainly aren't run up on a Singer in the back room; she looks like a beauty queen!'

'I've heard rumours.' Johnnie frowned. 'I know Melton is a village and rumours are part of life there, but there's usually a grain of truth in them. I may take a drive up there to have an ask around.'

'You'd better not be thinking about the Hobarts again.'

'Oh, come on, Rubes.' Johnnie sighed. 'We've been over that one. I'll shelve it for the moment, especially as there seems to be a bit of truce between her and the boys. Maggie's making a bit of an effort, and I don't want to rock the boat, but I still think we need to check it all out. Don't you have to go and see old Herbie again? And we do need to check the house is OK.'

Ruby stared at her husband. 'You're just looking for reasons to get there and ask about the Blythes.'

'Well, of course I am,' he said with a laugh, 'but seriously, I think we need to. Maggie is prime for having her heart broken by this boy, and we can't have that on top of anything else. Can you imagine?'

'You're probably right on that one, though it's bound to happen at some time. It always does, to all of us!' Ruby laughed and winked at her husband. 'Especially us!'

'OK, I'll give you that one, but not right now for her, eh? She's enough of a problem as it is.'

'She's not the problem; it's everything that's happened to her. OK, we'll arrange to go to Melton, but don't tell anyone. Promise?'

'Promise! How about one Sunday? Preferably when the boys will all be with Betty and we can bribe Jeanette to come over and keep an eye out for Maggie. You have no idea how much I'd like to get away for a day with you – just you, Rubes. No rowdy boys, no sullen Maggie. We could have lunch out and pretend we're still teenagers.'

'I dunno about that. Can I just remind you, Mr Riordan, it was a day out at Melton all those years ago when we were teenagers that got us both into so much trouble.' Maggie smiled and shook her head. 'If we'd known then what we know now . . .'

'We wouldn't be in this mess. I know,' Johnnie said quickly.

'But, I wouldn't change any of it. You, Maggie, George and Babs, the boys . . .' Ruby stood up and went over to Johnnie; she sat on the arm of his chair and kissed the top of his head. 'I love you Mr Riordan.'

'And I love you too, Ruby-Rubes. Oh, the arrogance of youth eh?' Johnnie sighed as he reached up and took her hand. 'We thought we were so clever that day, bunking off on the train and then getting up to no good on the way home. And that's what worried me about Maggie and that Andy. Can you imagine the hoo-ha . . .?'

'Not from us, because we wouldn't dare, that'd be a bit too hypocritical, but I imagine the Blythes would go bananas!'

They laughed together, and Johnnie enjoyed the feeling of them being a couple who were in agreement instead of at war as they had been for the past few months. He loved his wife as much as he always had, and from the very first moment, when he'd spotted her walking despondently down the road on her way back to the Blakeley family home after her evacuation was over. Little did he know then the route their relationship would take and the traumas they would both have to overcome.

As Ruby went back to her chair and book, Johnnie leant back in his chair and closed his eyes. But he wasn't dozing; he was trying to analyse his feelings for Maggie, his daughter by birth but not by nurture.

Deep down he was still convinced that Maggie should be back in Melton where she wanted to be but, knowing that he still had the Hobarts in reserve, he was prepared to wait and see. He had decided that Christmas would be the key, and if Maggie spoilt it for everyone then he knew he would have to overrule his wife, probably for the first time.

When Ruby had first told him about Maggie, it had been an emotionally charged time. She was five years old and had just been kidnapped, albeit temporarily, by a local who had a vendetta against Ruby. It was all strange and shocking and too much for him to take in at first. He had two small sons by his first wife, and he'd known and understood his paternal feelings towards them, and then suddenly he had a daughter who he wasn't allowed to acknowledge to anyone because she had been adopted by the Wheatons. She was their daughter, and because of that he had never been able to build a relationship with her other than that of a distant brother.

After George and Babs Wheaton had both died so unexpectedly and she had come to live with them, he had had no idea how to deal with a teenage girl, let alone one with so many problems, so he'd found it easier to stay at a distance. Ruby, meanwhile, had dived right in and tried too hard. He knew that between them they'd both probably been wrong, but Johnnie still couldn't see a way to change the brotherly relationship he had had with Maggie Wheaton into one of father and daughter. He just couldn't do it, and because of that he genuinely thought she would be happier away from the family she didn't want to be part of.

'You're off in a trance; where are you?'

He shook himself back to the room. 'Not that far away. Just imagining a day out with my wife.'

'How about imagining another day out as well? I asked Maggie if she'd like to go to Walthamstow to meet my ma and your Betty, and she didn't say no like she did last time . . .' Ruby paused. 'But then again she didn't say yes so who knows? I just thought she might be ready.'

'I don't know if she'll ever be ready. She lost her family, and I don't think she wants another one just yet, especially one like ours.'

Sixteen

Maggie Wheaton was standing in the newly renovated kitchen of the Thamesview Hotel looking out of the window but not actually seeing anything; her mind was too far away and too confused. She was finding it hard to make a decision about Ruby's suggestion that she meet some of her extended family, especially her birth grandmother. Her natural curiosity made her want to go and meet the family she hadn't even known existed, both on Ruby's side and Johnnie's, but her anger at her betrayal was still so strong.

Over the months, both Ruby and Johnnie had given her bits of information about the family who still lived in Walthamstow in East London, Ruby's own birthplace. Although she feigned uninterest, Maggie had gathered the information in her head and tried to get a picture of them all. She found it hard to believe that there was a whole group of people who she was actually related to but had never met and who, until recently, had no idea that she even existed.

The Blakeleys and the Riordans were all part of her birth family, and yet she was as much a stranger to them as they were to her. In an instant she had gone from being an only child in a small village with no relatives other than George and Babs, her parents, to living in a busy seaside town on the periphery of a huge East End family.

But while she was naturally curious, there was that part of her that was still engulfed in grief and which didn't want any more involvement with Ruby and Johnnie and their extended families than she already had; especially as she had no intention of staying around long enough to get to know any of them. All she wanted was to be back with George and Babs Wheaton, her mum and dad.

But she consoled herself with the thought that soon none of them would matter any more because she'd be Maggie from Melton once again and it would be as if the past months hadn't happened.

Maggie Wheaton was being torn in more directions than she could have thought possible, and her emotions were more confused than ever. Sometimes when she was awake in the middle of the night, especially after one of the regular nightmares she still had about the crash, she thought about her and Andy's plans, and she was scared by the enormity of it all.

In the darkness, as she forced herself to stay awake for fear of the nightmare returning, she would decide she couldn't go through with it, she would promise herself that she would ring Andy and tell him as soon as she got up, but then once it was daylight and she felt so overwhelmed with the people and noise, both at the Riordan house and at the hotel, she couldn't wait to get away.

Without realizing it, she shook her head and tightened her arms, which were already wrapped around her body.

'Hello, you.'

Maggie jumped and turned around as someone touched her on the shoulder. 'Hello!' Maggie smiled, genuinely pleased to see Jeanette, Gracie's younger sister, standing there.

'You looked like you were miles away there, young Mags.' Jeanette laughed. 'But wherever you are, can I join you? I'd love to be miles away rather than completely knackered after another shift on nights! God, it takes it out of me, especially now I'm on the children's ward.'

'Is it hard working all night? Don't you fall asleep?'

'Not a chance. We don't even get to sit down and take the weight off our feet, and my weight is a lot to be dragging round all night!' Jeanette patted her rounded belly and tutted at herself. 'Look at this? See it wobble? Those stodgy canteen meals at the hospital have a lot to answer for.'

Maggie smiled, and Jeanette took that as her cue to relate several stories of night duties, medical students and linen cupboards. She was an excellent storyteller, and even though Maggie knew she was embellishing it for her benefit, she couldn't help but laugh out loud at the tales. Jeanette McCabe, Gracie's younger sister, was the only person she had found since her move to Southend who she felt comfortable with, the only person who seemed to have no hidden agenda and who, she felt, had her best interests at heart.

Maggie watched Jeanette as she gesticulated and bounced around the kitchen and wondered again at how unlike each other Jeanette and Gracie were in appearance. Gracie was as dark and slender as Jeanette was blonde and curvy. Maggie could imagine that, despite all her stories of life on the ward, Jeanette was an excellent nurse. 'Are you looking for Gracie?' she suddenly asked.

'I am, but I'm not in any rush, so do you fancy a cuppa and a bit more chat? I'm out of touch with everything. You can tell me all your news now I've told you everything about my whole life!'

'Gracie's locked away with Ruby somewhere while they talk about things that can't be talked about in front of the children – in other words *me*, the troublesome one,' Maggie said, unable to keep the sarcasm out of her voice.

'Oh, I doubt it's about you. That pair have always gone off into huddles to chat, it's what they do,' Jeanette said, laughing, 'and this time it's most likely about the moving. It's not long till they set sail for Africa . . . I don't know how the two of them are going to cope being away from each other when it happens. They're so close those two, closer than sisters, which is funny as Gracie and I *are* sisters!'

'Why should it matter so much? Maggie frowned. 'It's not forever, and Ruby's got Johnnie and the precious boys and the hotel, and Gracie's got Edward and Fay. I can't see why it would bother them that much.'

'Ooohh, that's a bit strong. I don't think you get it, do you, Mags me darling? Ruby and Gracie had a bloody awful time back then, it was horrible for them both, but being together afterwards got them through it. They understand each other like no one else can.'

'Well, then, they shouldn't have got pregnant, should they? That way they wouldn't have had such a bloody awful time, would they?' Maggie said sharply.

'Lordy, that's cynical from one so young.' Jeanette stared hard at Maggie until she blushed and looked away, but still she couldn't let it go.

'It's just the truth. If they hadn't done what they did, they wouldn't have been all alone with just each other, they'd have still had their families, and I wouldn't be standing here being neither one nor the other with a birth certificate that's a lie. A bloody lie.' Maggie reddened because she knew she was lashing out at the wrong person, but she couldn't help it. It still all seemed so unfair.

After a moment Jeanette stepped up close to Maggie, wrapped her arms around her and pulled her into a bear hug, ignoring the girl's resistance. 'Listen to me, me darling. I understand, I do, but I want you to let some of this stuff go because I want you to be happy again. There are things we can change and they're worth bothering about, but the things you can't change? Let it go. None of us can turn back time.'

They stood for a few moments in silence until Maggie relaxed, and Jeanette let her go.

'That's better. Being angry never did none of us any favours,' Jeanette said with a smile. 'Do you think you can try and understand them just a bit?'

'Maybe, but they won't leave me alone! They just want to play happy families, but they're not my family, not in the way Mum and Dad were. And now they want me to go and meet the rest of the so-called family, you know, let's pretend we all love each other, but I don't know any of them,' Maggie said, desperate for someone to understand, desperate for advice but not wanting to ask.

'Are you going to go? Do you want to go?' Jeanette asked lightly.

'Of course I don't want to go. It'll be awful . . .'

'Well, how about asking Ruby to invite them here? And not all together, just in dribs and drabs. If they came to the house you'd be on your own territory and could run away if you wanted to.'

'Run away? Why would I want to run away?' Maggie asked sharply, fearful that Jeanette had somehow found out about her plans.

'I meant you would be able to go off and do something else . . . leave them to it.' Jeanette looked at her. 'What did you think I meant?'

'Nothing,' Maggie said sharply, turning away. 'Do you want that cuppa now?'

'Oh yeah, I'm gasping. Thought you'd never ask.' Jeanette laughed, easing the tension. 'By the way, did you hear anything about the record you made? Did it go any further?'

Maggie was back on alert, aware that whatever she said could be a clue to finding her after she'd gone. She clattered around with cups and saucers and didn't look at Jeanette. 'No, nothing. But I've changed my plans now, anyway. I want to be an air hostess.'

'Oh, that's interesting. How old do you have to be for that? They always look so elegant and ladylike on the news. I've never been on a plane. My parents live right near the airport; Dad works there.'

As Jeanette started to tell her stories about the airport, Maggie smiled, feeling pleased that she'd managed to divert Jeanette so easily.

Jack Blythe walked into the vast kitchen that dominated the back of the Manor House and looked around before walking up to Anna, the housekeeper, who was standing by the huge kitchen sink peeling vegetables. He stood very close to her, and his stance was aggressive enough to make the woman take a slight step sideways.

'Good afternoon, Mr Blythe,' she said. 'Can I help you?'

'Where is she? Where's my wife?' he snapped.

'I don't know, Mr Blythe. She didn't tell me what she was doing today, but I think she went out.'

'Out?' he asked incredulously. 'Why is she going out when I'm due home? And without leaving a message!'

'I don't know, Mr Blythe, but Andy is playing tennis; he'll probably know where Mrs Blythe is.'

He looked the middle-aged woman up and down dismissively, making no secret of his distaste, then, without another word, he pushed past her and pulled the back door open so hard that it slammed against the wall. He walked out, leaving it open, and stormed across the kitchen garden and out through the wrought iron gate in the wall into the main grounds.

'Andy? Get yourself over here,' he bellowed.

The young man, who had been banging tennis balls against the garage, dropped his racket and ran straight over to his father. 'Dad! When did you get back? We thought you weren't coming up till later . . .'

'Yes, I can see that. How come you've got time to piss about out here playing tennis? I thought you'd got phone calls to make for me, you lazy little tyke,' Jack said. 'And your mother's nowhere to be found; that bloody thick as shit Anna is covering for her, I know it. And there was me going to surprise you both. Well, I got a surprise alright! While the cat's away . . .'

'But she's only gone into the village to the hairdresser. She didn't know you were coming back so early. You don't usually,' Andy answered quickly, his panic all too obvious.

'She should have checked before buggering off, shouldn't she, then. What about Lil? Where's the old bat? Up in her room with a bottle of gin and her stack of out-of-date seventy-eights on the radiogram, I suppose.'

'No. She went with Mum,' Andy said, frantically wondering how to calm his father down before they got back.

'In that case there must be something going on. That crazy bitch doesn't go into the village, and neither does your mother, for that matter.'

'She does, she often does. She—' Andy stopped himself just in time, and because his father was nurturing his rage he didn't notice.

Both his mother and her sister had been going out and about and becoming part of village life when Jack was ensconced in the flat in London. Andy like seeing his mother with a bit of a life of her own, so he never said a word about it to his father; he knew that Jack Blythe wouldn't like it one bit.

Andy could sense the underlying anger bubbling away in his father, and he was alert, not for himself but for his mother. He'd seen it too many times – the irritation that quickly built into irrational anger which only needed the slightest trigger for it to end in his mother being hurt. Jack Blythe had never laid a finger on his son other than the occasional clip around the ear when he was a child, and he'd never laid a finger on his wife when his son was around, but Andy knew. As far back as he could remember he'd heard the sounds, felt the fear and seen the bruises.

'Oh, darling, don't be silly. I banged it on the wardrobe door; you

know how clumsy I can be,' she'd say if he asked about a black eye or the finger marks on her arms, but instinctively Andy knew. He knew all the signs of both before and after, and he could see them now and was scared for his mother for when she came home.

Jack Blythe was spoiling for a fight. With his wife.

'Dad, she won't be long, honestly. The hairdresser is at the top of the high street; do you want me to drive down to the village and find her? I can tell her you're back, and she'll be so pleased to see you.'

'No. I'll see her when she gets back. Meanwhile, you and I can have a talk about your pretty little piece of skirt Maggie and her singing.' He paused. 'Oh, and her inheritance. Priorities, son, priorities. I'll deal with your mother later.'

Andy's heart sank when he heard the tone that accompanied his father's words; he knew he was going to hear derogatory things about Maggie that he didn't want to. Despite his father's failings, Andy Blythe looked up to him both as his father and as a businessman, and he adored him unconditionally; all he wanted was for his father to feel the same way about him. But no matter how hard he tried, Jack Blythe always ended up dismissing his efforts and making him feel inconsequential. Now he knew that Maggie would be his target, and all because he'd noticed that his son really liked her. It was always the way.

'I told her what you said about a job after Christmas,' Andy said as they started to walk back to the house together. 'She's so pleased; she can't wait. And I told her about the room she can have.'

'You did tell her this opportunity wasn't going to be a free ride? That she's going to owe me? I mean, really owe me . . .'

'Of course I did. She's happy to work for nothing until she gets on her feet. She just wants somewhere to live so she can get away from Southend and the money-grabbers.' Andy looked up at his father. 'It's wrong, isn't it, Dad? That they can do that to her over her inheritance? That is what you said, isn't it?'

'It is, son. It sure is.' Jack paused for a few moments. 'Any idea how much is involved in this family fraud? The kid's got to be worth a few bob for it to be worth their while to take her into the family.'

'But she is sort of family to them.'

'Don't give me sentimental guff, son. You and I both know they don't want her, they want her money. Happens all the time. Come twenty-one it'll be bye-bye to her. She'll be on her way with the few pennies left they haven't embezzled. So . . . do you know what she's worth, our little heiress?'

Andy forced himself to ignore the sneer in his father's voice. He wanted so much to believe that his father really did have Maggie's best interests at heart. 'I did have it all written down. Maggie found the details in their office and copied them out. It's a lot – I mean, the doctor's house and surgery must be worth a fair bit, and then there was other money and stuff . . . I've still got it if you want to have a look.'

'Yes, let me take a look. I'll do what I can to help the girl; she looks like she needs someone to take her under their wing. But to help her, we have to make sure that her so-called family never get wind of where she is when she escapes them, so not a word to anyone. Especially your mother.'

Side by side, father and son continued to walk together. There was no disputing that Andy Blythe was his father's son. Both were tall, attractive and well-groomed and wearing obviously expensive clothes. They walked in step and both had their hands clasped behind their backs as they did so.

Both were also unaware that Eunice and Lily Blythe were apprehensively looking out of the first-floor landing window, watching them and dreading the moment Jack Blythe got back to the house.

Seventeen

Christmas Day

'Good morning,' Ruby said with a wide smile as Maggie finally came downstairs and followed the noise into the sitting room where the whole family was already dressed and ready for the family outing to church. 'Happy Christmas.'

'Happy Christmas, Mags . . . We did call you. You've missed breakfast, but you can have something when we get back from mass,' Johnnie echoed.

Maggie stared hard at the couple, who were sitting side by side on the sofa, unsure how to reply. She was shocked they would even think she could ever again have a happy Christmas. She also wondered how they could bring themselves to even say the words to her. She managed a faint smile but said nothing; she just stood in the doorway waiting.

It suited her to let them think she had overslept, whereas in reality she had been awake all night, dreading the moment she would have to join in the Christmas celebrations and make an effort in front of everyone – Ruby and Johnnie and the boys, Gracie and Edward and their daughter Fay. It was going to be a crowded dinner table, and she was expected to be there. She knew she couldn't ignore it because the boys were still children and eagerly anticipating their presents and the turkey dinner with all the trimmings, but she had every intention of running off to her bedroom at the first opportunity and waiting for Andy to ring, as he had promised.

She looked around the room, which was decorated with tinsel and paper chains, and tried to ignore the tree, which had appeared a few days earlier while she was in town and which was now in the centre of the bay window.

It was simply too painful for her to bear.

'Do you want to help us decorate the tree, Mags?' Johnnie had asked when she'd first seen it.

'Not a chance,' she'd said. 'I don't want anything to do with Christmas; how can I? It's not right, and you shouldn't expect me to.'

'I didn't expect you to – I was just giving you the option. I understand how hard this is going to be, we both understand . . . Ruby brought some decorations from the house in Melton; they were in the attic. Do you want us to use them?'

She'd shrugged. 'Up to you. Do what you like. They don't mean anything any more.'

Now though, on Christmas morning, she couldn't stop looking at it. It was a beautiful tree, and it was now covered in a collection of ornaments, old, home-made and even downright ugly. Then her eyes were drawn to the fairy that was standing on the middle of the mantelpiece. Every Christmas that she could remember she had stood with her feet on the seat either side of George Wheaton's knees, as he sat in his wheelchair, and ceremoniously placed the fairy at the top. He'd held her ankles, and every single time he'd let go and pretended to let her fall, only to grab her at the last second.

'We left the fairy for you, Maggie,' Ruby said. 'It's yours, and we want you to put her up there, in memory of your mum and dad.'

Before she could react, she was engulfed in the whirlwind that was three overexcited young boys jumping up and down and shouting.

'Put the fairy on the top, put the fairy on the top . . .' they repeated over and over, and much as she wanted to just run and hide, she couldn't do it to them; she made herself accept that they were just children anticipating Christmas.

She carefully picked up the fairy and then, without thinking, held it straight up to her face. She could smell her mother on it, just a hint of the Tweed perfume that she always wore, and along with that aroma she could remember her last family Christmas as if it had happened yesterday.

The last place she wanted to put the precious fairy doll was on the tree; she wanted to go up to her bedroom and hold it in her hands forever.

But she forced herself to do it, because she knew it was what her parents would have wanted. Standing on a chair, she placed the fairy on the empty top branch, then slowly and carefully pulled the lace and net skirt out, straightening the creases and gently fixing the arm that held her wand into the right position. Lastly, she moved the angle of the tiny tiara, which had been replaced several times over the years.

She could feel the tears prickling at the back of her eyes, so she opened her eyes wide and climbed down again.

'Shall we turn the lights on?' Ruby asked gently. 'Do you want to do it, Maggie?'

'No, let Russell do it, he's the youngest,' she said, without looking at anyone. She blinked again, not wanting anyone to see her tears, but she could feel Ruby's eyes on her as Johnnie and the three boys crowded around the switch.

'One, two three . . . ON,' they all shouted in unison. Except for Maggie, who just stood there silently.

The bedecked tree lit up, and the fairy looked as if she was aglow with the solitary small white bulb at the very top shining through her skirt. Maggie felt a physical pain in her chest as she looked and remembered, but the moment was gone when Martin, Paul and Russell all started talking at once.

'Father Christmas has been, but we're not allowed to open anything until we get back from church—'

'I've got more presents under the tree than you—'

'No, you haven't, we've all got the same. I counted—'

'You can't count—'

'Enough!' Johnnie clapped his hands and shouted over the top of the noise. 'We're going to church right now. We're meeting Gracie, Edward and Fay there, so we can't be late or we won't be able to sit together. Shoes and coats on, all of you.'

As the boys darted off to the hallstand, Ruby went over to Maggie and put her arm around her. 'I'm so proud of you. I know it's hard.'

Maggie shrugged her off. 'Christmas is for kids; so long as they enjoy it. I never want another one in my whole life – not without Mum and Dad, and certainly not with you.'

As they walked to church, Maggie kept her focus by counting down to the day when she would be away from them all forever. The day when she would be with Andy and she would have a career doing what she loved most, singing. The single thing which kept her from going mad in the lonely hours she spent in her bedroom or walking the streets alone.

Maggie Wheaton did what she'd promised herself and played the Christmas game. She'd written cards, bought presents for everyone and managed to look pleased when she opened hers from Ruby and Johnnie, which was a new record player and the smallest transistor radio she'd ever seen. It was a thoughtful present, and she wished she could be genuinely pleased, but the big black cloud hanging over her head meant it might as well have been a bar of chocolate. She didn't feel a single thing, so she faked it.

'Phew, I'm stuffed,' Johnnie said as he leant back in his chair after a long and noisy dinner and made a great show of patting his belly. 'That was great, Rubes, especially the pudding. Beautiful. It was the best, wasn't it everyone? The best . . .'

'Well, that's good, because Gracie, Maggie and I did all the work, so now all of you boys are going to do the washing up.'

'But we've got bikes . . .!' Martin said.

Ruby pretended to think. 'OK then. The two biggest boys, Johnnie and Edward, will do the washing up, and the rest of you can come with me and Gracie. We're going down the seafront.'

'Can we bring our bikes?' Russell asked.

'Of course you can.' Gracie laughed. 'Come on then – and you as well, Maggie. We need you to help. Three bikes and a doll's pram is a bit much for the two of us.'

'I'm going to my room. I don't feel well.'

Ruby and Gracie exchanged glances, and then both looked at her at the same time.

'No, Maggie, that's not fair. You've got to—' Johnnie started to say, but Ruby shut him down with a fierce stare.

'You've probably eaten too much; I know I have. You have a lie down, and we'll see when we come back. We won't be long; we're cutting it a bit fine for the Queen's Speech,' Ruby said as they all crowded through the front door into the porch. She looked at her husband. 'Johnnie, can you just help me and the boys get the bikes out of the garage?'

Maggie looked the other way; she knew that Ruby was going to talk about her, tell Johnnie to go easy on her, but she wasn't interested. She'd had too much of Christmas jolliness already, and she just wanted to be on her own.

As the front door closed, she ran up the stairs and watched from her bedroom window as they all marched off towards the nearby seafront.

Martin and Paul, Johnnie's boisterous two sons, were close in age and so similar in appearance that they were often mistaken for twins. Both had light brown hair, were tall for their ages, and loved rough and tumble play, while Russell, the baby of the family at five, was a gentle natured, blonde-haired little boy who had yet to find his feet alongside his brothers.

Martin and Paul rushed ahead, leaving Russell to try and catch up, while Fay, Gracie's daughter, trotted along importantly with Gracie and Ruby, pushing her pram with the new doll inside. It was a family scene that Maggie felt a stranger to, and after she'd watched the group disappear from view she lay down on her bed and closed her eyes. She couldn't wait to go to London and leave them all behind.

With the door ajar, Maggie lay there waiting and listening. She was scared to listen to music, despite the new record player and transistor, in case she missed the call from Andy. She heard them all come back from the walk, the clattering of crockery as tea was prepared, but he didn't ring, and she was too scared of upsetting Jack Blythe to phone the Manor House. Three times the phone rang down in the hall, and Maggie hurled herself off the bed and down the stairs, only to discover it wasn't for her.

'I think we should make her come down, make her join in something. It's not right her locked away upstairs like this . . .' Johnnie whispered to Ruby as she stood at the kitchen sink, pretending to be busy. It had been a strange day for her. Her daughter was in the family fold, just as she had wanted every Christmas since Maggie was born, but the circumstances were all wrong, and she didn't know how to make things right.

'And it's rude,' he continued.

'There's not one person here other than you who thinks that. The boys are happy enough playing draughts with Fay, and Gracie and Edward have far more important things on their mind than Maggie in her bedroom. Leave her alone.'

'It's not healthy. We should make her come down.'

'I said, "No!"' Ruby hissed.

'OK, whatever you want, but come the New Year, if things don't improve . . .'

'Don't even say it.'

Johnnie looked at his wife for a moment, and then, without another word, turned on his heel and walked out.

A few minutes after he'd left the kitchen, Gracie wandered in. She perched on the edge of the kitchen table and for a few moments said nothing – she just let Ruby take her frustration and anger out on a burnt oven dish.

'Everything OK?' she asked eventually. 'Stupid question. Of course it's not. But we all know why! It's the first Christmas for her without George and Babs, so of course she's going to be miserable as sin, but everyone forgets that you feel their loss also. Yes?'

'Yes, I know that, and you know that, but Johnnie just doesn't understand, and it shocks me that he doesn't. I thought he was kinder than that. He expects her to just get over it and behave.'

'That's men, Rubes. They like to think they can fix everything and hate it when they can't. Johnnie's frustrated because he can't get through to her. So he's downstairs feeling useless, and she's upstairs feeling useless. Cut from the same cloth that pair.'

'He wants to send her back to Melton. I told him that if she goes then so do I.'

'Do you mean that? Would you really leave Thamesview?'

'If I had to choose between Maggie and the hotel then it would be Maggie, but it would be hard.'

'And if Johnnie refuses? What about the boys?'

'Oh, shut up, Gracie, I'm not in the mood for you being all rational and sensible.' Despite her tone, Ruby managed a faint smile. 'And anyway, who are you to talk? I'm thinking about Cambridgeshire, with telephones and things; you're off to the other side of the world leaving me without a friend to bare my soul to.'

'Oh, below the belt, girl, below the belt!' Gracie looked at her friend quizzically.

'Come on, you know I don't mean it. I don't want you to go, but I know it'll be a fantastic adventure for you all.'

'OK, I forgive you. But, trust me, it'll all come out in the wash eventually. You've been through worse.'

'I suppose so. It just seems so strange to look back at last Christmas and see how different it is this year. Everything has been turned on its head.' Ruby flexed her shoulders and shook her head around to relax her knotted muscles. 'Oh well, we can't go back, so we have to do the best we can with what we've got. Come on, back to the fray.'

'Yep, let's go. And tomorrow's another day.'

'Oh, my good God in heaven, I'd forgotten that for a moment. We're going over to Betty's. Will Maggie go? Won't she? Will we have another row? Will it snow and put an end to the decisions, decisions?'

Gracie laughed. 'I dunno. How do you fancy another gin and tonic?'

'Sounds like the best idea of the day. Make mine a large one. The little ones are all overexcited; they need to calm down a bit or none of them will sleep tonight.'

The two women went back through to the sitting room arm-in-arm.

The three boys and Fay were laughing and bickering as they tried to gather up the draught pieces that were all over the floor as Johnnie and Edward stood, oblivious, in the corner of the room deep in conversation. It was a homely, family picture, apart from Maggie, who was upstairs, and Ruby just wanted to cry for her daughter, the daughter she had loved unconditionally since the moment she was born, the daughter who she had inadvertently caused such pain to.

Maggie was tearful with relief when Christmas day, the first one she had ever spent without George and Babs Wheaton, was finally over and she didn't have to pretend any more. She'd done exactly as she was asked for as long as she could, but she was tucked up in bed by nine o'clock – albeit with her door still ajar just in case Andy rang.

The next day she stayed in her room until she heard the house go silent and she knew she was at home alone. When Ruby had asked her again to go with them to Hornchurch to meet Betty and her family, she'd pretended to hesitate and then offered the alternative that Jeanette had suggested. She'd been surprised that her decision had been accepted; she had expected at the very least an argument, but they'd accepted it.

She went downstairs and looked at the telephone on the hall table as if she could will it to ring. It was several hours before it did.

'I expected you to ring me yesterday . . .' Maggie said, unable to keep the sulk out her voice. 'I wanted to wish you Happy Christmas, and I thought you'd do the same.'

'Oh, I know, but it all got just too hectic. I didn't have a minute to spare. Another of my mother's parties.'

'On Christmas Day?' she asked.

'What's wrong with that?' Andy asked tetchily. 'We like that sort of thing. Dad invited a lot of important people, and I had to circulate.'

'Sorry. I know you're busy. And your dad. I was just impatient to sort out the date I can move in. I've got to arrange this really carefully so they can't find me.'

'Anytime, really. I'm back at work on Monday, so up to you. Dad doesn't like taking time off, so it's business as usual. He never stops.'

'OK. As soon as I know when I can get out of the house safely, I'll ring you. I don't want to get caught with a suitcase.' Maggie laughed nervously. She didn't want Andy to know that she was scared witless at the idea, which had seemed so good at the time. They chatted for a while longer, or rather Andy talked and Maggie listened, and then she heard his mother's voice in the background calling him.

'Got to go. Dad wants me.' He paused. 'But before I go . . . Have you done anything about your inheritance? Only, Dad says he'll manage it for you. It'll be safer than letting your family get their hands on it. He's good with money.'

Again, Maggie felt the twinge of discomfort at the mention

of her inheritance, but she ignored it. They were only looking out for her, which was more than Ruby and Johnnie had ever done.

'I'll try again before I leave.'

Eighteen

'Where the hell is she?' Ruby shouted as she ran from room to room. 'Most of her things are still in her bedroom, but Babs' suitcase has gone from the top of the wardrobe and her favourite clothes are missing. And the photo of Babs and George from beside her bed . . . Johnnie, Johnnie, she's run away, she's bloody run away! This is your fault. You pushed and pushed, and that row was the final straw . . .'

'Hang on, it was you who went berserk. You ranted at her, not me!'

'She was drunk!'

'Not that drunk that she couldn't remember what you said to her, it seems.'

'I hate you, Johnnie Riordan,' Ruby shouted as she went off around the house looking in all the rooms. 'You never wanted her here, and you've made her life hell.'

When Johnnie didn't respond, Ruby started issuing orders. 'The garage – you go and look in the garage, and the sheds. Look over every inch of the garden, and I'll do the bedrooms again. And the attic! She might have gone looking for something and fallen . . .'

Ruby was distraught and terrified. It had been hard for everyone in the months after the accident, but she'd really thought they were getting somewhere, and recently Maggie had been much less argumentative and a little easier to live with.

But the row two nights before had been really huge, and Maggie had pushed to the point where Ruby had finally lost all her self-control and turned into the type of screaming banshee woman she'd always hated. Afterwards, she had been ashamed of her outburst, but Maggie had stayed in her bedroom out of the way.

'I'll go and talk to her,' Ruby had said the next day when Maggie didn't appear.

'Just let her suffer in silence. She's got to show her face at the hotel tomorrow; that'll be soon enough,' Johnnie had said, so they had left her to her own devices until the following morning, and now there was no way of knowing when she had actually gone missing or where she might be.

Maggie had stayed out later than her curfew of ten p.m. many times before, but it had never been more than an hour or so, and she'd never stayed out past midnight. On that particular occasion she'd rolled up at two o'clock in the morning and not even tried to come in quietly. It had been her first evening out in town since before Christmas, and she'd only gone to the Capri for a coke, but then things had escalated and a group of them had gone back to someone's house to a party and she had drunk alcohol for the first time since the sherry.

A girl who lived nearby had walked back with her, but then she'd gone off in the opposite direction leaving Maggie to try and find her key and get it into the lock. After much fumbling she'd managed, but then she'd accidentally slammed the front door so hard that the glass had loosened. As several pieces of lead-light glass had fallen out, landing on the tiled floor of the hallway with a crash, she'd started to giggle and feel sick at the same time.

The noise had been loud enough to wake Ruby and Johnnie, and Johnnie had run downstairs in his pyjamas to find Maggie crunching over the broken glass giggling and smelling of alcohol.

'Are you drunk?' Johnnie asked incredulously.

'I dunno, am I drunk?' Maggie slurred, just as Ruby appeared behind him, followed closely by Russell, rubbing his eyes and looking bewildered.

The little boy was a miniature of his father; he had blond hair, wide blue eyes and a smile that charmed everyone, but there was also enough of Ruby in his genes for him to also look just like Maggie, his blonde-haired sister.

As Maggie giggled even more, she stepped forward and stumbled on the corner of the rug. She didn't go right down, but it was enough of a trip to make Russell laugh.

'Shut up, brat, it's not funny,' Maggie mumbled as she reached out for the banister pillar to try and get her balance. 'It's not funny. It's not funny! Brat brat brat.'

'OK. That is enough,' Ruby shouted. 'I don't know where you've been, but just get yourself off to your room and to bed and we'll talk about this in the morning. This is a step too far, even for you.'

Johnnie touched his wife's arm to calm her in front of Russell, but Ruby had reached the end of her tether. She was fuming.

'Don't Johnnie. I've had enough. If she wants to wreck her life we can't stop her, but she's not going to visit her troubles on the boys. I'm not having it! I'm not.'

'Oh, shut up, woman . . . you're such a bloody old nag.' As Maggie giggled, she bent over and clutched at her stomach.

'Bed!' Johnnie said, his tone as angry as Ruby's. 'Just go. Now. You should be ashamed of yourself.'

'Ashamed? Me?' Maggie slurred as she tried to stand up straight.

Johnnie looked at her. 'Go to bed, Maggie, and if you're going to be sick there's a bucket under the sink in the bathroom.' He didn't berate or shout, he just said the words quietly and calmly.

Maggie looked at him curiously for a few moments before she turned and walked clumsily up the stairs.

Ruby moved forward to help her, but Johnnie put out his hand to stop her following. 'No, let her go, she's . . .' When he saw Russell sitting quietly by the understairs cupboard he paused. 'Go on, Russ. Off you go now. Maggie will be fine in the morning; she's just upset.'

'I want to listen,' he whined.

'There's nothing to listen to; now go,' Johnnie said.

He waited until he heard their son's bedroom door click shut before he looked at Ruby and nodded in the direction of the kitchen. They went through together, and Johnnie pulled the door closed behind him.

'It's time we stopped pussy footing around her. Little madam. From now on we're going to stand firm and together,' Johnnie said. 'She's going back to Melton to the vicarage. She might take notice of the Hobarts; it'll be for her own good. We need to go to Melton as soon as possible, talk to the Hobarts. And we can find out about the Blythes at the same time.'

'But it's not her fault . . .'

'Well, of course I know that, but we can't carry on like this. Sixteen years old and coming home drunk? And, even worse, we don't know where she's been or who she's been with, or even how she got home at this time in the morning. This is going to stop, and if we have to lock her up and stand guard then that's what we'll do.'

'Well, don't say I didn't warn you, Johnnie Riordan. If she goes, I go. I'll sell up and go back to Melton with her.'

'No, you won't. You're too sensible to wreck this family. Now, let's get back to bed.'

'I knew this would happen.' Ruby said. 'Oh God, I hope she's not doing anything stupid. Please tell me she's not. She must have heard you talking about sending her to Melton.'

Johnnie Riordan pulled his wife into his arms and held her tight to calm her. 'Stop for a minute and let's think about this. Chances are she's actually gone back to Melton of her own accord. Underneath all the nonsense she's a sensible girl. She'll be OK; she's just making a point. Now, you go round to the hotel and check she's not gone there, and I'll phone the Blythes. I'll bet she's gone looking for that boy again. He's been a bit of a constant since she had to leave there, her only link to the place.'

'No, it's all over, she lost interest in him. She told Gracie she had no one, no friends . . . . why didn't we see this coming?'

'Well, just to be sure, I'll phone them,' Johnnie said, 'and for the moment let's keep this to ourselves, eh? There have been enough shenanigans in this family already.'

Ruby Riordan was terrified. She had done everything she could to make Maggie feel welcome, to make her an integral part of the family, but now it seemed she had made things worse instead of better.

Maggie had run away. Ruby could sense it, but she just didn't know where she had run to.

Despite her fears, she could still easily understand how the girl felt, how traumatic it was to have had her life turned upside down and her whole identity stripped off her, but it still hurt Ruby, who was doing her best by her birth daughter. Doing her best was all she'd ever done, but Maggie just didn't seem able to forgive them all for getting it wrong. There had been an uneasy truce for a while, but the problems were still there, and the unhappy teenager was taking her frustrations out on everyone.

'I spoke to the boy's mother,' Johnnie said when he came back into the kitchen. 'She said Andy is in London working with his father. She's going to ring Andy and ask, but she says Andy hasn't mentioned Maggie since she left.'

'I'm not surprised. I always thought it was all one-sided. That boy was too old for his age for Maggie; she spent half her time sitting around waiting for him to phone, and he rarely did,' Ruby said. 'A nice enough boy, but completely under his father's thumb.'

'That's what I think.' Johnnie nodded. 'When I asked Mrs Hobart, the general gossip was that there's something wrong about the father, that he's a bully to his wife and Andy . . . The housekeeper said they're all scared of him.'

'But that's not the boy's fault.'

'That Andy's a spoilt brat, though; he reminds me of someone I used to know back in Walthamstow. He's just hanging on Daddy's coat-tails and waiting for his inheritance – if there is an inheritance. More gossip is that he's mortgaged up to the hilt and not really worth a bean. Fur coat and no knickers, if you ask me.'

'That's not fair, Johnnie, that's just the village gossips. She may be the vicar's wife, but Mrs Hobart is one of the worst . . . But it doesn't matter, anyway. If Andy's with his father in London, then Maggie won't be with him.'

'Probably not, but . . .' Johnnie's voice faded as he thought about the worst scenarios. 'We need to talk to everyone she may have spoken to. Gracie! Gracie might know something.'

'I doubt it. She'd have told me. Let's face it, we've not done right by her, have we? We don't know where she's been going or who she's been seeing . . . Oh God, Johnnie, what are we going to do?'

'Not panic is the first thing. Then you should talk to Gracie; she might have confided in her,' Johnnie said.

'Maybe she said something to Jeanette . . . I'm going to look again.'

With that she rushed around, checking every single space over and over again and searching Maggie's room for clues. She wondered if Maggie had really gone on the spur of the moment or if she had planned it and the night out was her final defiance.

As she searched, her mind was back to 1945, when she herself had run away. Ruby could still clearly remember the planning and subterfuge she had to go through beforehand: the lying to her family, the nonchalant way she had had to behave despite her inner turmoil, all so she didn't raise the suspicions of her mother and brothers. And then the final moment of getting out of the house and running as fast as she could until she was out of sight. No one had noticed a thing, the same as she and Johnnie hadn't.

She could also still remember how she'd felt sitting quiet and scared in her seat on the train, waiting to get caught but also trying to imagine what her future would hold if she did get away.

When she'd made the decision to run away from the family home in Walthamstow and go back to the Wheatons in Melton, she hadn't known what sort of welcome she'd get in her condition. Babs and George Wheaton had been good to her in the five years she'd been with them during her evacuation, but then she'd had to go back to Walthamstow to her family: she hadn't wanted to go back and the Wheatons hadn't wanted her to go, but there had been no choice, especially after her brother had been to visit and demanded that she return. Going back had been enough of a nightmare for her, but then she'd met Johnnie Riordan and accidentally become pregnant, leaving her with no alternative but to run.

With her brain in overdrive, she suddenly had a thought. She ran out on to the landing and shouted over the banisters. 'Johnnie, Johnnie, you don't think she's pregnant, do you? She spent time with that Andy, and she was besotted with him. Maybe she had to run . . .'

'I doubt it. She's not that daft – she's a difficult little mare, but she's not silly, and—' Johnnie said.

Before he could finish the sentence, Ruby erupted, 'Silly? You're saying I was silly? Me? So it was nothing to do with you, then, Johnnie Riordan? It was me being silly that got us into this mess? I got pregnant all by myself, did I?' Her anger was boiling over as she glared at her husband; she couldn't believe what he'd just said.

'Oh, come on, Rubes, you have to stop this . . . You're launching yourself off into the deep end every five minutes. You know that isn't what I meant at all. It never even entered my head, so cut it out! You're going to drive yourself round the bend if you don't calm down . . .'

She took a deep breath. She knew he was right and that she was becoming increasingly erratic, but she couldn't stop the terrible thoughts she was having about Maggie.

Her daughter. Their daughter.

She sat down on the top stair, and once she burst into tears she just couldn't stop. She cried for Maggie, she cried for herself, and she cried for her family. She cried until there were no tears left, and then she phoned Gracie, the only person who would understand. 'She's never coming back! She's taken the fairy . . .' she said to Gracie.

'I'll be straight round.'

Nineteen

As the overcrowded train from Southend pulled into Liverpool Street Station in London, Maggie looked again at the address on the piece of paper she had pulled out of her pocket. She had already looked at it a dozen times and memorized it, but she needed to check it just once more, along with the directions she would need to find her way to the Blythe offices. She'd been there before but only with Andy, and she was finding the thought of getting across London on her own far more daunting than she'd originally anticipated.

'You can find your own way to the offices, can't you?' Andy had asked when they'd made the final arrangements. 'Only, Dad says I've got to let you find your own feet. He doesn't want me to meet you. He says I'm in danger of looking like your nursemaid.'

'Of course I can find my bloody way! I'm not stupid. I've done it before,' she'd answered sharply with a confidence she didn't feel. Less than a year before, Maggie Wheaton had been living a sheltered life in a small village, so the thought of finding her own way across London on the underground trains terrified her, but she wasn't going to admit it.

'Just go into reception and ask for me, and I'll show you up to your room. We've saved the best one for you – it's on the floor below where we live in the penthouse and above the studio and our office. Oh, Maggie, we're going to have such fun in London, especially after that bloody awful village. And Dad reckons he can make you a star, especially if you do exactly as he tells you. He knows these things, does Dad.'

Andy's enthusiasm was catching, and she couldn't help but get caught up in it. He seemed to really want her with him in London, and after months of feeling isolated and unhappy she was raring to go.

Maggie waited in her seat until the carriage load of commuters had emptied on to the platform before gathering up her belongings. When she eventually stood up and retrieved her case from the rack above, she hesitated for a moment before stepping out on to the platform herself. Her stomach was rumbling with hunger after creeping out of the house with no breakfast, and she felt quite nauseous with nervousness, but she forced herself forward in the direction of the entrance to the underground, clutching the precious cream leather suitcase that had belonged to her mother.

Whenever they'd gone on holiday, Babs Wheaton had always taken the same suitcase for her own things. This time it was packed with a selection of Maggie's essentials; she'd picked the most grown-up clothes in her wardrobe, a few mementoes of her previous life in Melton and the bare minimum of cosmetics and toiletries. Other than that she just had her handbag, which contained her purse and a few pieces of her mother's jewellery and, carefully wrapped in a piece of tissue paper, the fairy from the Christmas tree that she'd snatched at the last minute.

Everything else was back in her bedroom at Ruby and Johnnie's house, the house that had never been, and never would be, her home. The house she never wanted to go back to. She was off to start a new life and didn't need any of the things that would remind her of the old one.

Maggie successfully made her across London to Oxford Street and then followed Andy's precise instructions to the offices. Just before the entrance she stopped and straightened her coat, patted her hair and licked her lips, a tip she'd picked up from a magazine. Then she swung the door open, took a deep breath and did her best to look mature and confident. 'Good morning! I'm Maggie Wheaton. Andy Blythe is expecting me . . .'

The immaculately turned out young woman behind the reception desk at the agency smiled. 'I'll tell him you're here. There's someone auditioning at the moment, but they won't be long. Take a seat.'

Maggie sat down on the only empty chair in the room and tucked her case under her legs, which she crossed at the ankles, another tip she'd picked up from the same magazine article, and then looked around curiously at the assorted group sitting around her. Next to her on one side was a middle-aged man who looked so ordinary that she wondered what he could possibly be auditioning for, and on the other was a young man with very tight trousers, a stringy tie and a guitar on a strap. Maggie just knew he was going to go in and sing a Cliff Richard song, same as she knew the other young man with what looked like a rather large picnic basket was probably a magician. She wondered if he had rabbits in the basket and stared at it for longer than was polite.

As she looked around and made up assorted scenarios for everyone else, she nearly missed Jack Blythe quietly opening the door behind the desk.

'Maggie. This way,' he said, without altering his expression one iota.

She jumped up and followed him as he went back through the door and walked ahead of her up the stairs. On the second floor he stopped and opened a door near to the stairwell. 'This is your room; we'll discuss the rules and conditions later. You go in and unpack, and I'll send young Andy to see you when he's free.'

Jack Blythe stood back and left just enough room for Maggie to pass. Again she couldn't help but notice what a very attractive man he was for his age. He was probably not much older than Johnnie, and he was a similar height, but his shoulders were broader, his hair was thicker and she again noticed the air of danger which he seemed to exhale as he breathed.

'Thank you, Mr Blythe, for the room and everything. I'm going to work hard and do my best. I'm so grateful for this opportunity.'

'Well, just you remember that when you hate me for working you so hard. You get nothing for nothing in this business, and luck is bloody well overrated. The toilet and bathroom are at the end of the hall. They're shared, but the others are away on tour in Blackpool at the moment so it's just you on this floor. You've got today and tomorrow to settle in and acclimatize, and after that you'll belong to me, hook, line and sinker.' He took a step towards her, slid his hand behind her and patted her on the backside. 'By the way, there's a fire escape out back for when the office is closed, but I don't want any young men traipsing up and down.'

'Andy's the only young man I know,' she said, hyper aware of his hand.

'He's got a key, but I still don't want you distracting him from his job.' He patted her again; she was still trying to get over the shock when, without another word, he turned and left, pulling the door closed behind him.

Maggie looked around the cramped room which housed a single bed, a bedside table and a narrow tallboy with no hanging space for dresses. Once again she felt the flutterings of doubt started to rise in her chest; it was more basic than anything she had ever seen, and it was so very cold. She clicked the switch on the one-bar electric fire and stood in front of it as the bar started to glow red. After the comfort and warmth of the Riordan house, this little room seemed like an icebox. It wasn't what she had expected at all.

She waited a few minutes to make sure that Jack Blythe had gone and then tiptoed out on to the landing. She checked out the bathroom, which was cold and forbidding with a filthy toilet bowl and handbasin and bath, which all looked as if they hadn't been used for months. The next room was the kitchen, which looked out on to the house next door. There was an aged gas stove with two rings, one of which had a kettle on top and an oven door that was too congealed to open.

Maggie was horrified, but at the same time she wasn't intending to spend much time there. She was hoping that, as she was Andy's girlfriend, when she wasn't working she'd be up in the penthouse flat.

She went back to her room and unpacked her case. With no hanging space, she looped her dresses one on top of the other on to the solitary hook on the back of the door and then folded everything else and put it in the tallboy. All her knick-knacks and precious belongings she left in the suitcase and pushed it under the bed.

Apart from the fairy and the transistor radio.

She perched the fairy carefully on the bedside table, where she knew she could see it when she went to sleep and when she woke up, and put the transistor in her dressing gown pocket. It was far from luxurious in the room – in fact, it was just one step up from a tenement room – but Maggie breathed a sigh of relief as she lay back on the bed. She had made the first step to a new life, and she had a plan to keep her focused;

she had already decided that when she was rich and famous she could go back to Melton and live in the old house once again, inheritance or not.

The electric fire barely took the edge off the chill in the room so, fully dressed and with her dressing gown on top of it all, Maggie had climbed into the bed and pulled the grubby eiderdown up around her neck. Her head and stomach still hurt from the alcohol so it wasn't long before she dozed off.

She awoke with a start to a loud knocking on the door.

'Are you there, Maggie? I've come to take you out for something to eat. Bloody hell it's cold out here, so open the door quick . . .'

She jumped up, threw the door open and flung her arms around his neck. 'I've missed you.'

'I've missed you too . . . but you're here now, and so am I. Let's go to the Italian place down the road. They know Dad well in there, and we can catch up. I've got lots to tell you; it's all so exciting what's happening.'

'I need to get ready . . .'

'OK. Downstairs in ten minutes; that long enough?' He smiled, and Maggie remembered why she was there. They were going to have so much fun together in London.

The small Italian restaurant was warm and inviting and the food so welcome that she had to force herself to eat slowly.

When they got back, Maggie was a bit surprised; she had expected to be invited up to the penthouse, but instead Andy walked ahead of her to the door of her room and stood to one side while she unlocked it. Then he kissed her briefly and said goodnight. She didn't say anything, she just opened her door and again jumped straight into the cold bed fully clothed.

During their meal she'd tried to tell Andy about her own thoughts and reservations, but he hadn't been listening. All he wanted to talk about was her inheritance and how his father thought she was being defrauded. It was strange and disappointing, even more so when he grandly told the waiter to charge the meal to his father's account.

That night she couldn't sleep. She was cold through to her bones, despite having everything she could find piled on her bed. The room smelt of mildew, and she was terrified to turn the light off. It hadn't seemed bad in daylight, but in the dark the building reminded her of something out of a horror movie, with creaking window frames and floorboards.

It was a long weary night, and she looked forward to getting up and doing something. Anything rather than stay in that room.

'Well, young lady, let's see what you can do.'

Maggie physically jumped, and her heart banged hard in her chest. She was in the middle of getting changed and was sitting on the edge of her bed putting clean stockings on when the door flew open. In a panic, she jumped up and snatched at her dressing gown and quickly pulled it around herself without even putting her arms in the sleeves.

'I didn't know I was doing anything today. I thought you said tomorrow . . .' she said, backing away from Jack Blythe, who was standing just inside the door staring at her. He had a large tape recorder under his arm. 'I'll get dressed and meet you in the studio. I'll be as quick as I can.'

'No need for the studio. We can do a bit of a sample down here, save you having to get dressed.'

Maggie Wheaton was an intelligent girl, and suddenly all her senses were on alert, but she knew her budding career could be in danger if she didn't handle the situation properly. She wanted to know why he had a key to her room, why he hadn't knocked and, most importantly, why he wanted to make a recording in her room when there was a perfectly good studio upstairs. But she didn't say so. 'I have to get washed and dressed. I can't sing like this; I'm too cold . . .' She smiled as best she could as she slipped her dressing gown on properly and pulled the cord tight.

Jack Blythe moved a step closer, and she saw him glance down at the small single bed pushed against the wall. 'Of course you can. We can sit together to keep warm and go through the words. I know you know them, I've heard you sing them, but just to be sure we'll do a quick run-through. I'll do some recording, and then we can listen to the playback in peace.'

As he spoke, his steely blue eyes never left her face, and against her will she could feel herself being drawn in; his charisma as he smiled at her momentarily overrode everything.

Maggie smiled back nervously. 'Alright, but I just have to go to the bathroom . . .'

Slipping past him, she went out on to the landing and ran barefoot along the freezing linoleum to the shared bathroom. Shivering from the cold she leant against the closed door and breathed deeply as she tried hard to think. She didn't want to upset the man who was promising her fame and fortune, and who had given her somewhere to live out of the goodness of his heart, but at the same time she was scared – both of his intentions and of her own reactions to them.

She looked at herself in the grubby mirror that hung crooked over the washbasin. Her unbrushed, but still backcombed hair stood out at all angles, and she had black rings around her eyes from where she'd gone to bed with her mascara on. She looked a mess, but she had none of her washing stuff with her. She pulled her hair back from her face, forced it down flat with her hands and knotted it into a bunch at the nape of her neck and then, with a handkerchief she found in her pocket, she tried to rub the smudged mascara off. Just as she'd made herself look as respectable as she could, she heard footsteps outside the door.

'Maggie?' a voice shouted. 'Maggie, are you in there? I've changed my mind. Get yourself done up and I'll see you up in the studio in half an hour. Don't be late.'

Leaning her head back on the door she started to cry, a combination of relief and frustration. Jack Blythe had scared and confused her, but at the same time she'd felt a shameful frisson of excitement at the possibility that the handsome and successful older man had shown more than a little interest in her.

Half an hour later, on the dot, Maggie went into the empty room and walked over to the microphone. She stood in front of it and tried to imagine herself singing to an audience – a large audience, if Andy was to be believed. She looked around and wondered where he was; she had expected him to be there to lend her some moral support.

'Pleased you could make it.'

She spun round to see Jack Blythe sauntering into the room with a girl on each arm.

'Meet my girls, Angel and Marnie.' He looked from one to the other and kissed them on the lips in turn. 'You're going to be singing with them down the club on Saturday night, so I want you all to get to know each other. Go for a coke or something over the road, kill a couple of hours while I see the next couple of young girlies who are snapping at your heels.'

The two young women didn't even glance at Maggie – both of them were gazing at Jack – but he was focused on Maggie, his words aimed at her.

'The competition is red-hot at the moment so you need to be good, you need that something special, a sort of *je ne sais quoi*; you also have to do exactly as I say and keep the boss happy.'

'OK, Mr Blythe,' she answered cautiously, unsure what he was expecting her to say.

'Call me Jack; now, off you go. We'll have a bit of a rehearsal after lunch.' He looked at Maggie and paused. 'But, thinking about it, I want a word with you, Maggie, before you go. The girls can wait over the road for you.'

Without a word, the two young women picked up their coats and walked out just as Andy walked in. She noticed a flash of puzzled irritation in his eyes, but it was gone as quickly as it arrived.

'Dad, I just wanted to—'

'Get your arse back downstairs, son, and get those new applications sorted. You're not wanted in here right now.' Jack Blythe smiled at Andy, but his eyes were steely and his stance aggressive.

'But . . .' Andy stammered.

'No buts. Go. Now.'

As his face reddened and his shoulders drooped, Maggie could feel Andy's shame as if it was her own. His adored father had shot him down in front of her without a thought for his feelings. She was mortified and also deeply ashamed of herself, because instead of speaking up in his defence, as the Maggie of old would have done, she simply watched as the young man turned and walked silently out of the door.

'I want you to come through to my office. I've been thinking about a change of direction from what we discussed before,' he said as Maggie walked alongside him across the room. 'And also we have to discuss your inheritance and your thieving family. Eunice and I are thinking about applying for guardianship, so we need all the details of this solicitor who's in on it. I know you're not happy with how it is, and if I'm your agent and manager then it seems right.'

Maggie was instantly alert at the words; she didn't want to think it, but she suddenly wondered if she had made a huge mistake. If Jack Blythe was in charge of everything, she would be as beholden to him as she was to Ruby and Johnnie. But still she followed behind him like a puppy.

Once she was inside the office, Jack Blythe pushed the door to and removed his jacket before carefully hanging it on the hook on the back of the door. As he turned towards her, he loosened his tie. 'Ah, that's better. Come on now, Maggie, get yourself comfortable as well. Take that silly cardigan off. It makes you look frumpy, like someone's granny, not the sexy young woman you really are.'

She stayed standing where she was. 'I'll keep it on. I'm cold; I got cold in my room downstairs, and I haven't warmed up yet . . .' was all she could think to say. At that moment she felt uncomfortable to the point of threatened, and she really wished Andy was there with her. Jack Blythe's demeanour had changed; it was as if as he'd pushed the door to, he'd left his charm outside.

'Come on, be a grown-up. I need to see what you really look like. You never know, I might even be able to get a bit of modelling work for you if you play your cards right. Your face is pretty enough, but I want to see your body.'

'I can't . . .' she said, wrapping her arms around herself. 'I'm not like that.'

'Look, just sit on the sofa and relax. I don't bite, you know.' He paused and smiled. 'Well, maybe just a little when I'm confronted by a pretty little thing like you. It'd take a stronger man than me to resist.'

As she slowly perched on the very edge of the long sofa that was positioned against the wall behind the door, he walked over and, without a word, picked her bag up from beside her and dropped it on the floor, before sitting down next to her.

After a few seconds he leaned back and crossed his legs so that his knee touched hers, and his hand slid along the back of the sofa until his fingers rested gently on the nape of her neck. Maggie could feel every muscle in her body tighten as he gently ran his fingertips through her hair and along her hairline.

'Now relax, and I'll show you how all this works. It's very much a case of you scratch my back and I'll scratch yours, because you don't get nothing for nothing in this business.'

She was scared rigid, but she didn't want him to know. Andy had already told her that Jack Blythe was looking for sophisticated grown-ups to turn into stars, not scared little girls. She moved a little, and then leaned cautiously back on to the sofa.

'Young Andy told me about your financial woes; when are you going to able to get your hands on what's rightfully yours?'

'I don't know if I am. Not till I'm twenty-one, I don't think.'

'Then we're going to have to find another way for you to fund your career, aren't we? As I said before, young Maggie, nothing for nothing.'

'But I don't . . .'

'If you *don't*, as you say, you wouldn't be camped out in the room beneath my flat. Come on, stop playing games. We both know the rules . . .'

Maggie tried to stand, but he pulled her back down. He leaned over, and before she could react he'd forced his tongue in her mouth and had his hand up inside her blouse. He pinched and squeezed her breast so hard that she yelped, but he seemed to enjoy her discomfort; it made him pinch even harder.

Maggie was scared. She couldn't believe what was happening, and she had no idea how to extricate herself from it.

Jack Blythe stood up and swung a leg over so he was standing astride her on the sofa and, holding her down with his forearm across her throat, he started to unbutton his flies.

'Don't!' Maggie started to cry. 'Please don't . . .'

'You'll love it, Maggie, you'll love it. Now relax . . .' His breathing was shallow and fast, and she could see his face reddening.

The man was so engrossed in what he was doing that he didn't notice when the door opened a fraction – but Maggie did. She could see through the crack in the door that it was Andy. They locked eyes, and she nearly cried with relief, but then, to her horror, she saw him watch for a few seconds and then back away and pull the door closed as quietly as he'd opened it.

It dawned on her in that second that he wasn't going to help her.

By that time, Jack was tugging at her knickers, trying to get them off.

Maggie came to her senses. 'Get off me! You can't do this. You're Andy's father, and I'm his girlfriend.'

Jack looked bewildered. 'So what? What's his is mine, and that includes you. Andy's a Blythe; he knows how it works.'

'Oh God, he's outside, I heard him . . .' Maggie said, trying to wriggle free from underneath him. She was frantic to get out of the situation. 'Please don't let him catch me in here. He'll hate us.'

Jack's eyes changed, and he was suddenly back in the room. He stood up and straightened his clothes before he opened the door an inch and peered out into the studio. 'He's not here, you daft cow. There's no one there at all. Oh, go on, get out. You've spoiled it now. Go on . . . out. We can continue this another time, after you've rehearsed. Nothing for nothing, remember.'

Maggie grabbed her bag and ran out into the studio and sat on one of the chairs under the window. She didn't have a clue what to do.

It seemed like hours before the door opened again, and Jack Blythe came out of his office and acted as if nothing had happened. 'Aren't those bloody girls back yet? You'll have to go and find them, Maggie. It's rehearsal time . . . Oh, hang on, here they are.' He waved his hand in their direction. 'Come on, I haven't got all day. Microphone.'

Maggie had no idea what to do, so she decided to carry on as if nothing had happened. She walked over to the other two girls and stood alongside them at the microphone.

'Here you go, girls.' His voice echoed across the sparsely furnished room. 'Lights down, music ready to go. It's time for you to show me what you're made of Maggie . . . a one, a two, a three and . . . SING.'

Despite breathing deeply and digging her fingernails into the palms of her hands, Maggie was so nervous that she thought the pounding of her heart would be heard over the backing music, which was blaring out of the two tinny speakers balanced on the floor on either side of her and the other girls.

As they started to sing, Jack Blythe pulled the heavy curtains at the long narrow windows across and blocked out much of the light before clicking on a solitary spotlight, which shone from the other side of the room straight at them.

Maggie couldn't see anything or anyone, and the fierce light hurt her eyes, but she knew it was her one chance to impress the show-business agent sitting alone on the other side of the room. She told herself that all she had to do was sing her heart out and stay in sync with the others, who were experienced dance-hall singers. She had to ignore what had happened in his office. He knew now she wasn't like that. He wouldn't try his luck again.

Although she had only just met Angel and Marnie, she knew what to do. Andy had briefed her well the night before. She knew all the words already, so all she had to do was sing in tune as she'd practised over and over so many times, to sway her hips and click her fingers in time to the music. Just like she'd been told.

'And another one,' Jack Blythe's voice snapped as the first track of music faded. 'One, two, three . . .'

After four more songs, Maggie heard footsteps going across the room and then the spotlight went off and the curtains were pulled back. She had spots before her eyes for a few moments until she could refocus in the daylight.

'You can go now,' he said.

Grateful it was over, Maggie started to follow Angel and Marnie.

'No, not you Maggie,' he said. 'Back in my office now.'

She glanced sideways at the man. This was the moment of decision, the moment she would either have to get up and run and throw her dreams away or close her eyes and accept that this was the way it was in show business.

Nothing for nothing.

Twenty

'Hello, Mum?' Andy whispered down the phone with his hand cupped around the mouthpiece. 'Mum, I don't know what to do. I need you to help me.'

'Calm down, baby, whatever's wrong?' Eunice Blythe said. 'Has something happened to you? To your father?'

'Mum, it was horrible. Dad was . . . Dad was . . .' As he tried to get the words out, it all got the better of him and, to his embarrassment, he started to cry and couldn't disguise it. 'I went into Dad's office, and he was . . . he was . . .' Andy stuttered and stopped, finding it hard to say the words. He started to sob loudly.

'Tell me, Andy,' Eunice said. 'Has something happened to Dad?'

'No, it's not like that. He was in his office doing things to Maggie! He was trying to make her do things . . .'

'I don't know what you mean, Andrew. You'll have to speak slower; you're gabbling. Now, start again, darling,' Eunice Blythe said gently.

Andy took a few deep breaths and tried to calm himself; he already felt better just hearing his mother's gentle voice. He told himself he didn't need to cry like a girl, that she'd know what to do. She always did.

He was crouched down behind his bedroom door with the cord of the telephone stretched under it. He was terrified his father was going to come up and spot the cord and catch him in the act of phoning his mother and betraying him, but he couldn't help it. He had to talk to her. 'I opened the door to Dad's office, and he was on top of Maggie. He was . . . he was . . . Mum, she looked so scared, and I didn't say anything. What shall I do?'

'Nothing, baby, do nothing, that's what you should do,' Eunice said forcefully to her son. 'But you know that, don't you, darling? Do nothing! You don't want to upset your father, especially not when you're in London with him on your own . . . Are you in the office or the flat?'

'The flat,' he whispered.

'Now, I want you to stay up there and keep out of the way. This will blow over; it always does. These silly girls are forever throwing themselves at him. It's part of his job, and it'll be part of your job. Tomorrow the girl will be gone and everything will get back to normal. It's nothing to worry about.'

But you don't understand! It's Maggie, Maggie Wheaton . . .'

There was a pause.

'Are you still there?' Andy asked in panic.

'Yes, I'm here. Do you mean that young girl who used to live in the village?' Eunice asked sharply as she realized what he was saying. 'Whatever is she doing in your father's office? Her parents are looking everywhere for her; they're really worried.'

'She wants to be a singer, and Dad's managing her. He wants to make her a star, and he's been helping her try and get her inheritance from Ruby and Johnnie. Dad said no one was to know where she was, and he's given her one of the rooms downstairs. He's trying to help her, he really is, but . . .'

Andy's voice faded, but Eunice Blythe didn't answer. All her married life she'd watched from the sidelines as her husband Jack had affair after affair. In the beginning it had demoralized her, but at the same time it kept him happy, and that meant that her life was happy. She'd known from the start that her husband would never be faithful, it wasn't in his nature, and if she wanted to stay married to him she would have to turn a blind eye. She had submitted to him on everything in their life to keep him happy, because she loved him and she loved her affluent lifestyle and didn't want to jeopardize any of it, but at the same time she adored her precious only child with a passion she never knew she had.

The day they'd moved into the Manor House, Eunice had felt as if all her Christmases had come at once. It was a beautiful house with extensive grounds, plenty of room for her sister to live with them, and just far enough away from London. The thought of Jack staying up in London during the week, every week, was the icing on the cake. The only downside was having her precious son living with Jack without any supervision, but although she worried about her husband's influence over the boy she knew there was nothing she could do about it.

'Mum? Are you there, Mum? What shall I do? She's my girlfriend, and she's only sixteen.'

'What did Jack say when you went into the office?'

'He didn't see me . . . I didn't say anything. I just left.'

'What about Maggie?'

'Mum, she saw me, and I didn't help her! I just ran away. I'm so ashamed of myself.'

'You did the right thing – the last thing you want to do is upset your father. Stay in the flat, go to bed, and if he comes up tell him you feel ill, you've got a fever, anything, but whatever you do, don't let him know you saw him.' She thought for a moment. 'I'm on my way. Don't say a word to anyone.'

After she'd put the phone down, Eunice quickly got ready and then went into the orangery where her sister was sitting reading. 'Lily, I have to go to London and get Jack out of another fix.'

'What's he done this time?' Lily looked up and raised one eyebrow at her sister.

Eunice gave her the outline. 'So I have to get to London and rescue Andy. Oh, and I'll probably have to pay the girl off. These stupid young women are costing me a fortune, one way and another. I hope Jack appreciates it.'

Lily stood up. 'I doubt he does for a minute. You're a doormat, Eunice Blythe, and I'm ashamed of you. All you can think about is keeping that bastard happy and out of trouble. How would you feel if that was your daughter? Or, heaven forbid, your son? Jack doesn't seem to be selective; they just have to be in the same room.'

'That's not very nice. You're happy enough to live in his house!'

'Because you want me here! Listen to me, Eunice. You can't turn a blind eye to this. He's taking advantage of her, and he's trying to get her money.' Lily looked her sister in the eye. 'And let's face it, Eunice, you and I both know it's not the first time he's fleeced some poor heiress either.'

Eunice frowned. 'We can't afford another scandal. I'm going to go and persuade her to go home. I'm sure she'll keep quiet for Andy's sake.'

'But you said her parents are looking for her. Shouldn't you tell them she's safe?'

'So long as she goes home they'll be happy, and Jack will just think she's gone off. Same as they all do, eventually, once I've had a little word.'

'And Jack'll pounce on the next poor girl that goes through his door all starry-eyed. Come on Eunice, you can't keep digging him out of the shit.'

'He's my husband, and—'

'And Andy?' her sister interrupted her. 'He's your son. Do you want him to turn into his father? Do you want that lovely sweet boy to behave like him? He's a good boy, but it wouldn't take too much for him to follow in his father's footsteps.'

'Andy's his father's heir. We can't have him upsetting Jack and losing all that, can we? Now, I'm going to London. The taxi will be here in a minute, and if I hurry I'll just catch the next train. I'll ring you later.' She smiled and kissed her sister on the cheek. 'Don't worry, it'll be fine. It always is. These silly girls just don't realize that you can't lead a red-blooded man on like that and not expect trouble. Jack just reacts.'

When the phone rang, Ruby snatched it up quickly, hoping against hope that it was Maggie.

'Hello.' The voice on the other end was tentative. 'Is that Ruby Riordan?'

'Yes, it is. Who's calling?'

'This is Andy Blythe's Aunt Lily. Eunice Blythe's sister. We met in the summer when Maggie Wheaton had her little accident in our garden? Well, I understand you're looking for her. I know where she is . . .'

'Johnnie, I know where she is,' Ruby screamed at full volume. 'Quick, we've got to go to London as soon as we can.'

Johnnie ran down the stairs to where his wife was standing with the receiver still in her hand. 'Tell me!'

'Seems she ran away to London to be a singer. She's staying at that agency place that Jack Blythe owns, where Andy works. That was Eunice Blythe's sister on the phone.'

Johnnie looked at his wife for a moment as he tried to understand what she was saying.

'She said Maggie's too young to know what she's letting herself in for . . .'

'They lied to us, they all lied to us! I knew there was something wrong about that bastard.' Johnnie clenched and unclenched his fists, his anger and frustration written all over his face.

'I don't think Eunice or Lily knew she was there until just now,' Ruby said. 'Lily rang as soon as she did. Andy lied, that's certain, but that doesn't matter; we know where she is now. Lily gave me the address, but we need to hurry before Maggie finds out we're on the way and disappears again.'

Ruby and Johnnie looked at each other fearfully for a few seconds before jumping into action.

After calling Gracie and Isobel to hold the fort at the house and the hotel, Johnnie and Ruby jumped into the car and raced straight up to London. The traffic was reasonably easy, so Johnnie put his foot down and they got there in record time.

'There . . .' Ruby pointed. 'That's the place.'

Johnnie screeched to a halt outside the office and just left the car where it was. 'Where is he?' Johnnie demanded as they both ran into the office.

'Who?' the receptionist said, looking nervously around the room.

Johnnie noticed her eyes linger for a split second on the door behind her. 'Forget it. I'll find him.' With a cricket bat in his hand, which he'd grabbed from the hall before they left, and Ruby hot on his tail, Johnnie went straight round the back of the desk and through the door.

They raced up the stairs and spotted the open door to the studio.

'Blythe? Where are you, Blythe?' he shouted as they looked around.

'What's going on here?' Jack Blythe came out of his office and looked calmly at the couple standing in the doorway to the empty studio. 'Who are you, might I ask, and how did you get up here?'

'Where's Maggie?' Johnnie snarled. 'We know she's here! Where's my daughter?'

'I've no idea what you're talking about,' Jack Blythe said calmly, although there was a beading of sweat forming on his upper lip. 'I don't appreciate being interrupted when I'm mid-audition, so please leave or I'm calling the police. You're trespassing.'

'Where's Andy? Is he with her?'

'He's not here, and she's not here . . . Look, what is going on? What's this all about . . .?'

'I know all about you, you dirty bastard. Maggie is a child, she's our daughter, and you're taking advantage of her. You're trying to screw a child? I should break your fucking neck.'

Jack Blythe stood his ground, but as the colour drained from his face, Johnnie knew that it was all true.

'Look, the girl wants to be a singer. I was helping her. *You* signed the agreement. *You* gave consent. She just asked us not to tell you she was here.'

'Consent? Never in a million years have we signed consent for anything.'

'Well, I'm sorry, but you did. I'll get it . . .' Jack Blythe went back into his office and came out with a slim folder. He pulled out a piece of paper. 'Here . . . You've happily handed me quite a lot of authority over the girl you claim to be worried about.'

Ruby snatched it from him and studied it carefully. 'This isn't my signature,' she said, staring at him.

'Prove it.' He smiled. 'Oh, and here's another one – Maggie Wheaton declaring she wants me and my wife to be her legal guardians. Now, I have work to do, so if you'll excuse me? I've had enough people wasting my time.'

Johnnie took a step forward.

'Don't, Johnnie, don't! Let's find Maggie first.' Ruby paused and looked at the man in front of her. His suit was expensive, his tie probably cost more than the average wage and he was groomed to perfection. He looked like a movie star. '*Then* you can beat the bastard to a pulp.'

As Jack Blythe grinned and turned to walk away, Ruby heard a movement out on the landing. She ran out and saw Andy crouched on the stairs looking terrified.

'I'm sorry,' he muttered.

'Where is she?'

'Downstairs.' He stood up slowly. 'I'll show you.'

'Andy! Andy, you keep out of this, out of it, or you'll regret it,' Jack Blythe bellowed at his son. 'This is all your fault. You brought her here! You wanted me to help her. You brought that little prick-teaser here . . .'

'This way,' Andy said, ignoring his father. He led them back to the stairs and to the floor where the bedsits were.

'I think she's in here; she ran away from him. Again . . .' he said, his eyes focused firmly on the floor.

Ruby tried the handle, but the door was locked. 'Maggie? Are you in there, Maggie?' she shouted. 'It's me, Ruby. Let me in. Please? We just want to know you're alright.'

Slowly, the door opened, and they realized that the girl had moved the tallboy over to block the door.

Ruby slid through the gap and grabbed Maggie with both arms. Her daughter.

For a few moments, no one said anything.

'You're freezing cold. Here, put this on.' Johnnie took his coat off and wrapped it around her shoulders. 'You go down to the car with Rubes; I've got something I must do.'

Ruby looked over Maggie's shoulder and shook her head. 'Don't do it,' she mouthed.

But instead of going after Jack Blythe, Johnnie grabbed Andy by the scruff of the neck and spun him round until he was hanging head-first over the banisters. 'Tell me what Maggie was running away from. Tell me!'

'Please don't! It wasn't my fault . . .'

'TELL ME.'

'From Dad. She was running from Dad. He tried to—'

At that moment there was a clatter of feet on the thinly carpeted stairs, and two policeman appeared. 'We had a call from the office downstairs. There's a disturbance, we understand?'

one of them said, looking carefully, trying to assess the situation.

Johnnie let go of Andy. 'Nothing for you to bother about . . . eh, Andy?'

Andy's shoulders dropped as Johnnie let go of him. 'No,' he said.

'This is our daughter, officer, and we've just come to take her home. She had a barney with the boyfriend, this young man here. I'm sure he'll tell you all about it.'

The policeman looked at Andy. 'Well?'

Andy looked at his feet, the ceiling, anywhere but at the officer standing on the landing. 'Yes, I'm Andy Blythe, and this is my father's building.'

'And you, miss? You are?' the young policeman asked Maggie.

Throughout the exchange Maggie had said nothing, but then it was as if she shook herself back to life. 'I'm Maggie Wheaton. These are my parents, who have come to collect me. Andy is my boyfriend. My *ex*-boyfriend. Jack Blythe is his father; he's upstairs in his office if you want to ask him anything.'

'We'd better, just to be sure. Where did you say his office is?'

'Through the studio and then the door straight in front of you, but I think you'll probably bump into him on the stairs,' Maggie said.

She looked at Andy, staring straight into his eyes for a few seconds before shaking her head and looking at Ruby. 'I'm so sorry, Ruby. I'm really sorry. I believed him. I believed both of them.' Again, she stared at Andy.

'I'm sorry too,' Andy said. 'I didn't know what he was going to do, truly I didn't. I thought he wanted to help you, and you said you wanted him to help you. It's not my fault.'

'Yes, it is, because when you did know, when you saw what he was doing, you didn't help me, did you? They were right – you are just a spoilt little boy. Daddy's office boy.'

'I did try to help. I phoned . . .' He paused and looked around to see if his father was somewhere listening.

Maggie smiled for the first time and shook her head. 'You're such a drip.'

Throughout the exchange, Ruby could see Johnnie itching

to join in, itching to get to Andy and his father. But he didn't.

Maggie looked away from Andy. 'Can we go now, please? I want to go home, if you'll have me.'

Johnnie put his arm around her shoulder. 'Home it is; I'll get your things.'

'Don't forget the fairy. I must have the fairy . . .'

As they walked out of the front doors, Eunice Blythe, wearing a fur coat and lots of perfume, was wafting in. She frowned. 'Is everything OK? I was just going to go and see young Andy; he said he's not well.'

Ruby stared at her. 'You knew exactly what was going on in there, but you lied to us. As a mother, how could you?'

'I don't know what you're talking about . . .'

'Do you know what, Mrs Lady of the Manor? I envied you. You're beautiful, you have a beautiful house, and I thought you had a beautiful life, but I wouldn't swap with you for a million pounds.'

Again Eunice frowned. 'I don't know what you mean, darling.'

'Yes, you do, and I despise you for letting your son think that this is the way to behave. Now, excuse us, we're taking our daughter home. You should close your eyes and thank God that we got here in time or your husband would be coming out of there in a wooden box.'

Eunice smiled and shook her head. 'You're wrong, you know. Jack's a good man, really. He just lets himself get taken advantage of sometimes.'

As Maggie, Ruby and Johnnie climbed into the car parked outside, Andy came to the door. His mother kissed him on the cheek, and they both walked in arm in arm, for all the world as if nothing had happened.

Ruby looked over her shoulder at her daughter, huddled in the back seat against the door. 'Are you OK? There's a travel rug beside you; put that over your knees. It's a long drive home, and it's blooming freezing today.'

Maggie shivered and pulled her coat around herself. 'Thank you.'

'That's OK. Wrap it tight around your feet as well.'

'I didn't mean the rug. I meant thank you for rescuing me.'

'That's what families are for.' Ruby smiled and then looked at her husband. 'Isn't it, Johnnie?'

'It sure is . . . I just wish I'd got one swipe with the bat round his smug face before the police got there.'

'Don't talk like that.'

Johnnie looked in the mirror and Maggie locked eyes with him.

Then they both smiled.

Epilogue

A few weeks later

'I feel a bit old to be here,' Ruby said, looking around the crowded ballroom at the Kursaal.

'Nonsense!' Gracie laughed. 'But blooming heck, this place brings back some memories. Seems like only yesterday I was working my fingers to the bone in those hotel rooms upstairs.'

'Before Aunt Leonora rescued you and introduced you to a life of leisure in the classy little joint up the road.'

'Oh, leisure, my eye!' Gracie shook her head and pulled a face. 'Slave-drivers the both of you!'

At that moment Johnnie and Edward arrived back from the bar with a tray of drinks.

'Well, here we are,' Johnnie said holding his glass of beer up. 'The beginning of new times for everyone. Cheers.'

'Cheers. I was starting to think it would never happen after all the delays, but we're finally going. Just three more days and we'll be sailing past the Thamesview en route from Tilbury docks . . .'

'Don't forget to wave as you go past. We'll be looking out for you.'

They all clinked glasses and murmured, 'Good luck,' all round. The mood was a mixture of happy and sad at the same time.

'Oh, look, there's Jeannie.' Gracie pointed and waved. 'Over here . . .'

'What time does it start? Do you know?' Edward asked.

'Seven thirty. Just a few more minutes.'

'Shall we grab a table while they're still free?' Jeanette said. 'Look over there, right near the stage. And we'll be able to watch the dancing. I love a bit of rock 'n' roll!'

The group of five went and sat down.

'I really appreciate you all coming to support Maggie. It's

been so awful for her, one thing after another, but now there's a light at the end of the tunnel at last.'

'It's been awful for all of you,' Gracie said. 'I don't know how you've got through it, but here we are, and everyone's in one piece. Though I do wonder at everything we've all been through over the years. Do you think we all attract trouble? All of us have had more than our fair share.'

'Too right we attract it.' Johnnie laughed. 'Must be because someone somewhere knows we can cope with it.'

The group of five all clinked glasses again.

'Here's to Maggie's success and Jack Blythe's failure. It was the icing on the cake to see him fail so spectacularly. The Manor House is up for sale, and they've already all moved out.'

'And without any help from me.' Johnnie laughed again. 'He brought it all on himself. Well, not much help from me . . . just a few words in the right ears. Reputation is everything in his business, and his has gone for a lovely long sail down the old Swanee.'

Maggie Wheaton was standing out of sight behind a large pillar at the side of the dance floor, just watching the group who had gathered together to hear her sing for the first time. It was just two songs as a warm-up for the main singer, a short fat man who called himself Mario, and who sang loud and strong and pretended to be Italian, but who was actually Pete, a car mechanic from Chelmsford.

It wasn't what she had expected when Jack Blythe had promised to make her a star, but it was a start. A real start.

They had gone to a lot of trouble to get the booking for her, especially Gracie, as she'd worked there in the past and knew people. After everything that had happened with Jack and Andy, it was more than she had expected. It had been a horrible experience, but it had made her see that they were all on her side after all.

She watched them for a few minutes before going back behind the curtains that edged the area where the band were already in place.

It was all too surreal. Then the lights went down in the ballroom, the lights over the band went up and the first few notes echoed.

It was her cue to go and stand by the side and wait for 'her' music.

She pulled a hand mirror out of her pocket and checked her hair and make-up, straightened her skirt and wiggled her toes in her new pointed stilettos which were pinching her feet already. She tried to see herself from top to toe but it was hard, so she ran around the back to where there was a wall mirror just to be sure.

Her long blonde hair was scooped up into a beehive, and her new bright-green frock fitted tightly around the top with a flared skirt that floated just above her knees.

As she was looking she suddenly heard her cue.

'And now, a couple of tunes from a new local talent who I'm sure we're going to be hearing a lot more of . . . I give you . . . MAGGIE.'

She stepped out to the microphone and then, in a flash, it was all over and there was applause ringing in her ears. Applause for her.

'How did I do?' she asked tentatively when she went over to the table.

They all jumped up and one by one hugged her.

As she sat down, she locked eyes with Ruby, who had tears streaming down her face. 'Oh Maggie, Maggie, Maggie . . .' she sobbed, unable to hold back any longer. 'You were fantastic and so beautiful. I'm so, so proud of you. George and Babs would have been bursting with pride if they could see you right now.'

Johnnie smiled. 'Like mother like daughter.'

At that moment it was as if there was no one else in the room, just the three of them, mother, father and daughter. They all knew it wouldn't be easy, but they also knew they'd broken through and it could only get better.

Lightning Source UK Ltd.
Milton Keynes UK
UKOW04f1438190915

258863UK00002B/15/P